Volume Five

AIRSHIP 27 PRODUCTIONS

AN AIRSHIP 27 PRODUCTION

Sherlock Holmes: Consulting Detective, Vol. 5

The Adventure of the Other Man © 2013 Chuck Miller
The Adventure of the Stolen Centennial © 2013 Aaron Smith
The Abominable Merridew © 2013 I.A. Watson
The Adventure of the Invisible Assassin © 2013 Andrew Salmon
The Napoleon of Crime © 2013 Ron Fortier

Cover illustration © 2013 Mike Fyles
Interior illustrations © 2013 Rob Davis

Editor: Ron Fortier
Associate Editor: Gordon Dymowski
Production and design by Rob Davis
Promotion and marketing by Michael Vance

Published by
Airship 27 Productions
www.airship27.com
www.airship27hangar.com

ISBN-13: 978-0615935812
ISBN-10: 0615935818

Printed in the United States of America

10 9 8 7 6 5 4 3 2 1

Sherlock Holmes
Consulting Detective
Volume V

The Adventure of the Other Man
When Holmes is arrested for attempting to seduce the wife of a married man, Dr. Watson begins to worry that his friend has truly lost his mind.

The Adventure of the Stolen Centennial
Why would someone cruelly murder a man only a few months before he turns one hundred? That is the mystery put before the Great Detective and his loyal companion in a truly bizarre affair.

The Abominable Merridew
A murderous fiend is loose on the streets of London and is pursued by two very different hunters, Sherlock Holmes and his nemesis, Prof. Moriarty.

The Adventure of the Invisible Assassin
When a cunning murder attempt leaves Sherlock Holmes incapacitated and at death's door, it is up to Dr. Watson and Mycroft Holmes to bring a fiendish plot to an end.

The Napoleon of Crime
Being a commentary on Professor James Moriarty and his place in the Holmes stories.

Sherlock Holmes

in

"The Adventure of the Other Man"

By
Chuck Miller

I had seen but little of my friend, Mister Sherlock Holmes, in the months since my marriage, though I made a habit of calling at 221-B Baker Street whenever I found myself nearby with an hour or two to spare. Relations between Holmes and myself were such that no prearranged appointments were necessary. Indeed, owing to the erratic nature of his schedule, planning a personal call in advance was quite useless. If he happened to be in, which was not often, I was received with as much warmth as he was capable of displaying, depending upon his mood. He might be distracted by some investigation to the point of brusqueness, or he might be touchingly effusive. But we had, inevitably, drifted apart. After my marriage to Mary Morstan, I had moved out of our digs in Baker Street and busied myself with my new wife and my medical practice, leaving Holmes to his own devices.

Such news as I had of his investigations came to me through the public press. His name appeared two or three times a month, in connection with some celebrated criminal case. It had never occurred me to wonder about his personal life. The concept seemed irrelevant where Sherlock Holmes was concerned. His personal and professional lives were one and the same.

One morning in the late spring of 1889, as I was sitting down to breakfast my wife said, "Have a look at this awful news item."

The newspaper she was waving in my direction was one that I recognized, but had always made a point never to purchase or read. It was one of those miserable sheets that catered to the lowest common denominator amongst the British reading public. The dubious reportage consisted in the main of highly sensationalized accounts of the most appalling crimes and natural disasters. Several pages were devoted to "society news," a lurid catalog of rumor, gossip and innuendo involving royal personages and other celebrated figures, actors, writers, and other luminaries.

"Mary," said I with a frown, "when did you start reading this trash?"

"Never. It was brought to my attention by someone, and now I am bringing it to yours," she said, handing the thing to me and pointing to an item in the middle of an inside page.

This is what I read:

"We see that one of London's wisest and best men has been playing the fool of late. Rumors surrounding the doings of a certain consulting detective have been confirmed by this reporter, who witnessed a rather touching scene at a popular restaurant this Monday evening past. It seems that this intellectual paragon has taken it into his head to pay court to a young woman. The lady in question has made no comment upon the situation, at least not within earshot of any member of the press. One must wonder what sort of an accounting of herself she gives to her husband."

"Of all the damnable calumny!" I exclaimed, tossing the offensive thing onto the floor. "What twaddle! If I were Holmes, I would sue them for libel!"

Mary nodded. "It does seem an unlikely tale. They were careful not to use his name, you'll have noticed."

"Cold comfort! It could refer to no one else. Why, Holmes would no more conduct himself in such a manner than would... why, the Archbishop of Canterbury!"

"That's a bit much, don't you think?" Mary said, amused. "He took your departure from Baker Street rather hard. Perhaps he's lonely and it has driven him to behave foolishly."

I shook my head. "Absurd. Why would Holmes pay court to a married woman?"

"Irene Adler was married, was she not?" Mary countered. "In fact, Mister Holmes witnessed her wedding. That must have been quite a blow in itself, and not so very long ago."

"Holmes had no romantic feelings toward Mrs. Norton...Irene." I protested. "He was in awe of her intellect and ability."

Mary laughed. "Don't tell me you actually believed him when he said that!" She shook her head. "You men may be able to fool one another, but a woman is not so easily gulled. A man does not cherish a photograph of a woman, as Mister Holmes does Mrs. Norton's, because he admires her thought processes. You wrote that he once described her as 'the daintiest thing under a bonnet on this planet.' That goes somewhat beyond the academic, wouldn't you say? I swear, John, you have such a blind spot where he is concerned. You see only what he wishes you to see. You must keep in mind that he is a human being with human foibles.

"And," she continued, eyes shining with emotion, "since you are his best, and possibly only, friend in the world, you might want to pay a call on him to see if you can be of assistance. You have been apart from him long enough now that you may be able to look at him with fresh eyes. I hate the thought of him suffering in his loneliness, and perhaps behaving rashly in an attempt to alleviate it. I will admit that it is difficult to picture Mister Holmes as the 'other man' in a love triangle, but his is a complex

"...you might want to pay a call on him to see if you can be of assistance."

nature, John, and we both owe him a very great deal."

She was right, of course, and I found her concern for my friend touching. I was ashamed that I had failed to display the same attitude. I realized that it had been more than a month since I had last paid Holmes one of my impromptu visits. I resolved to speak with him that very evening.

After I had finished with my patients for the day, I made my way to Baker Street and that familiar house which had been the starting point for so many great adventures. Though it had been no more than half a year since I had lived here with my friend, it seemed already a relic of some bygone age, and it was with an acute feeling of nostalgia that I tugged at the bell pull. In less than ten seconds, the door swung open, and there stood my former landlady, Mrs. Hudson.

"Oh, Doctor Watson!" she exclaimed, before I could so much as say hello. "Thank goodness it's you! Look at this message I just wrote down." With that, she thrust a scrap of paper into my hand. I read what was written there and frowned.

"This message must be in error, Mrs. Hudson," I said. "There is a mistake in the wording, surely."

"I thought so too," she said. "So I asked the gentleman who telephoned here to repeat it. Three times. There was no mistake. I took it down word for word."

I looked once more at the note in my hand:

"Mister Sherlock Holmes is being held at the Dorset Street police station, charged with malicious mischief, assault with intent, and wanton destruction of private property. No bond has been set at this time."

"Mrs. Hudson," I said reassuringly, "I am sure this is a misunderstanding, probably related to a case he is investigating. He does employ unconventional methods, you know, from time to time."

"He commits crimes, you mean," she said knowingly.

I cleared my throat. "Well, he might only in a very good cause, you understand, if it is necessary to see true justice done step outside the strict letter of the law now and again."

In fact, he made quite a habit of it. This I knew full well, having been his accomplice more than once. But he never acted without good reason. I was quietly grateful that my friend was not being held on a charge of grand larceny, burglary or manslaughter. I also felt a small pang of guilt.

Had I been available to assist him.

"Oh, I understand how the world works," Mrs. Hudson said. "The law and morality are often two very different things. I would not cast aspersions on Mr. Holmes' character, you know that. I have complete faith in him. That's why this troubles me so. I always thought he was much too clever to be caught at anything."

I sighed. "One may press one's luck only so far, I suppose."

"Circumstances may turn against anyone, no matter how clever he is," the landlady said worriedly. "And if I may say so, Mister Holmes has not been himself lately. I fear that a public scandal might be his ruin! Thank goodness you rang the bell when you did! I had only just hung up the telephone and was wondering what to do. Coming on the heels of that queer incident last night... I considered calling on you then, but I didn't think it was my place. But this..."

The poor woman seemed on the verge of tears. It was plain that there was more than this brief communiqué weighing on her mind. "You must tell me everything, Mrs. Hudson, and I shall see what I can do to help him."

After the distraught woman had led me into her small parlor and onto a divan, with a cup of tea in my hand, I asked her, "What was the queer incident you referred to?"

My question quite obviously caused the poor woman a great deal of discomfort. She squirmed in her seat, took a large swallow of her own tea, and said, "I suppose I can tell you, as you are his closest friend. You've been more a brother to him than Mister Mycroft Holmes ever has. It's rather embarrassing, but... Two nights ago, Mister Holmes had what I can only describe as a drunken row with a woman in the middle of the street in front of this house!"

"My dear Mrs. Hudson!" I was taken aback, and scarcely knew how to react.

"I know, Doctor, I know!" she said, with a stricken look on her face. "You've no idea how painful it is for me to utter those words."

"The woman was drunk?"

"She may have been. Mister Holmes certainly was."

"I cannot believe it!"

"Nor could I, but there it was, right in front of me! He was staggering drunk! I saw and heard the whole thing myself."

This was troubling, to say the least. Holmes' use of cocaine had been of great concern to me, as his friend and as a physician, but I had never known him to drink to excess, and had never seen him even mildly inebriated. He had always seemed a model of self-control. But the autumn of 1888, I knew, had been a taxing time for my friend. In the month of September, he had achieved happy resolutions to the perplexing case of the Sign of the Four and the dark and deadly affair of the Hound of the Baskervilles.

He had exerted himself to the utmost, and had much to be proud of. But Holmes was unable to rest and savor his triumphs. He felt that those successes were overshadowed by his failure to capture the fiendish murderer known as Jack the Ripper. The faceless madman had butchered at least five women in the East End, and in spite of Holmes' Herculean efforts to bring him to book, the monster remained at large. I knew this had cut him to the quick, and I felt certain that he had turned to cocaine for solace.

I thought about everything Mary had said to me that morning. I knew that I must heed her advice and keep my mind open to all possibilities, no matter how unpalatable they might be.

"Tell me what happened, Mrs. Hudson."

She composed herself and began her narrative.

"I know that Mister Holmes is given to some very eccentric behavior at times," said she. "But I have never before seen him conduct himself as he did last night, and would not have believed him capable of it. He seems never to take what I would call a healthy interest in women, but he is never anything less than a perfect gentleman around them.

"At about ten o'clock, a hansom cab stopped at the front door. I was in the front parlor replacing some curtains, and was in an excellent position to observe the events. Mister Holmes climbed out, unsteadily, onto the pavement, then leaned back into the compartment. The other passenger, a young woman, placed her hands on either side of his face and kissed him full on the lips! This went on for no less than three minutes, perhaps longer. Then Mister Holmes stood up straight and extended his hand to help the woman alight from the cab. She shook her head. They exchanged a few words, too softly for me to hear, and she shook her head again, more vigorously this time.

"This seemed to incense Mister Holmes. He loudly demanded that she accompany him up to his rooms. There was no doubt about what he had in mind." Mrs. Hudson's cheeks reddened. "When she refused, he proceeded to berate her, using some of the most shocking words, I am sure, that have ever been uttered in this street. Then he reached in with both hands and attempted to bodily remove her from the vehicle.

" 'Don't be a fool!' the woman shouted. 'A cafe is one thing, but if my husband caught me in there with you, it would be both our necks!'

" 'You do not care for me!' said Mister Holmes, in a voice that tore at my heart.

" 'I do care for you, Sherlock,' was the woman's reply, 'but I cannot afford to jeopardize my marriage.'

" 'You care only for money!' he accused.

" 'That isn't so. You must know that. I shall leave him, as I have told you, but it must be in my own time and on my own terms.'

"At that, Mister Holmes made one more attempt to drag her out, but lost his grip and fell sprawling onto the pavement. As the cabbie made haste to depart, Mister Holmes got to his feet and stood swearing and shaking his fist.

"Thank goodness there was no one about to see, save for a shabby-looking loafer idling in front of Camden House across the street. Mister Holmes eventually fell silent, dusted himself off, and let himself into the house, cursing all the while. It took him several tries to get his key into the lock!

"I stood stock still where I was, holding my breath. I did not want to embarrass him by letting him know I had witnessed that awful scene. He made it up the stairs and into his rooms, and that's the last I've seen of him. And now, this!"

We sat in silence for several minutes, sipping our tea and thinking our own thoughts. What could I say to Mrs. Hudson to comfort her, or her to me? I finished my tea and awkwardly took my leave, patting the dear woman on the shoulder and assuring her that all would be well. Part of my mind believed that to be true, while another part fretted and wrung its hands.

There was nothing for it but to go to the Dorset Street police station. It was small and dingy. A uniformed police sergeant sat behind a desk in a small reception area. Behind him, a doorway opened onto a narrow corridor that ran the length of the building, no more than twenty feet, leading to a single cell. As I entered, I caught a glimpse of a solitary, shadowy figure behind the bars.

"Excuse me," I said to the man. "I believe you have a Mister Sherlock Holmes here."

The sergeant looked up from his paperwork with an expression of annoyance on his face. "I've already told one representative of the press that we are not..." His voice trailed off as an expression of recognition dawned upon his face.

"I know you, don't I?" he said, squinting at me.

"Possibly. I'm Doctor John Watson."

"I thought I recognized you," he said with a smile. "You won't recall it, I'm sure, but I met Mister Holmes and yourself some six years ago, when I was a green young constable. I was most impressed with his manner and the way he managed to cut to the heart of a very knotty problem."

"Yes," I said, "I remember you now. Perkins, isn't it?" It had been a puzzling matter indeed, involving a prominent banker, a Member of Parliament, and a homicidal madman. The case is recorded in my archives under the title, "The Problem of the Third Twin." Holmes had worked one of the miracles of deductive reasoning that he performed as routinely as most men lace up their shoes. The lives of six children had been saved, two men had gone to the gallows, and Scotland Yard had, with Holmes' blessing, taken full credit.

"Yes, sir!" beamed Perkins. "I am touched that you didn't forget me. Well, I'm a sergeant now, and this small station is my responsibility."

"My congratulations," I said, genuinely pleased to see him doing well.

He thanked me and explained that this was an auxiliary station, and prisoners would not ordinarily be held here for any great length of time. It had been decided, however, that because of Holmes' notoriety, he should be kept here, further from the public eye, until his case could be adjudicated. The news of his plight had been kept from the press...for now.

"Tell me what happened," I said.

He seemed hesitant, so I added, "I am a doctor. I have grown accustomed to giving and receiving unpleasant news."

He nodded and told me the tale.

Sherlock Holmes had shown up at the residence of Mr. and Mrs. Walpole and created a shameful disturbance. He had shown up at the house early in the morning, hammering on the front door and demanding to be let in. He appeared to be quite intoxicated. A servant was sent to the window to order Holmes to desist and leave the premises at once. He responded by hurling a flower-pot at the window, shattering both. At this point, a sudden shower of rain commenced. The occupants of the Walpole house hoped this would dissuade Holmes from any further mischief, but he began to tromp to and fro on the pavement in front of the house, getting soaked to the skin and bellowing Mrs. Walpole's given name, Stella, at the top of his lungs.

This was too much for Townshend Walpole to bear. He rushed out of the house with a riding crop in his hand and confronted Holmes. Angry words were exchanged, and an altercation ensued.

However impaired he might have been Sherlock Holmes was still master of a dozen esoteric styles of physical combat. The outcome of their scuffle was thus a foregone conclusion. In a matter of seconds, Sherlock Holmes fled the scene, leaving Walpole unconscious and bleeding on the pavement outside his own front door. The police were alerted, and Holmes was seized on the street as he was making his way back to his rooms.

My friend had come before a magistrate that very morning. His manner had been sullen and defiant, and had refused to accept counsel or to enter a plea. The magistrate had no choice but to order him to be held in custody pending further investigation of the charges against him.

"They had the devil of a time bringing him in," Perkins said. "But he's been calm and collected ever since. Do you wish to see him now?"

I nodded. Perkins rose, and I and followed him down the corridor. He unlocked the door, and Holmes, who was sitting cross-legged on the narrow bunk, with his back against the wall, looked up at me with a wan smile.

"Watson," said he.

Holmes' manner was languid and carefree, to a degree that his current circumstances scarcely warranted. At the same time, his physical appearance was shocking to me, someone who knew him well and was familiar with his customary fastidiousness. He was disheveled, tieless, with his collar undone and his dark suit dreadfully wrinkled and haggard, his chin and cheeks covered with dark stubble. His grey eyes were as bright and intelligent as ever, but the dark half-circles beneath them told their own tale. He smelled faintly of gin.

Once Perkins had ushered me into the cell, locked the door behind me, and returned to his desk in the front lobby, I spoke:

"What the devil is going on, Holmes? I assume, of course, that you are practicing some deception in order to pursue an investigation, but I confess I cannot fathom it."

"For the love of God, Watson," said he, clapping a hand to his forehead, "tell me you have some cigarettes on you. I have been many hours without tobacco, and my nerves are becoming frayed."

Once I had supplied him with cigarettes and matches, I pressed him for an explanation:

"What the deuce are you playing at, Holmes?" I asked, my voice trembling with urgency. "This is surely the most grotesque and scandalous charade you have ever undertaken. I must assume that the stakes are very high indeed if you're resorting to such excesses."

"It looks bad, does it not?" he drawled. "Perhaps it is, Watson. Your faith in me is quite touching, I assure you, but might it not be that your assessment is inaccurate? Have you not chided me time and again on my celibate life? How often have you told me that I should benefit greatly from a woman's influence? I look to you as an authority on such matters."

"I did not mean you ought to chase after a married woman," I said reasonably, "fight with her in public, and attack her husband!"

"One must take great care in what one asks for, Watson. I mean to have that woman for my own. If I cannot, then I do not care to continue living."

"Holmes!"

"She is trapped in a loveless marriage," said he, leaning forward with an expression of painful earnestness on his haggard face, "with a brute of a husband who cares nothing for her. He married her for her dowry, and is ignorant of, and indifferent to, her true nature. She is sweetness and light personified, and that man is not fit to touch the hem of her garment."

"Be that as it may," I remonstrated, "your behavior has done nothing to calm the troubled waters. Indeed, you have created a tempest, one which may swamp both you and Mrs. Walpole. You assaulted her husband in his own home! This is no trifling matter. You could very well go to prison."

He shrugged and pouted, a curiously Gallic gesture. "What of it, Watson?" he said mournfully.

"How did you become involved with her?"

"There was an attempt on her life."

"By whom? Did she consult with you?"

"Never mind all that, Watson," said he, shaking his head. "That man will do her to death yet, one way or another. What does it matter if it is done with a single blow or by a process of attrition." He slumped over and placed his head in his hands. After a moment, I saw that his shoulders were trembling.

Sherlock Holmes was weeping!

I scarcely knew how to react, so I moved to sit beside him and patted him awkwardly on the shoulder. I arranged my face into what I hoped was an expression of confidence and reassurance, but I was shaken to my core. I tried to provide such comfort as I could, but the words felt grossly inadequate to me even as I uttered them. He thanked me for coming, and I stood and made ready to take my leave.

"Don't lose hope, Holmes," I said. "I shall do whatever I can on your behalf. I must be off, but I shall return."

I called down the hall for Perkins.

"Fear not, Watson," he said mournfully as the sergeant opened the door and I departed. "I shall be out of here by the end of the week, that much I can guarantee. Mycroft will use his influence on my behalf. What happens after that is in the hands of the gods and the British criminal courts."

❖ ❖ ❖

On the street outside the station, I was approached by a man of thirty or thirty-five years, who looked both vaguely respectable and marginally seedy at the same time.

"Sir, may I ask your name?" he rudely asked.

"Of course," I said coldly. "You may do as you like, but you will not receive an answer." I was in no humor to suffer this ill-mannered stranger.

"My name is Albert Pinch," he told me, as though the information might carry some weight.

"You have my sincere condolences," said I, turning from him and walking purposefully toward the corner.

Loping along beside me, he told me that he was a newspaper reporter, and named the very scandal sheet Mary had shown me that morning.

"Are you a friend of Mister Holmes?" he pressed, as I attempted to outdistance him without actually breaking into a run. "His solicitor, perhaps? I know he is in a cell, sir, and I am aware of the nature of the charges. Can you tell me anything?"

Coming to a halt, I gave him a stern look and said, "I can tell you I have no idea what you are talking about. Further, I can tell you that my name and my business here are no concern of yours. I have nothing to say to you on this or any other subject. And that is an end to it, my good fellow." I nodded curtly and proceeded to cross the street. He did not follow.

Thus taking my leave of the infernal pest, I returned to my home in Kensington to ponder the things that I had learned. I gave an account to Mary, who listened to me with much head-shaking and many expressions of shock and dismay.

"He may well be playing a part in order to pursue an investigation, "she said when I had finished. "But what if he isn't, John? What if he isn't?"

❖ ❖ ❖

The following morning, I went to 221-B to offer such meager reassurances as I could to Mrs. Hudson, and to pick up a few items of clean clothing to take to Holmes in his cell. I reassured her as to his health and safety, and told her that he expected to be back home within a few days.

I gathered up some clothes and made them into a bundle. As I prepared to take my leave of the familiar place, I had a look around the sitting-room. It was much as it had been when I lived there. The place was in a greater state of disarray than was usual. The orderliness of Sherlock Holmes' remarkable mind had never extended to his environment. I had been well aware of this when we roomed together, but his housekeeping appeared to have deteriorated even further in the recent past. The coal-scuttle overflowed with unanswered correspondence and the Persian slipper that contained his tobacco was affixed to the mantelpiece with a jackknife. It was plain that he had forbidden Mrs. Hudson to tidy up, even in his absence. One might have supposed from these surroundings that London had been struck by an earthquake.

Something caught my eye. On the table before Holmes' customary chair was a small pile of photographs. Most of them were of people and places that were unfamiliar to me, but in one, a much younger Sherlock Holmes,- he appeared scarcely out of his teens, posed with a very striking young woman. I felt for a moment like some archaeologist who had unexpectedly discovered an incredibly rare and precious artifact. Holmes had never been forthcoming about his early life, and I was unaware that he retained any mementoes of the past. The photo had an undated inscription on the back, in a neat, feminine hand:

"To Sherlock, 'We are such stuff as dreams are made on, and our little life is rounded with a sleep.' Affectionately yours, Stella."

I turned it back over and studied the image. Holmes and the young woman were attired in costumes of some kind, and the setting seemed to be the backstage area of a theater. I very gently replaced it in the exact position in which I had found it before quitting the familiar yet strangely alien sitting-room.

No sooner had I made my farewells to Mrs. Hudson and set foot on the pavement outside the front door than I was accosted by a stranger. This one was of a different cut than the journalist who had approached me in Dorset Street. The man who stood glaring at me now was young, perhaps five and twenty, clean-shaven, with chestnut hair and a fierce expression in his dark eyes. His attire told me he was a man of means, while his soft-looking hands had certainly never been turned to manual labor.

"You are Mister Sherlock Holmes?" he demanded in a most impertinent manner. He was a large man, very formidable-looking. His hands clenched and unclenched, and his eyes flashed cold fire as he fixed me with a murderous glare.

"I am not," I said as calmly as I could manage, tucking the bundle of clothing under my arm. "My name is John Watson. Doctor John Watson. And who might you be?"

"Where is Holmes, then?" he rudely demanded.

"He is presently indisposed," I coldly informed him. I saw his gaze move to the door of 221-B, and I quickly added, "And you will not be admitted to this house."

His eyes narrowed. "You're the scribbler who chronicles the so-called adventures of that coxcomb Holmes, are you not? Well, if I cannot confront the man himself, his lapdog will do. You tell your master that he is to refrain from harassing my sister immediately, unless he is keen to receive a thrashing. The law has already been brought into the matter, and if Holmes does not desist, he will have to answer to me personally."

My first impulse was to respond to this ruffian in kind, but I gained control of myself, and when I spoke, it was with the voice of calm reason.

"My dear fellow," I said. "Mister Holmes is my friend, but he is not my employer, and he is certainly not my master. I would very much appreciate it if you would change your tone, introduce yourself properly, and explain to me the nature of your difficulty. Perhaps I can be of some assistance, but I do not respond well to threats and bluster."

At this he seemed somewhat chastened, though not entirely mollified. His mood changed from violent to sullen, and I sensed that he was at least manageable. He introduced himself as Thomas Bowyer, and said he was the brother of Mrs. Stella Walpole. Well, this might be an interesting development. The lady's name was certainly intriguing. I resolved to learn whatever I could from this man, and I wondered if he knew of Holmes' arrest, or the circumstances behind it.

Adopting a friendly manner, I guided him away from the doorstep of 221-B, to a small pub a block and a half up the street. Seated at a table with a whiskey and soda in hand, he proved more reasonable.

"As I told you," he said, "my sister is Mrs. Townshend Walpole. Stella is her Christian name. Her husband's family claims descent from the

"*Where is Holmes, then?*"

first Earl of Orford, though I shouldn't wager any money on that. They have rather gone to seed in recent decades; risky business dealings with unfortunate outcomes, and so forth. I was a bit suspicious of him when he began courting Stella some years ago. We were orphaned young, Doctor Watson, my sister and I. When we came of age, a considerable amount of money was settled upon us from our parents' estate. We inherited almost equal amounts, though a bit extra was set aside to serve as a dowry for Stella whenever she should marry.

"We shared our family home in Mayfair, which is large enough that we each maintained a private suite of rooms, separate residences, in effect, though we shared the household staff. It was a comfortable arrangement for both of us until Stella took up with Mister Townshend Walpole." He said the name as though it were a curse.

"As I say," he went on, "Stella entered the marriage with a considerable dowry, and she has some of her own money, too. She has retained control over that, though Walpole has of course had the use of her dowry. Walpole, too, is an orphan, with no close kin living. He inherited a considerable estate, but I gather he has been rather free with his money over the years. It is whispered that he was on the verge of some very dire straits before he married my sister. It is the money, not my sister, that commands Walpole's 'loyalty.' One of the first things he did after they were wed was to purchase an expensive house in Mayfair. I live close by, and am in and out of their home frequently, though my brother-in-law has never made me feel particularly welcome. My sister he sees merely as another piece of his own private property. I thought he would remain content to oppress and browbeat her, but there was a disturbing incident not long ago that set me to wondering.

"Mister Sherlock Holmes was called in to investigate the incident. I was abroad when it all began, and have not been made privy to all of the details. But your friend seems to have developed a strong attraction for my sister. And now he seems bent on creating a perfect scandal for her. She claims to be mystified by his attentions. To be frank, Doctor, I don't believe her."

I said nothing of the scene Mrs. Hudson had described to me, or of the photograph I had so recently seen.

"I hate to say this," Bowyer went on, "but my sister has a bit of a past, I'm afraid. So I cannot be sure. But her husband knows nothing of this. Should this scandal blossom into a divorce action, it will mean her absolute ruin. Townshend Walpole will leave her with nothing. It would be an awful tangle. They have already had three or four fearful rows on the subject.

Threats have been exchanged. He says he will divorce her, but I believe he is so deeply aggrieved that mere separation will not suffice. I believe that Townshend Walpole intends to murder my sister."

"How did all of this come about?" I asked. "What was the disturbing incident?"

"There was an attempt on my sister's life. That is what brought Sherlock Holmes into the picture. One of God's angels must have been looking after her, because she escaped what should have been certain death. It seems a paid assassin was engaged to do the job. The fellow had a spot of ill luck, though. He had made his way into the house through an upper-story window and crept into my sister's room. Stella and her husband maintain separate bedchambers, you see. This fellow entered her room, knife in hand, only to discover that the bed was empty. My sister had gone downstairs for a glass of milk.

"She returned to her room to find a strange knife-wielding man standing next to her bed. His back was to her, so Stella, who has excellent night-vision, and had not carried a candle with her, quietly slipped into the room, lifted a very heavy lamp from her night-stand, and brought it crashing down on the intruder's head. He dropped his knife, but remained conscious and attempted to subdue Stella. A fearful struggle ensued, which ended when my sister managed to propel him through a window. He fell two stories, landed atop an ornamental wrought-iron fence and was horribly impaled. Quite dead, and he left no clue as to why he had endeavored to attack poor Stella. Oh, Doctor, it is a tangled web, and Sherlock Holmes has done nothing but make it worse."

I wondered about that. I knew there had to be some method to Holmes' apparent madness, and now I thought I was beginning to see what it was. He would not hesitate to place his person or reputation in jeopardy to help a woman whose life was in peril.

"The newspapers carried a much tamer account of the incident than the one I have just related to you," Bowyer was saying. "The story was given out that the man was a burglar. But he had a great deal of cash on his person that had not come from the house. I believe somebody hired that man. Who could it have been? I put it to you, Doctor. There is nobody in the world with a motive for harming my sister apart from her husband."

"But this murder attempt predates her association with Holmes," I pointed out. "If her infidelity was her husband's motive..."

"It pains me to say so, but Holmes was not the first tomcat to come sniffing around my sister, nor was he the first to receive encouragement from her."

"Was it your sister who engaged Holmes' services?"

"I do not know," said Bowyer with a shrug. "Neither my sister nor my brother-in-law would speak of it in detail to me. I learned what I know of the murder attempt from a neighbor, and what he told me was more surmise than fact. Perhaps Stella wanted to spare me the worry. As for Townshend Walpole, however... Well, I have nothing more than my suspicions, and they are not enough for the police or the courts. He means to divorce her at the very least, but would, I believe, prefer to kill her."

"Well," said I as we parted company, "I can tell you that you need not fear any further difficulties from Holmes. He is incarcerated, and likely to remain so for the next two or three days."

It was distasteful to me to admit this to him, but it seemed the right thing to do under the circumstances.

The news seemed to come as a relief to him. He was considerably more relaxed as he said, "Yes, well, I appreciate your speaking frankly with me, Doctor. I bear Holmes no personal ill will. I hope that things can be resolved more genially when cooler heads prevail."

"Just so," said I. "Oh, before you go, would you happen to be carrying a photograph of your sister and brother-in-law? Perhaps I have seen them before. I should like to refresh my memory."

"Certainly," he replied, taking a large bill-fold from his jacket pocket and thumbing through it. "Ah, here we are." He produced a small photographic print depicting a well-dressed, prosperous-looking couple. A rather fierce-looking man with a full beard stood next to a chair which was occupied by a more mature version of the striking young lady who had posed many years ago for a photograph with a young Sherlock Holmes.

Bowyer's hoped-for resolution seemed remote indeed that evening, as one of my most immediate fears was realized. On my way home, I had purchased a copy of the offensive periodical that had earlier made such sport of Holmes' reputation. On page three of the society news, I found an item that made my blood boil. Under Albert Pinch's byline was an account of the scene in front of 221-B Baker Street that had been described to me by Mrs. Hudson. How had this confounded reporter obtained the information? Could he have listened in on our conversation somehow? Or perhaps he had been nearby when the dreadful scene was enacted. I remembered Mrs. Hudson's remark about a loafer in front of Camden House.

This time, Holmes was mentioned by name, though Mrs. Walpole was not. But the writer indicated that a revelation of the lady's identity would be forthcoming.

I decided to pay a visit to Albert Pinch upon the morrow.

Early the next morning, I went to the editorial offices of the scandalous publication where Pinch had his employment. They were not to be found on Fleet Street. I found them on a side street, occupying a small suite of offices on the first floor of a dreary, nondescript building that could have been either residential or commercial, with no joy in it either way.

A number of people scurried about in the smallish lobby as I walked in unchallenged and made my way up the stairs to the news-room. No one paid me the slightest attention as I emerged into a large space that must have taken up the entire floor. Desks were scattered about, some with bored or harried-looking men seated behind them, pens flying across sheets of yellow foolscap.

Looking around the room, I spotted my quarry, seated at a desk in the far corner of the room, deep in conversation with another man. This individual's appearance, stooped and aged, with white side-whiskers, and a pair of tinted spectacles perched upon his nose, was peculiar, but in a strangely familiar way. This impression grew stronger as I approached. He looked so unlike Sherlock Holmes, I knew instantly that was who he must be.

Detouring around an unoccupied desk to come up behind the man, I clapped a hand on his shoulder and said, "Broken jail, have you?"

Startled, the disguised detective whirled around, took a good look at me, and laughed.

"My dear, Watson!" said he, "This is a red-letter day! You have taken me by surprise!"

"Never mind all that," I said in a low voice. "What is going on here, Holmes?"

And then an awful thought struck me. What if my friend were here practicing some kind of a deception on the reporter? I may have just spoiled his game, ruined whatever work he was up to.

"Not at all, dear fellow," he said, as though in direct response to my thought. "Pinch here is in on my secret. You've done no harm."

"How..?"

"The sudden look of horror on your face could have had no other cause. But it is completely unfounded. Don't let it mar your moment of triumph!

"Once again, I have used you as a barometer for a piece of pantomime I essayed upon the stage of the real world. ... For that, you have my sincerest apology, but not my promise never to do it again. You must understand the necessity. You see, I knew that if I could gull you, the rest of the world stood no chance. You are the standard, Watson, and there is none higher."

This compliment made it impossible for me to continue taking him to task, as he had known full well that it would.

"Very well, Holmes," I said. "You are forgiven, naturally." I was not nearly as nettled as I might have been just a year earlier. I had become accustomed to moving in circles where I was most often the ultimate authority. My ways were as inscrutable to my patients as Holmes' were to me. It had been quite some time since I felt that my intellect was thoroughly overshadowed by that of my companion. The niggling sense of my own inferiority that I had sometimes experienced in his presence had evidently withered and died. I no longer felt a need to prove my worth to him or to myself. It had finally dawned on me that Holmes would have made as poor a doctor as I did a detective.

"However," I added wryly, "since you have raised the subject of promises that cannot be made, I cannot promise to refrain from striking you the next time you play of this sort of game on me."

He laughed and clapped me on the shoulder. "If that is the price I must pay for your invaluable presence, then I shall accept it gladly."

"If it's any consolation, Doctor," said Albert Pinch, "he did the same to me. Of course, we were not allies to begin with; at least, not that I was aware of. I didn't know that the little scene with the lady in front of 221-B was staged for my benefit. I was surprised when he made contact with me earlier today and let me in on his scheme. Any credibility I might have lost will be more than made up for by the exclusive story I shall have once this business has been concluded."

"I have been ably, if unwittingly, assisted by Mister Pinch," Holmes said to me. "His surveillance of me at 221-B was prompted by an anonymous tip I sent his way. I felt it appropriate to bring him into the scheme before it reached its climax. After my arrest, I decided to confide in him and request his assistance in the next phase of the thing.

"It was Pinch here who telephoned Mrs. Hudson with the message that ultimately brought you to Dorset Street. I knew that you would eventually see some mention in the press of my activities, and I wanted to usher you into the inner circle. I knew that a message to Mrs. Hudson would swiftly find its way to you. Pinch, having trailed me, unaware that I was aware of him, approached me when I was brought in. I promised him an exclusive interview later on if he would make the call for me. And now, you see, I have proven to be a man of my word."

"A gentleman through and through," said the reporter.

"Mister Pinch is now composing a story that will appear on the stands this very afternoon," said my friend. "It details the tragic circumstances in which the once-brilliant Mister Sherlock Holmes now finds himself. Smitten with Mrs. Stella Walpole, he has thrown away his good name and reputation to pursue her, going so far as to vandalize her home and make a vicious attack upon her husband, a cruel brute who stands in the way of his wife's happiness. Walpole has vowed to press charges, and Mister Holmes is being held by the police. Bail is expected to be set within the next two or three days, once the date has been set for a trial. It is expected that he will spend at least two years in durance vile. And, in the meantime, Walpole has expressed his intention to divorce his wife and is quite confident that, when all the facts are revealed, he will leave her with nothing."

I nodded. "That fits with some information I recently received."

"Information?" he said, eyeing me keenly. "You've been busy, old fellow! Pray tell me about it."

I gave Holmes an account of my meeting with Thomas Bowyer. He listened in silence, eyes closed, fingers steepled before his face in a prayer-like attitude. I omitted, of course, to mention the photograph I had seen in Holmes' sitting-room.

"That is most interesting," he said when I had finished. "He was quite agitated, you say?"

"Furious would be a more apt word. Champing at the bit to take some kind of action."

"Very good," said Holmes, nodding and smiling. "Most gratifying."

Holmes did not elaborate on this peculiar response, and I did not press him. "Do you think he is correct?" I asked. "Would Walpole really murder his wife rather than suffer public cuckoldry?"

"It has been known to happen, my dear fellow. I have told you many times that there is nothing truly new under the sun. Every crime that is committed today contains echoes of earlier ones. So it has been since the day after Cain slew Abel.

"I can tell you this: Mrs. Walpole is in great danger from a certain man in her life, one she ought to be able to trust without reservation. His motive is money, the love of which, while it is not the root of all evil, produces more than its fair share. He has made one attempt on her life already, and will make another very soon, if my recent performance has been effective."

Holmes then bid Albert Pinch good-bye, and the man went to work on his story.

"So you are acting on behalf of Mrs. Walpole?" I asked, once we had left the building. "She is a willing participant in this charade?"

"Indeed, Watson, and a fine performer she is."

"I can see how this course of action would prevent Walpole from making another attempt on her life," I said. "Now that he is to be under public scrutiny, it would be madness on his part. But could it not have been achieved in some less dramatic way?"

"All will be made clear, and soon, if I have not misread my man. I have a few matters to attend to today, and then I think a bit of relaxation would not be out of order. The past few days have been rather trying. Do you fancy a night on the town, Watson? I know of a delightful little bistro where we might while away a pleasant hour or two."

"A capital idea, Holmes," I agreed readily. "It has been too long since I enjoyed an evening in your company. I should welcome the opportunity to discuss this matter in greater detail. Just tell me when and where."

"This evening is as good a time as any. Call for me at 221-B at eight this evening. Come to the rear door, and take care not to be followed. Oh, I should mention that the place is a most exclusive club, and has a rather strict dress code. Do not trouble yourself about it just now. I'm sure I have something on hand in my wardrobe that will fit you."

Just before nine o'clock that evening, Holmes and I arrived, on foot, at the "exclusive club" he had spoken of. It was everything he had promised, and more. Appropriately attired, we walked through the front door without drawing undue attention from the patrons. Holmes' remarkable sense of fashion had served us well.

I was dressed to the nines, in a pair of filthy, threadbare trousers, a ragged grey shirt, a stained and malodorous overcoat and an aged, dented derby. On the backs of my hands, I sported a pair of crude, simulated tattoos, executed by Holmes in non-indelible inks. My right hand proclaimed my deep love for someone called "Rosie Redd," while my left was adorned with a leering skull. A false set of side-whiskers and some dirt rubbed into the skin of my face, and Doctor John H. Watson was no more, his place taken by a nameless and depraved hooligan with a wicked, if entirely imaginary, past.

My companion was arrayed in similar style, and cut a decidedly menacing figure, with an artificial scar that traveled diagonally across his left eye and down his cheek almost to the chin. The eye itself was hidden behind a thin glass lens of a milky, yellowish-white color, which Holmes had applied directly to the eyeball, so that it appeared quite dead. A masterful touch, I thought. One of those small but significant details, the study of which Holmes had made himself master.

Thus transformed, we could blend into our noisome surroundings; a dark, dirty and nameless public-house on the fringes of the Whitechapel district, which would forever be associated in my mind with the atrocious deeds of Jack the Ripper.

Though it was a dangerous, and somewhat absurd, position into which we had put ourselves, I must admit that I felt a rush of the old excitement. The game was once again afoot, and I stood side-by-side with the most wily and tenacious hunter I had ever known.

"I have learned that our quarry has visited this place once before. With a bit of luck, he will do so again tonight. I have made inquires among some of my contacts in London's criminal underworld. Specifically, I asked them where and how one might go about commissioning a murder, if one were so inclined. This place was mentioned prominently by all of them. It seems that there is a new organizer or broker of some kind who is making a reputation for himself. None of them have the slightest idea who he is, but this establishment serves as one of his contact points."

As my eyes adjusted to the dimness, I took a look at my strange surroundings. The place was populated with a motley collection of individuals who had only one thing in common: an almost palpable air of menace and corruption. As far as attire and physical characteristics were concerned, they might have been creatures brought to earth from a dozen alien worlds. Some of the men busied themselves with card games, a few held furtive discussions in corners and at tables, while others conducted earnest negotiations with ladies of a certain sort. Several sat alone waiting, perhaps, for the arrival of some unsavory acquaintance, or possibly just seeking intoxication for its own sake.

Somewhere in the stygian recesses of the place, a piano player was torturing his instrument, producing a vaguely musical din. This, I reasoned, was not meant to serve as entertainment, but rather to make it impossible for the patrons to overhear other people's conversations.

Every pair of eyes in the place swiveled in our direction when we entered, and just as quickly went back to what they had been doing. Evidently, we were acceptable.

"This is a most insalubrious place, Holmes," I remarked, as we seated ourselves at small, rickety table. "Can there possibly be a more wretched hive of scum and villainy?"

"Oh, I know," said my companion with a nod and a smile. "Wonderful, is it not? Though the word hive is perhaps inappropriate. Bees are orderly, purposeful creatures, and quite altruistic toward their fellows, unlike the denizens of this establishment. There is no better place in London to observe members of the species homo criminalis in the wild. I understand that it has recently come under new management. I have learned that this place may have a connection with the current troubles in the Walpole household."

"Which you still have not explained to me in any detail. It seems that we once again find ourselves in very deep waters."

"No," said Holmes, "the waters are not deep, but they contain quite a number of obstacles and invisible dangers. We must tread carefully, and be alert to avoid an undertow."

We had been there for two hours when Holmes caught sight of a man coming in through the street entrance.

"There he is, Watson," hissed my friend, inclining his head toward the front of the room

When I saw Thomas Bowyer making his way toward the bar, I was surprised. I had been expecting someone else altogether. I experienced another sensation that had become familiar to me during my days in Baker Street; that of being utterly at sea. The picture I had been constructing in my mind was shattered. I decided to relax and follow Holmes' lead, as usual. He did, or soon would, know everything. He would share it with me when he was ready, and not a second before.

"When you made mention of the man in Mrs. Walpole's life, I took it to mean her husband."

"No," said Holmes, shaking his head. "I referred to the other man in her life. Her brother. I have learned much about him in the recent past, and his presence here is exactly what I was expecting."

Bowyer sat down on a stool at the bar, ordered a mug of beer, and spoke with the barkeep at some length. We could hear nothing of what was being said. The barkeep nodded and disappeared through a curtained doorway behind the bar. Bowyer sat staring into his beer, as though the liquid contained the answer to some great mystery that he might divine if he were only patient enough.

"He seems familiar with the place," Holmes observed, "though not what one would call at home. He's been here before, but not more than once or twice, I think."

Bowyer sat for some little time, glancing nervously at his watch every five or ten minutes.

I do not know just how much time passed in this fashion. At least two hours had passed when a development manifested itself in the form of a whippet-thin, rat-faced individual who sidled into the establishment and took a seat on the stool next to Bowyer. The two of them ostentatiously ignored one another as the newcomer ordered a drink. As this transaction took place, the newcomer reached into his pocket and removed a folded slip of paper. He placed it casually upon the bar, and pushed it toward Bowyer, who surreptitiously placed his hand over it.

After the rat-faced man had finished his beer and left, Bowyer unfolded the paper and studied what was written upon it. After three or four minutes of this, he tore the paper into small fragments, dropped it into an ash-tray, and set it alight with a match. When it had burned to ash, which he crumbled between his fingers, he placed a coin on the bar and made for the door. Holmes and I quickly rose to follow.

Once he was on the street, Bowyer headed west. We followed him on his meandering course around London. He seemed to have no aim in mind; just a young man with time on his hands, casually enjoying the sights and sounds of the great city. At length, he made his way into Kensington, the very district in which I made my home. Once there, he made his way to Mortimer Street, where his stride became more purposeful.

Holmes ducked into an alcove between two buildings and shed his outer layer of clothing. I followed suit. Underneath the rough attire we wore dark-colored suits of a more respectable appearance. Holmes peeled away his false scar and removed the colored lens from his eye. Tossing our original disguises into a rubbish bin, we resumed following our quarry.

We were less than a quarter-mile from my own house when Bowyer, who had slowed his pace in order to start reading the house-numbers, turned up the walk of a large, rambling house. I knew this to be a very respectable boarding-house. It was my understanding that several army coaches resided there, receiving pupils in their rooms. Bowyer knocked at the door and was admitted by the stout, grey-haired landlady.

"What now?" Holmes asked rhetorically. "Let us just have a look at the house from all sides, shall we?" The grounds were not at all spacious in this residential area where the houses were all situated in close proximity to their neighbors. We walked around the dark, three-story structure, gazing up at the windows, several of which showed lights.

"No way of knowing where he has gone," Holmes muttered, then stood deep in thought for several moments. Suddenly, his eyes lit up and he said, "Hello, what have we here?" He pointed toward a spot at the bottom of one wall of the house.

I looked down and saw rectangular window, the bottom edge of which was almost flush with the ground. A light had appeared in the cellar, a rather feeble glow that danced upon the window-panes.

"Come," said Holmes, gripping my arm, "Let us just have a look."

We dropped to all fours and crawled through some shrubbery to take up a position at the small window. Crouching there, we peered through the glass into a gloomy cellar.

Down the steps came Thomas Bowyer, preceded by a most curious-looking individual. It was a man of some sixty or seventy years, holding the lantern whose light had drawn us here. This individual was slender and stooped, with sallow skin, sunken eyes, thinning hair, and a great dome of a forehead. His movements, which were lithe and economical, belied his elderly appearance. He reached the packed-earth floor of the cellar and moved nimbly in the direction of a large steamer trunk, passing close below our window, Bowyer trailing awkwardly behind him. They were so near that I could have reached out and touched them had the glass not been there. Holmes, I saw, was subjecting them to intense scrutiny. They were conversing, but the window-glass was too thick to allow the sound to reach our ears. Of course, that seeming handicap worked both ways. At least Holmes and I could communicate freely.

"Who is the older man, Holmes?" I whispered.

"I have no idea," replied my friend, sotto voce. "But he intrigues me. I took in every detail of his appearance that I could as he passed the window, quite a good view, actually, under the circumstances, and what do you suppose I have deduced about him?"

"Quite a bit, I should wager."

He chuckled grimly and shook his head. "You would lose. I have not deduced a thing, Watson. Not one blessed thing. He might as well be a manikin in a clothing store. It is as though he has deliberately shorn himself of anything that might hint at his occupation, personality, or past. He does have a rather professorial air about him, but that could well be a contrivance. Absolutely fascinating. What sort of a creature is this?"

The old fellow placed the lantern upon a table, then squatted down and opened the trunk. He took from it a small morocco case, perhaps six inches long and three wide, which he handed to the younger man. The old man watched Bowyer keenly, his head swaying from side to side, as though he were stricken with a mild form of palsy; an innocent enough mannerism in itself, but for some reason it struck me as loathsome and repellent. His deep-set eyes glittered with intelligence and something else besides; something dark, implacable, and malevolent.

"He seems almost inhuman," I muttered.

"Perhaps," said Holmes, in a thoughtful voice. "He is rather singular, is he not? Hm. Inhuman? People have said the same of me..." His voice trailed off, and we watched the rest of the proceedings in silence.

Bowyer ran his fingers over the little case, then pulled it open. Inside, resting on blue velvet, was a hypodermic syringe, with a needle attached. After a brief examination, he nodded and slipped the case into a jacket pocket.

The old man reached into the trunk once more. This time, he produced a revolver, and passed it to Bowyer, who weighed the gun in his hand, looked at it from several different angles, said a few words, and placed it into his hip pocket.

Bowyer produced his wallet and extracted a thick stack of banknotes. These he handed to the old man, who tucked them away in an inner pocket of his black frock coat. Their business evidently concluded, the pair went back to the stairs and ascended.

Holmes and I backed out of the bushes, stood up, and crept away from the window.

"Well, what do you make of all that?" I asked.

"A syringe and a pistol," said he. "Interesting selections; seemingly incompatible, but all the more telling for it. Yes, it makes sense."

"I don't follow," I said.

"I am not leading just yet," he said. "Merely moving my facts and theories about to see what might fit where."

We loitered in a dark alcove across the street until Bowyer emerged from the house and headed back the way he had come.

"I do not think there will be any further drama tonight, Watson. I shall follow Bowyer, just to make certain, but I expect he is heading home to bed. I recommend that you do the same. I have preparations to make, Watson. I should be most grateful if you would come to the Walpoles' residence at ten o'clock this evening, where I believe I can write the finish to this sordid

"A syringe and a pistol. Interesting selections..."

business. Here is the address. When you arrive there, please go to the rear door and knock. My regards to Mrs. Watson."

◇ ◇ ◇

The eastern sky began to lighten with the coming dawn as I walked the quarter-mile to my own home, where I managed to get three hours of sleep before I had to rise once more to attend to my practice.

It was almost a quarter after ten that night when I arrived at the home of Mr. and Mrs. Townshend Walpole. The impressive house was situated in Mayfair, not far from Grosvenor Square. Remembering Holmes' instructions, I made my way through the garden to the rear door.

Before I could knock, the door swung open and I found myself facing Inspector Lestrade.

"Doctor, it is good to see you," he whispered, shaking my hand. "Your presence in Baker Street is sorely missed. We are awaiting developments. Do please be as quiet as you can, and follow me. These are Mister Holmes' instructions, and you know how he is. We mere mortals can only carry them out."

Lestrade gave me a wink and I fell in behind him. The interior of the house was dark and quiet. We crept up the rear stairs to the second story, and down a short hallway. Lestrade went to a door on the left-hand side, twisted the knob, and pushed it open. Turning to me, he whispered, "Mister Walpole's bedroom. Let us just crouch down in that dark corner next to the armoire."

As my eyes slowly grew accustomed to the darkness, I made out a few small details.

The window curtains were pulled nearly shut, allowing only a wan sliver of moonlight into the room. I could hear the heavy respiration of two sleepers. One, light and feminine, came from the four-poster, while the other, deep and masculine, came from an armchair situated at the foot of the bed. I could not see the woman at all, as she had the covers piled on top of her, covering her head. Of the man, all I could make out was a dressing-gown and night cap.

As Lestrade and I sat on the floor in the shadow of the armoire time crawled by with agonizing slowness. Midnight, I was sure, had come and gone before something finally happened.

The bedroom door had been left slightly ajar, and I heard muffled footfalls in the hallway outside. They stopped just outside the door, which slowly swung open.

Thomas Bowyer crept quietly into the room and advanced upon the figure slumped in the armchair. In his hand was a hypodermic syringe. The needle caught a stray bit of moonlight coming in between the curtains and glittered briefly as it moved toward the shoulder of then sleeper in the chair. I felt Lestrade tense beside me, and I held my breath, my hand moving involuntarily to the jacket pocket in which I carried my revolver.

Suddenly, Townshend Walpole sprang from his chair with a shout: "Now!"

Lestrade raised the shutter on a dark lantern. Another officer hidden in the shadows on the other side of the room did the same, and the stalker stood illuminated in the sudden glare.

Thomas Bowyer looked wildly about him, dropped the syringe, and made a grab for an object stuck in his belt.

"Never mind that," said Walpole, swiftly producing a riding crop from within his dressing-gown and bringing it down on Bowyer's gun hand, causing him to drop the weapon. By this time, Lestrade and the uniformed man had dashed to his side, and they gripped him by the arms and held him immobile. Lestrade swiftly removed the pistol from Bowyer's belt and put it into his own jacket pocket.

The man who had so abruptly risen from the chair threw off his dressing gown, then did the same with his beard and his thick, black hair, to stand revealed as Sherlock Holmes! I had been more than half-expecting it, rather counting on it, actually, but it took me by surprise just the same. Age could not wither, nor custom stale his infinite variety!

Behind Holmes, the still figure on the bed rose up, the bedcovers slipping away to reveal a rather formidable-looking police matron whom I recognized. She was wearing a one-piece coverall of some sort, and it was plain that there was some kind of padding beneath it.

"Lestrade," my friend said, "I should be grateful if you would fit our friend here out with a pair of bracelets, before he takes it into his head to have another go at me."

"Right you are, sir," said the smiling inspector. "Casey, shackle this lad here and stand with him to keep him out of mischief." One of the uniformed officers hastened to carry out Lestrade's instructions. Bowyer put up no struggle.

❖ ❖ ❖

"Mister Walpole and his wife came to me shortly after the first attempt on his and his wife's lives," said Holmes, once the lights had been put on. "Accompanied by Lestrade, I had a look at the corpse of the would-be killer, and recognized him immediately: Ichabod Grace, a criminal of the vilest sort, with a long history of mayhem and depravity. There are men in this great metropolis, I can put names to four of them, who make their living from murder and mayhem. For a price, one may have a rival crippled for life. One might even have a sister and her husband murdered and in such a way that no suspicion whatsoever falls upon the party responsible for setting the plot into motion.

"Grace, of course, had no personal motive for attempting to murder Mr. and Mrs. Walpole. What he did have was a note pertaining to both Walpoles, which one slept in which room and pencil sketches of them."

"Bowyer did not mention those items to me when we spoke," said I.

"He may not have known they were found. Even if he had, he would not have mentioned them to anyone. You said he told you that his sister's room was the assassin's first target, though. That was significant because it was a lie. The scene he described to you did indeed occur, but it was Townshend Walpole who fought with the man and put him through the window, not Stella."

"Why should he tell such a tale?" I wondered.

"The original plan required Townshend Walpole to die first," said Holmes. "Thus, there would be no problems with the will. His property would pass to his wife, who would die next. A few days later or a few minutes, it would not matter. When she was no more, it would all go to her brother. He was using you as a sounding board, my dear Watson, a position you seem to find yourself in with some regularity! Indeed, almost everything that he told you, in what might be called excessive detail, one of the hallmarks of the industrious liar, was the tale he would tell the world once there were no living witnesses to refute it. Thus it would appear that the mystery assailant didn't care about the order in which his victims perished."

Bowyer uttered a filthy word. Lestrade's man gave him a sharp elbow in the ribs.

"At any rate," Holmes continued. "I examined the room Grace had occupied in a disreputable boarding-house, and found almost nothing of interest. The only fact I gleaned was that Grace had recently become a habitué of a questionable drinking establishment in the East End. This caught my attention. When a man like Grace suddenly changes his habits, he does it for a reason. But that is where the trail ended, and I could not make my way any deeper into the man's history."

Holmes paced about as he spoke, taking great pleasure, as always, in making an oration to a rapt audience.

"I then started at the other end of the problem. I questioned Mister Walpole at length about his family and business associates. The only one among them with a possible motive was his wife's brother. Walpole himself had no heirs, and were he and Mrs. Walpole to perish at the same time, a considerable fortune would be settled upon Thomas Bowyer. My suspicions were strengthened by the fact that Bowyer had been on holiday in France for two weeks, and was expected to return to England very soon. Bowyer had never taken such a holiday before. It was plain that he wished to establish an unshakable alibi.

"I was certain of my surmises, but had nothing in the way of proof. Bowyer returned from the Continent on schedule, shocked and dismayed, no doubt, to find his sister and brother-in-law alive and well.

"It was pure luck that the first attempt was unsuccessful. Had Mister Walpole not felt in need of a glass of milk when he did, things might have taken a much darker turn. And now the originator of the plot had been put on notice. He could bide his time for a little while, and find the proper moment eventually. For my client, it was a situation that could not be borne. We needed to force Bowyer's hand.

"To do that, we had to present him with an immediate threat to his ambitions. What form could it take? Were his sister to disgrace herself publicly and be divorced by her husband, Bowyer's hope of inheriting anything would be forever ended. After much thought and discussion, we settled upon the course of action that Mrs. Walpole and I carried out. She was not absolutely convinced of her brother's guilt, but knowing him as she does; she had to admit that it was possible. Subsequent events must have seemed both a curse and a godsend to Bowyer. It gave him the raw materials for a plausible death scenario, but also imposed a deadline."

"What was his motive?" I asked. "Financial gain, yes, but he had money of his own. Which, I of course understand, would not preclude his wanting still more. But why now? Why take such risks?"

"He had gambling debts," Holmes said gravely. "The oldest and most tedious of murder motives, next to sexual jealousy. I made my inquiries, and learned much. Bowyer was an exceedingly poor and utterly obsessed whist player. He had received a considerable inheritance from his father, and was for many years quite profligate with it. He recently reached a crisis point. He had enough money to continue the routine to which he had grown accustomed for no more than six or eight months. And he owed every penny of it and more to individuals who would not hesitate to resort to grievous bodily harm, or worse, to collect the debt. He had fallen in with some exceedingly bad companions—at the Bagatelle Card Club, I believe—and he had to do something quickly. It occurred to him that the easiest course was to eliminate his brother-in-law, whose sole heir was Stella, and his sister, preferably in that order.

"I suggested a stratagem to Mr. and Mrs. Walpole. They agreed to it, and we staged our little drama. I was arrested and taken to Dorset Street. But I had taken Lestrade into my confidence already, and my surreptitious release was soon arranged. That cell is currently occupied by an actor made up to resemble me. And, of course, Sergeant Perkins was delighted to be brought into the scheme."

Holmes eyed the prisoner coldly. "Bowyer would be afraid to act so long as I was at liberty. But act he must, and be sure of the result this time. He was rather clever in his way. Clever enough to know that he would require a bit of help. I represented a danger to him, untenable though my position relative to his sister seemed to be. He must act while I was still safely locked away. He returned to the place where he had first met his failed assassin, which he had learned of from some of his gambling connections, and made further inquiries. This time, he was provided with a plan and the means to carry it out."

Holmes turned to Lestrade and said, "Have a good look at the revolver you got off of him, Inspector, and unless I'm in error, you will find the name, or the initials, of Mister Townshend Walpole somewhere on the barrel or the grip. Further, you will find that the engraving has been done very recently, though someone will have taken pains to make it appear otherwise, creating the impression that Walpole had owned the weapon for some time."

Lestrade nodded.

"Bowyer's plan was to inject his sister and brother-in-law with the poison," Holmes continued, "so they would cause him no trouble while he staged a murder-suicide. Given the couple's recent and very public difficulties, no one would question it, and Mister Thomas Bowyer would soon find himself in possession of another fortune to squander."

"But, Holmes," said I. "In this murder-suicide scenario, the sister would of necessity have died first."

"Well, it really wouldn't have mattered, since Walpole had no other heirs. The estate would ultimately have gone to Bowyer, though there might have been something of a tangle in the courts. He would have preferred to avoid anything that might invite additional scrutiny. Undoubtedly, Bowyer would have arranged things so that his sister lingered awhile after her husband was unequivocally dead. A smaller dose of the poison for her, coupled with a grave but not immediately fatal gunshot wound, probably in the throat, to prevent her making any problematical remarks, would have served."

"Diabolical," I said, as Lestrade scowled blackly at the prisoner.

"An interesting word," said my friend, fixing Bowyer, who had stood sullen and silent throughout Holmes' discourse, with his penetrating gaze. "Is our friend here capable of planning such a master stroke? What of it, Bowyer? You don't look the type to me. Nothing to say? Probably the wisest course you could take at this stage."

Holmes turned back to me. "Lying to you about the murder attempt for no good reason, Watson, was a capital mistake on Mister Bowyer's part. One that his mysterious patron would not have committed and would not countenance in a subordinate." He whirled back upon the handcuffed criminal. "Anything to say about that, Mister Bowyer?"

"I've no idea what you're talking about," he said defiantly, though I was sure I saw a glimmer of fear in his hooded eyes.

"Oh, of course not," said Holmes, nodding. "Leave him out of it, then. Your life may be preserved, if not your liberty."

"Excuse me," said Lestrade, scratching his head. "What is this about a patron?"

Holmes was silent for a moment. A significant glance passed between him and Thomas Bowyer.

"I was speaking metaphorically, Inspector," said my friend with a shrug. "The Spirit of Evil. The Devil, if you will. I think Mister Bowyer here has learned a very expensive lesson about his own limitations. I fancy he is now prepared to take full responsibility for his crimes, rather than plead the influence of some sinister bogey-man, eh?"

Bowyer would not meet my friend's gaze. He stared at the floor and spoke not another word.

"Have the contents of that syringe analyzed, Lestrade," Holmes went on, "and you will find some lethal compound that is difficult or impossible to identify in a post-mortem examination. Potassium chloride is common in such cases, but you may find something a bit more exotic here. As for where Bowyer obtained it, you shall have to ask him. Appearances to the contrary, I am not omniscient, Inspector."

❖ ❖ ❖

After Bowyer had been taken away, I was finally able to meet Townshend and Stella Walpole, who had remained in a small room, under police guard, until any danger had passed.

Walpole was a cheerful, gregarious fellow, as unlike the cold brute described to me by Bowyer as the sun is unlike the moon. I learned later that the man's finances were in excellent shape.

Receiving Holmes and myself in his study, he wrung our hands warmly and professed his sincere gratitude. Mrs. Walpole, who was also present, was an extraordinarily attractive young woman, with a magnificent head of reddish-blonde hair and arresting green eyes. The photographs I had seen of her did not, could not, do her justice.

"Not at all," said Holmes modestly. "You owe no more to me than you do to your desire for a glass of milk in the night. For want of a nail..."

"Be that as it may," said Walpole, "you have my undying gratitude."

Holmes made a slight bow. "I assure you, sir, it was my... pleasure."

I could not help noticing that, although he was speaking to Mr. Walpole, Holmes was looking at the man's wife as he spoke those words.

"It is too bad that your brother has turned so wrong, my dear," said Walpole, placing an arm around her shoulders. She took his free hand in hers and smiled sadly. The affection between them seemed both unfeigned and unequivocally mutual.

Stella Walpole sighed and said, "Perhaps I should have seen it coming, Town. He was always greedy, and seemed to have little or no regard for the rights and feelings of others. Still, I would never have thought him capable of such an outrage as this."

"He might never have been," said Holmes, "had he not come under the influence of evil company. Be thankful that the only death involved in this business was that of the hired killer."

"Though the tidings are sad," said she, "I thank you from the bottom of my heart for coming to our aid... Mister Holmes. I am glad I thought to call upon you." There was something in the air between Holmes and Mrs. Walpole, but its exact nature was not clear to me.

"Think nothing of it, Mrs. Walpole," my friend replied, his voice betraying no emotion.

"Of course," said Townshend Walpole, "your fee will be paid promptly, and with something extra for a job well done. Oh, do not demur, Mister Holmes, I must insist upon it. Now, is there anything further that I may do for you?"

"Well," replied Holmes, "since you mention it, it is my custom to collect small mementoes from clients who have benefited by my efforts. I wonder if I might trouble you for a copy of that photograph of you and Mrs. Walpole that hangs on your wall there."

At this, I smiled inwardly; I knew full well that Holmes practiced no such custom.

One evening some weeks later, I dropped in at 221-B and found Holmes in his rooms. Soon we were seated on either side of the fireplace with drinks and cigars. Holmes' fall from grace had been exposed for what it was, and all was once again right with the world. We discussed the case, and I asked him about the singular stratagem he had devised.

"Like myself," Holmes said, "Mrs. Walpole once considered a career on the stage. As far as Bowyer was concerned, I had met his sister during the course of my investigation, and become infatuated with her, but it may interest you to learn that she and I in fact knew one another many years ago."

"You don't say," I replied innocently.

"I do. We appeared together in The Tempest. Her Ariel was sheer perfection."

"She didn't play Miranda?"

"No," said Holmes. "She was quite good at certain male roles, particularly the more fey and ethereal ones. I myself essayed the part of Caliban. That production is among my fonder memories, Watson. Miss Bowyer, as she was then, was a joy to work with. And I quite enjoyed our 'curtain call' in the middle of Baker Street the other evening. I daresay we would both receive good reviews were we to enact that little drama upon the stage."

"You did receive a review of sorts," I said. "Your pièce de résistance struck poor Mrs. Hudson as quite genuine. As I mentioned before, she gave me a most vivid and detailed account. I would not hesitate to pay a shilling or two to see it. Tell me something, though. Mrs. Hudson said that when you kissed Mrs. Walpole after you got out of the cab, it went on for upwards of three minutes. I should think a quick peck would have served your purposes well enough. I have remarked before upon your penchant for the dramatic, but was it absolutely necessary for you to make such a production of it?"

Holmes looked at me with no expression whatsoever on his face, and blandly said, "No, my dear fellow. It was not necessary at all."

He fell silent and his face remained a blank. I smiled, then laughed, wondering just what had passed between "Ariel" and "Caliban" all those years ago, and what sort of experience Holmes had drawn upon to lend such verisimilitude to his recent performance.

Perhaps Mary's insight was superior to mine after all. It occurred to me then that Holmes was anything but the cold, logical thinking machine he professed to be. That was one facet of his personality, to be sure, but there was also a deeply sensitive and artistic, even romantic, component that he never bothered to suppress or hide. And these two sides of his character, which one might at first suppose to be polar opposites, forever in conflict, actually worked together in perfect harmony. Curious that I had never seen that as clearly as I did now. I'd been taking him at his word, rather than at face value.

And it was at that very moment that I noticed a curious new addition to the decor at 221-B. In a small gilt frame propped up on the mantelpiece was the photograph of Mr. and Mrs. Townshend Walpole. Or half of it, at any rate. Holmes had evidently cut or folded the portrait in half, so that Stella Walpole alone occupied the frame.

I refrained from commenting upon it.

"And what of the other man we saw in the cellar of that house?" I asked. "The one who provided Bowyer with his murder tools?"

My friend sat back in his chair, his eyes fixed on some distant point in time and space that only he could see.

"What, indeed?" he said, in a strange, dreamy voice. "To all appearances, he is an ordinary academic, a humble professor of mathematics. That is all anyone knows, and I cannot prove anything more. But I think, Watson, that he may be in the process of setting up a very unique business of his own.

"Some years ago, you may recall, the idea of a consulting detective was quite a novelty. I saw the skepticism in your eyes when I informed you that I was the world's first practitioner of the trade. But, I think you will admit, I have more than proven my mettle, and created a respectable demand for my services among the police and the public alike."

"Of course, Holmes."

"I have been successful, my dear Watson, thanks in no small part to your own efforts. And success always spawns imitation. That being the case, it was only a matter of time before some enterprising soul made use of my principles on the other side of the law."

"A consulting criminal?"

Holmes nodded. "If you like. Our curious friend is building his trade, and he is devilishly clever at it. Were we to go to that house and confront him, we would find that he had removed every trace of his nefarious activities. If pressed, I do not doubt that he would produce a perfectly plausible and innocent explanation for the activities you and I observed. He might even deny it outright, and how could we prove otherwise?"

Holmes sat for a few moments with closed eyes and furrowed brow. I thought I detected the hint of a smile playing about his lips.

"He is operating under a false name," he resumed at length, "and no doubt has one or two other aliases prepared that he may quickly assume in an emergency."

"How can you know that?" I asked.

"Because it is what I would do. And I should prefer that he not bolt just yet. I left him out of the account that I gave to Lestrade. I shall keep an eye on him, and see what I may learn about his true identity and curriculum vitae. I made a very discreet inquiry of his landlady and his neighbors there in the house. Where he came from, nobody knows. He gives his name as 'Jay Ires Marmot,' an obvious fiction. The gentleman, it seems, is an army coach, a professor of mathematics. He has resided in that house for two months, during which time he has received a series of the most curious 'pupils.' 'Suspicious characters,' the landlady called them, and I could not help but think of your reaction to my motley succession of visitors during our first days in these rooms.

"At any rate, Bowyer remained mute about this man, denying any knowledge of him. He admitted to hiring the original assassin, but went no further than that. Since a creature like Bowyer cannot be motivated by honor, I conclude that he was impelled by fear. That sinister old man is not one to be trifled with, it seems."

"Well," I said, "at least Bowyer will not escape prosecution for his own crimes."

"That depends upon your point of view," my friend replied. "You haven't heard? No, it has not appeared yet in the public press. Bowyer hanged himself in his cell. I've had a wire from Lestrade."

"Dead?"

"Very much so."

I shook my head. "Not too surprising, I suppose. He may have been a scoundrel, but he came from a good family. He would have had a hard road ahead of him. But... do you think it happened that way, Holmes? Or do you think someone else got to him and..?"

Holmes shrugged. "Impossible to say. There was no doubt that he did the deed himself. As for possible influence from outside, we do know that he received a visit from a crony of his the evening before he was found dead. They prayed together, the warder said."

"Was the visitor a clergyman?"

Holmes gave a harsh laugh. "Hardly. He was an individual called Colonel Sebastian Moran. He is outwardly respectable, but there is talk. In addition to his military career, he has distinguished himself as a big-game hunter. He is also an inveterate gambler, Watson, a great devotee of gaming tables everywhere. That is how he came to make Bowyer's acquaintance.

"Moran is a man of considerable means who seems to live beyond even those. But no serious breath of scandal has thus far ever touched him. His visit may have been innocent. Or it may have been connected to the man in that cellar. Is Moran a confederate of his? Did the Colonel guide Bowyer in that man's direction to begin with? Did he arrange the first murder attempt? Was it he who suggested murder to Bowyer in the first place? Was a threat or a sinister promise passed along to Bowyer in his cell? There is no way to know any of that now. The Colonel was questioned, and revealed nothing, of course. But I fancy that he will bear watching."

My friend leaned forward in his chair, his hands clasped before him, eyes glittering. "I have developed certain suspicions, Watson, and made further and exceedingly discreet inquiries. All of this has led me to form an interesting hypothesis. You once wondered aloud how it would have been had I turned my talents to crime. This man may be the answer to that question. If he is left unhindered, he will go far in his chosen field. I believe he has great ambitions. Why, he might even have it in him to unite many of the disparate factions of London's criminal underworld into a single organization. Imagine it, Watson!"

I shuddered. "A ghastly prospect, Holmes."

"Not necessarily, old fellow," said my friend with a smile. He seemed strangely delighted. "Perhaps 'tis a consummation devoutly to be wished. Instead of rushing about putting out small, unrelated brush-fires here and there, the police could swiftly catch all the fish, from the minnows to the sharks, in a single net; if you'll forgive a dreadfully mixed metaphor. I shall keep an eye on our sinister professor and see what develops."

"I stand ready to aid you in any way that I can, Holmes."

He looked at me and for a moment, his piercing grey eyes softened with emotion. "And I thank you for that, Watson. But you have a wife now, and a growing medical practice. Mrs. Watson would not thank me for placing you in jeopardy, nor would I be able to live with myself should you come to harm through me. No, you mustn't protest, I won't listen. Put that man out of your mind. I shall not mention him again until his career has been brought to a close."

"Holmes, really, I..."

"Oh, very well, Watson," said he with mild asperity. "I promise you, should events reach a crisis point, and should your invaluable assistance be required, I won't hesitate to call upon you. Does that satisfy you?"

I allowed that it did, though I knew Holmes would follow his own course, regardless of any promises I might extort from him.

He was silent for several minutes after that. Finally, as though in response to some silent command, he stood erect and removed his jacket. Draping it over the back of the chair, he reached into an inner pocket and withdrew his revolver. Handling it gingerly, as though it were hot enough to scald his fingers, he walked to his desk, opened a drawer, and, with a look of mild disgust on his face, put it away.

Then his features softened, and he turned and lifted his violin from the sideboard where it had been carelessly placed.

"I think we have had enough talk of violence and murder for one evening, Watson," he said, tucking the Stradivarius under his chin and lifting his bow. "What say I entertain you with an interesting little air that only recently came to my attention? It is of uncertain provenance, but I believe it to be the work of Niederhauser, a Swiss composer who lived near Meiringen. He claimed to draw inspiration from the sounds of nature. In this particular passage, one does seem to hear echoes of the famous waterfall at Reichenbach. Have you ever been there, Watson? No? Well, one day, perhaps."

He began to play a stirring air that was both majestic and melancholy at once much like the man himself, I reflected. I settled back in my chair and closed my eyes, content and grateful to be enjoying a peaceful evening in the company of my most remarkable friend.

The End

A Long Ago Dream

I don't recall when I first became aware of Sherlock Holmes, but I was given a copy of the complete stories when I was eight years old. I already knew who Holmes was, of course, via movies and comics. The original stories were a bit much for the eight-year-old me. At least fifty percent of what I read went over my head, but I plugged away at it for years, until my ability to read and comprehend was equal to my fascination with the Great Detective and his world.

When I was twelve, I decided to try my hand at a Holmes pastiche. I think I managed a single handwritten page before I gave up. I didn't have much confidence in my ability to do it, nor did I have much ability in which to have any confidence. There the matter lay for 38 years.

I thought about it occasionally over the years, and even took one or two half-hearted stabs at it that never yielded more than three or four rather embarrassing pages; the kind of thing you do not file away, but dispose of as thoroughly as you can. I concluded that my ability was not equal to the task. Having finished all the Conan Doyle stories when I was young, and re-read them countless times, I started in on the pastiches. The first one I read was "The Seven Percent Solution" by Nicholas Meyer, and went on to devour as many more as I could find. And they are legion. I don't know how many I've read at this point, but it must be up in the triple digits. Some were good, some were bad, some were indifferent. All of them reinforced my conviction that I couldn't pull it off.

Last year, I finished up a novel called "Vionna and the Vampires," in which the villain is Professor James Moriarty, who has become Lord of the Undead. My Protagonists, Vionna Valis and Mary Jane Kelly, receive help from a ghostly Sherlock Holmes. At one point, Vionna finds herself mysteriously transported to 221-B Baker Street in the year 1888, where she shares a harrowing adventure with the Great Detective. I introduced that plot device mainly because I thought it would be fun to write a Sherlock Holmes story from Vionna's quirky point of view.

And I was right. It was fun. So much so that I started once again thinking seriously about doing a traditional Conan Doyle-style pastiche. My Vionna story had all of the elements one expects to find in a Holmes tale: Inspector Lestrade, Mrs. Hudson, malodorous chemical experiments, brilliant deductions, the works. I realized that I knew the character intimately, that he and his surroundings had been a large part of my mental life almost as far back as I could remember. And now I had done a Sherlock Holmes story. That boosted my confidence and resurrected my ancient ambition. If I could write one as Vionna, surely I could shift gears and put myself in the shoes of Dr. John H. Watson.

This time, I believed I could pull it off. I approached Ron Fortier with the idea, and he decided to give me a shot at a spot in an upcoming volume of the "Sherlock Holmes, Consulting Detective" series.

"The Adventure of the Other Man" is the result. In it, we see hints that the notoriously reticent Holmes has some sort of a past, but we don't learn too much about it. We see the beginning of what will become the most significant conflict of his life. We see his friendship with Watson survive another bit of chicanery on Holmes' part.

And, most significantly from my point of view, we see that my twelve-year-old self was right after all. It just took him a few decades to get it done.

CHUCK MILLER was born in Ohio, lived in Alabama for many years, and now resides in Norman, Oklahoma. He is a Libra whose interests include monster movies, comic books, music and writing. He holds a BA in creative writing from the University of South Alabama.

He is the creator/writer of TALES OF THE BLACK CENTIPEDE, THE INCREDIBLE ADVENTURES OF VIONNA VALIS AND MARY JANE KELLY, THE BAY PHANTOM CHRONICLES, and THE MYSTIC FILES OF DOCTOR UNKNOWN JUNIOR. He has also written stories featuring such classic characters as Jill Trent: Science Sleuth, Armless O'Neil, The Griffon, and others.

Miller received the BEST NEW WRITER OF 2011 Award from Pulp Ark. His first novel, the critically acclaimed "Creeping Dawn: The Rise of the Black Centipede" was published in 2011 by Pro Se Press. The second installment in the Black Centipede series, "Blood of the Centipede" was published in 2012. "Black Centipede Confidential" is slated for release in 2013. Also due in 2013 is "Vionna and the Vampires," the first installment of "The Incredible Adventures of Vionna Valis and Mary Jane Kelly."

http://theblackcentipede.blogspot.com/

Sherlock Holmes

in

"The Adventure of the Stolen Centennial"

By
Aaron Smith

herlock Holmes had always been immune to the tears of a woman. On occasions when that particular form of emotional expression occurred, it was most fortunate that Holmes, and not I, was the leading member, so to speak, of our partnership, for my resistance to tearful persuasion had never been of as much strength as his.

Miss Pamela Douglas, a young lady of perhaps twenty-one or twenty-two years of age, and a quite attractive one at that, had come to Baker Street on a particular spring morning to seek the advice of Sherlock Holmes. Mrs. Hudson had announced her and admitted her to the apartment which Holmes and I shared. Once introductions were made and Mrs. Hudson had made her exit, I implored Miss Douglas to be seated. Almost immediately upon her settling into her chair, streams of tears began to run down her cheeks.

I acted on instinct. A lovely young lady, obviously distraught, was seated only a few feet from my position. As I would have done in any similar circumstances, I stood, walked to a place directly in front of Miss Douglas, and offered her my handkerchief, which she accepted and used to begin wiping her eyes.

"Miss Douglas," I began to say, making sure to keep my voice at a gentle, soothing tone much as how I would speak to a frightened patient or the mourning relative of a patient whom I had been unable to save, "please try to regain your calm. I assure you that Mr. Holmes and I shall do everything we can to solve whatever problem is troubling you so."

Before I was able to continue and before the weeping young woman was able to reply, the only other person present let out a sharp cry of protest.

"Watson, stop!" Holmes shouted. "Do not make any guarantees, do not offer any promises that you are not certain can be kept. These tears and this gentleness will do us no good. What we must do is learn precisely what business it is that has brought Miss Douglas to see us on this day! Please, Watson, return to your chair and let us hear what our visitor has to tell us."

I did as Holmes asked and took my seat. Holmes' stern words seemed to have snapped Miss Douglas out of her fit and she now looked at him with readiness and the willingness to speak apparent on her face.

"I should begin by telling you something about myself I suppose," the young lady began, but Holmes once again interjected.

"You may omit the facts that you live on the west end of London, possess adequate if not spectacular skill with a typewriter, shared lodgings up until recently with an older relative of the male gender, adore the color blue, and were somewhat injured by a fall from a horse when you were approximately thirteen years of age. All those things are already known to me and I would prefer that you proceed directly to the details pertinent to your reasons for coming to see me."

Miss Douglas looked shocked and coughed softly once or twice. I, of course, had grown used to Holmes' bursts of deductions though I was still at a loss as to how he had managed to learn those facts with a few glances in the young lady's direction. When the surprise had passed, our visitor began to speak.

"The relative you mentioned, Mr. Holmes, was my grandfather, and he is recently deceased, having passed on only two days ago. That is the reason I have come to see you."

"Our sympathies on your loss, Miss Douglas," I said, polite instinct initiating the statement. Holmes, who had never been servant to such habits, said nothing but waited for Miss Douglas to continue, which she did after nodding to me in response to my acknowledgement of her state of mourning.

"My grandfather had been my sole living relative for the past five years, since my father's weak heart finally sent him to the Lord's kingdom. My mother died of an illness when I was a small child. My grandfather, my father's father, Cyril Douglas was his name, was much older than you might expect the grandfather of a woman of my age to be, for he married and sired my father rather late in life."

"And how old was he when he died this past week, Miss Douglas?" Sherlock Holmes asked.

"Ninety-nine years of age," was the reply, spoken in a tone that showed some pride in her grandfather's great longevity.

I was quite shocked by the number she stated and expressed my surprise aloud. "My word! To reach such an advanced age is quite a rarity! Tell me, Miss Douglas: was he in good health for most of that long life?" As I asked, I glanced at Holmes, hoping he did not too sternly disapprove of my medical curiosity causing me to interrupt. He gave a slight nod to indicate that my asking the question was not inappropriate.

"He was, Dr. Watson, indeed he was. He did suffer from some of the common infirmities of old age. His teeth were not his own and his nearsightedness was obvious when not wearing his spectacles and his bones tended to creak and knock when he walked at his slow, cane-aided

"Ninety-nine years of age."

pace, but he had his appetite and his sense of humor and was a happy old man in all ways."

"Most impressive," I said, clapping my hands together once.

"Of what then," Holmes asked as he once again silenced me with a raised hand, "did your grandfather die, Miss Douglas?"

"The doctor would tell you, as he told me, that Grandfather's heart ceased its work as a heart is wont to do at such an age, but I do not believe that for one moment!"

"I see," said Holmes. "And what is it, Miss Douglas, that causes you to doubt the judgment of a professional in the field of medicine?"

"A promise," she said, and as those two words left her mouth I glanced over at Holmes and saw him sigh, for Holmes had little patience for flights of fancy in the minds of women, particularly when they wasted his time. But Holmes said not a word; he allowed Miss Douglas to continue.

"You see, Mr. Holmes, Grandfather was quite adamant in his desire to be the first of our family and, indeed, the first among our social circle, to achieve the goal of living an entire century. The idea first came upon him when he celebrated his ninety-fifth birthday and he often boasted of his intention. In fact, a great party was being planned for the day he acquired the prize of such a number of years upon the Earth. He had put aside a sum of money for the occasion, had promised to buy me the most splendid gown he could afford so I'd be properly attired on that day, and his closest friends, although he'd reached a stage where those nearest him were in most cases the children of old friends, were all to be invited to the affair. It was to be the happiest day of his life, for he was to achieve something unheard of among all those many people he had encountered in his time."

"Hmmmph," Holmes grunted.

"If I may ask," I said, "how close did your grandfather come to reaching his hundredth birthday?"

"He had only a single month to go," Miss Douglas revealed, and once again lost control of her emotions as the rivers of tears resumed.

"Has he been buried yet?" I asked.

"The funeral is to be held tomorrow morning."

I looked in Holmes' direction. "Perhaps we should examine the body, Holmes."

"Yes, Watson," said Holmes, "I agree. Where is the body of your grandfather now, Miss Douglas?"

"At the undertaker's firm near to where I live," Miss Douglas answered.

"Then we shall go there at once!" Holmes said. "Fetch our coats and your bag, Watson. Miss Douglas, you should not accompany us on this errand. Return to your home and Dr. Watson and I will meet you there when we have finished what we must do."

Miss Douglas nodded. She reached into her bag, produced a card upon which was printed her address, and handed it to Holmes. "Thank you both," she said.

Holmes called for Mrs. Hudson to see our guest out.

❖ ❖ ❖

On the carriage ride to the undertaker, I questioned Holmes about the observations he had made when Miss Douglas had first arrived in our company.

"Watson," he said, "If you would only learn to use your eyes and ears and let them guide you, the things you'd discover would astound you! It was all quite simple.

"Her manner of speaking is what led me to believe she had lived on the west end of London for most of her life. Each region of the city has its own particular accent, Watson, although one who has travelled widely, as you have, for example, shows a certain alteration of speech due to the unconscious influence of encountering others of different areas of origin. Miss Douglas's accent is pure West End, meaning that she has lived in the area of her birth for all of her two decades of life. Although we now dwell here on Baker Street, which is, of course, in the western part of the city, we have both seen enough of the rest of England to have lost some of the peculiarities of speech that would immediately mark us as natives of this section to any observer astute enough to hear such signs in our words.

"As for who she has lived with, Miss Douglas's attire is conservative, that of one who dresses to please an older generation, modest and a bit quaint, not the modern fashions of a young married woman or one who is in the process of trying to attract a husband. Obviously she lived with an older relative. Had this older relative been her mother or grandmother, her clothing would be more neatly pressed and laundered, for older women tend to take more time with such things. While Miss Douglas is by no means shabbily dressed, she does not take the care with her clothing that a more matronly woman with lifelong habits might. This told me that her housemate was of the male gender. Her infatuation with the color blue was apparent from the shade of not only her hat, but her gloves and coat.

"A quick glance at the young woman's hands showed me calluses, noticeable though not severe, in places that correspond to frequent use of a typewriter, though probably for the writing of occasional letters rather than of the constancy of one who types professionally on a daily schedule.

"And I am surprised, Watson, that you did not take note of the small scar on the left cheek of our visitor. It is not an ugly, disfiguring mark at all, but a slight imperfection, faded now, but still visible. It looked to me like the remnant of a wound made by falling from a height of several feet and striking the face on some small twig or pebble. This I guessed to be the result of a fall from a horse. Having gambled on the possible source of the scar, I then judged by the degree to which the old injury has faded that the incident occurred the better part of a decade ago. There; I believe I have covered all my immediate observations."

"Splendid, Holmes," I said. Even after many years with the detective, the speed and accuracy with which he made his discoveries continued to impress me.

The short journey over, our carriage stopped in front of a building marked "J. Francis, Funerary Preparations and Caskets."

Inside the shop, we were greeted by Mr. Francis, a tall, stout man with one eye that floated haphazardly in its socket as if it could not decide upon what to focus. His other eye, the good one, looked straight into mine as he shook my hand.

"Aye, feel free to do what you must, Doctor. The old man's got till tomorrow to go into the ground. I'll have a rest while you do what you've come to do."

Mr. Francis led us down a set of stairs to the colder, subterranean room where he dealt with the dead. As Holmes and I approached the table whereupon rested the body of Cyril Douglas, the undertaker left, closing the door behind him.

I removed the shroud from the corpse and began the examination. I had never before encountered the body of a person who had survived nearly a century. For a man of science, it was a noteworthy experience.

"What have you to say on the condition of the body, Watson?" Holmes asked. He stood a short distance from me and puffed on his pipe, waiting for me to finish my inspection before he approached the cadaver.

"Aside from his obviously advanced age," I said, "I see nothing of interest, Holmes. I detect no signs of foul play, no wounds or other marks. But…look here!"

"What is it?"

"His false teeth, Holmes, seem to have been constructed of cheap wood!

These teeth would not be fit for grazing on grass, let alone chewing meat or bread."

"It is known," Holmes told me, "for undertakers to sometimes steal the teeth of the dead and sell them, and to replace them, assuming that the relatives of the deceased will have no reason to examine the mouth prior to burial."

The detective tore open the door and called out, "Mr. Francis, come here!"

The undertaker entered and Holmes, not one to remain quiet and docile when he'd caught the scent of a thief, grabbed him firmly by the shoulders.

"It would do you well, sir, to give us the part of this man's body, artificial though it may be, which you have so rudely taken from him!"

Francis stuttered a bit, but soon dropped the pretense of not knowing what Holmes referred to. Within moments, Holmes had in his hand the proper set of porcelain teeth which had recently graced the jaws of Cyril Douglas.

"Look here, Watson!" Holmes shouted. "The backs of the lower front teeth are stained with spots of blue! Do you understand what this means?"

I looked closely at the teeth and saw the stains of which Holmes spoke. "Lighter than the remains of blueberry pie," I observed. "What do you suppose it to be?"

"Watson," Holmes instructed, "go and have tea with Miss Douglas. Entertain her with trivial conversation for the next hour. I must return to Baker Street and engage in certain methods of chemical analysis. When I have the results, I shall join you in the company of our young client. As for you, Mr. Francis, you will make no extra profit from this man's burial. You may carry out the rest of the preparations. Consider yourself fortunate that I do not inform the police of your attempt at theft!"

And with those stern words, Sherlock Holmes ran from the cellar with the porcelain teeth in his hand.

❖ ❖ ❖

Miss Douglas proved to be a polite, considerate host. We settled in her parlour and drank tea. Her home was a small, neat, modest flat in which I could see the accumulation of objects acquired over the very long life of her grandfather.

"An odd assortment of objects, isn't it, Dr. Watson?" Miss Douglas said as she noticed my glancing back and forth across the room.

"Yes," I said. "I see the clutter of an old man's life, but accented by the presence of a woman's habits of cleanliness."

"My grandfather," Miss Douglas said, with a sweeping gesture of her hand, "travelled much of the world during the first half of his life. A soldier for many years, he saw the Americas, both north and south, as well as portions of the African continent and the Arab nations, not to mention most of the various regions of Europe. He collected souvenirs of his journeys and adamantly refused to part with any of them!"

I could see the great range of locations from which the objects of which we spoke had been acquired. There was a ceremonial mask that I suspected had been used by one of the tribes indigenous to what is now the United States; the head of an African gazelle mounted on the wall; a jar of currency among which I noticed the money of Mexico, Chile, Russia, China, and several other nations. Cyril Douglas had indeed lived a long and interesting life and I somewhat regretted having learned of him only after his death, for I would have liked to have talked with him and heard him tell of his experiences around the world.

As I pondered that, the door to the parlour was suddenly flung open from the outside. Miss Douglas gave a start and I turned to see the source of the intrusion.

It was Sherlock Holmes, which did not surprise me, bursting into the room without knocking, rudely marching in and flopping down into the chair opposite Miss Douglas's seat and several feet to the right of mine.

"Miss Douglas," Holmes said, his voice colored with the excitement that always accompanied the true beginning of a new case, "you were right in coming to see me, for your instincts in this matter have proven correct. Your grandfather did not die of his advanced age. He was, in fact, most certainly murdered!"

"Holmes!" I shouted, wishing that my friend should choose his words more carefully and deliver the news gently, but I was too late.

Miss Douglas let out a little shriek and fainted. Luckily, she was already seated.

When the horrified, grieving young woman had her senses back and we all had fresh cups of tea, Holmes began to explain what he had discovered during his brief return to Baker Street.

"Cyril Douglas was poisoned," Holmes said. "When I found those light blue stains on his false teeth, I had little doubt. But I could not be certain until I had conducted the proper tests. Your grandfather, Miss Douglas, died due to the ingestion of a rare chemical substance known in its land of origin as the Blue Eternity."

Miss Douglas stared at Holmes, nodded, and waited for more.

"What land is that, Holmes?" I asked.

"The Blue Eternity can be found in use among some of the primitive peoples of the South American continent, Watson. It is a mixture of the juices of certain shrubs and berries that only grow in that part of the world."

"Oh no," Miss Douglas suddenly said as she heard Holmes' words, "it can't be! Not Major Bellringer! He would never do such a thing!"

The poor woman looked close to tears again, but Holmes barked mercilessly, demanding to know of whom she spoke.

"And who is Major Bellringer?"

Miss Douglas breathed deeply, calming herself, and explained.

"Eustace Bellringer is one of Grandfather's oldest friends. At ninety years of age, he had known Grandfather longer than any man still alive. The two of them served in the army many, many years ago. Grandfather was the captain at the time and Eustace Bellringer was one of his lieutenants. They spent some time together in South America, which is why you startled me so when you revealed that the poison was of that part of the world. In fact, Mr. Holmes, Major Bellringer remained in that area for many years after his army days had ended. He only returned to England in the last decade."

"Do you know, Miss Douglas," Holmes asked, "in which nations of the South American continent this man lived for most of that time?"

"I believe it was Peru, Mr. Holmes. He married a native woman and remained in her country until she passed away, at which time he returned here, to the nation of his birth."

"Ha!" Holmes grew excited in a way I had witnessed many times before. "The precise part of that region I would have guessed! Had Major Bellringer spent much time among the native peoples of Peru, surely he would have heard of the deadliness of the Blue Eternity!"

"Mr. Holmes," Miss Douglas said, still somewhat shocked, "do you really think an old friend of Grandfather's could be the murderer? Why would he do such a thing?"

"I am not yet certain that he is the guilty one," Holmes said. "But I must ask you this: when was the last time he was in the company of your grandfather?"

Miss Douglas hung her head, stared at the floor as she answered, as if she had no choice but to face the terrible truth. "He visited Grandfather on the morning of the day he died. They had tea and some sandwiches I had prepared before leaving them to their talk of old times. Major Bellringer left around noon. Grandfather passed away in the early evening."

Holmes leaned forward in his chair, looked Miss Douglas in the eyes. "Do you know the current address of Major Bellringer?"

"Yes, he lives only a mile from here."

Holmes turned to me, "Watson, send a messenger to Scotland Yard. We'll need an inspector, preferably one of the usual men: Gregson or Lestrade!"

❖ ❖ ❖

Eustace Bellringer was taken into the custody of the police by Inspector Lestrade after Holmes explained the results of the tests he had done on the porcelain teeth. Holmes and I stood and watched as Lestrade's men guided the old major into a carriage and took him away. Bellringer was frail, walking slowly and squinting as he looked around. How such an elderly man could commit such an act as poisoning an old friend was dreadful to contemplate, but he said nothing in his defense. When the constables had taken him, Holmes, Lestrade, and I stood in the entryway of his home. Miss Douglas had, at my insistence, remained in her own flat, for I did not want to subject her to any further shocks on that day.

"It seems you've caught your criminal once again, Holmes," Lestrade said, "but you haven't yet answered the question of why he'd commit such a foul deed!"

"Perhaps," Holmes responded, "the answer lies within the major's house! Lead the way, Inspector."

Lestrade marched past us, into the residence of Major Eustace Bellringer, and Holmes and I followed close behind.

The interior of Bellringer's house was quite unlike that of the Douglas flat. Bellringer had lived alone despite his advanced age, and his situation was evident by the disarray of the place. Books lay in heaps and piles and in no particular order. Wrinkled clothing was strewn about the place without care. The rooms smelled of old age and failing health. It was very much the abode of a lonely widower facing his final years in solitude. I suspected that his living in close proximity to his old friend Cyril Douglas was perhaps the one positive element of Bellringer's life after his return to London. But why then would he want to kill Douglas?

As I stood guessing at the circumstances of the major's life, Holmes had thrown himself into the task of thoroughly searching the flat's contents, running from room to room, tossing objects about, sniffing the air and mentally cataloging details that would never catch the attention of other men. Lestrade, having grown used to Holmes' eccentricities and methods over the years, stood and watched with a sly smile on his lips.

A few moments had gone by when Holmes shouted, "Watson, Lestrade, I have found it!"

The inspector and I hurried into the kitchen to find Holmes holding a small vial of blue liquid.

"And that, of course, would be the infamous jungle poison," Lestrade said.

"The Blue Eternity," Holmes confirmed, with the sort of smile that shows on the face of a man who has read of some spectacular thing and now sees it and holds it for the first time. "This, gentlemen, is one among the great variety of means man has devised over the course of history for the dark purpose of killing his fellow man!"

"So there we have it then," I said. "Bellringer took the poison with him to Douglas's house and added some to the sandwich his old friend ate."

"Thank you," Lestrade said. "We've got our murderer under lock and key, the evidence in our possession, and that's all we'll need to put the old miscreant away for the little time he's got left to him on this earth!"

The inspector snatched the vial from Holmes' hand and turned to leave.

"Inspector," Holmes said, "we still have not..."

But Lestrade would hear no more. He stalked out of the kitchen, through the other rooms of the house, and out the door. Holmes and I followed.

"We still have not ascertained Bellringer's reason for killing..." I said, but Holmes put a hand on my shoulder.

"Let him go, Watson. There are questions other than the murderer's motive that must be answered. Let Lestrade proceed. We will pursue this mystery further when I have had time to think."

❖ ❖ ❖

I returned to Baker Street at seven in the evening. Holmes and I had gone our separate ways after Lestrade had run off with the Blue Eternity. I had returned to Miss Douglas's flat to see to her well being. She was resting, having mostly recovered from the shocking revelations of the afternoon. She offered me another cup of tea, but I declined. Satisfied that she would not need my attention any more that day, I was on my way back to Holmes.

I reached our address, greeted Mrs. Hudson, and climbed the steps up to our rooms. I found Sherlock Holmes seated in his usual chair. The air was thick with the smoke of his pipe. Holmes had his eyes closed, the pipe in one hand, the other hand tightly clenched in a fist as if it was a physical manifestation of the intensity with which his mind was working. Still, even in such a forest of thought, the sharp ears of the detective noticed my approach. The eyes opened, the head turned in my direction, and he was suddenly returned to the world of sight and sound and communication.

"Watson, there are too many pieces still missing from the complete picture of this sad affair of the murdered old man!"

"Yes, Holmes, we still don't know why Major Bellringer did it. I wonder if Lestrade has made any progress in interrogating him."

"And there is more, Watson. Where did Bellringer acquire his poison? According to Miss Douglas, he returned to London ten years ago. The Blue Eternity is made of the plants of the jungles of Peru. It does not last long, certainly not for a decade, so he could not have brought it with him on his voyage home. It was either brought to him or sent to him in the recent past. But from whom did he receive this deadly package? That is the important question, Watson!"

"Shall we go back and search his home again?" I asked. It would not have been the first time Holmes and I had done such a thing in the interest of discovering the truth. "The police need not know."

But before Holmes could reply to my idea, Mrs. Hudson appeared in the doorway and we could hear heavier footsteps coming behind her.

"Inspector Lestrade, sir," Mrs. Hudson said, even as the ferret-faced policeman stomped past her.

"Thank you, Mrs. Hudson," I said.

Holmes, eager to know more, spoke before a single phrase could leave the inspector's mouth. "What have you come to tell us, Lestrade? Has Bellringer explained his motives to you?"

"The old goat won't say another word on the matter, Holmes. He admits to poisoning Douglas, but won't tell us why he did it no matter what we say. And we can't get rough with him like we'd do with a younger prisoner, for fear of breaking his brittle bones or causing his heart to quit!"

"Allow me to speak to him," Holmes said.

"I can't do that," Lestrade argued. "You know my superiors at the Yard don't always approve of your involvement in matters like this one."

"Lestrade," Holmes tried again, "surely we can make an exception to the rules. You know I can be quite persuasive. And furthermore, if you fear for the old man's health under questioning, who better to be present at the event than Dr. Watson?"

"All right, Holmes," the inspector nodded, "but if the chief of detectives tells me to send you on your way, that's precisely what I'll have to do!"

Within minutes, taking only the time needed to don our coats and hats, the three of us were off to Scotland Yard.

❖ ❖ ❖

When Lestrade admitted us to Major Bellringer's cell, we found the elderly prisoner wide awake, sitting on his cot with his eyes trained on the wall and a scowl on his face.

Holmes, moving more slowly and gently than he usually did, walked over to Bellringer and sat beside him. I stood several feet away, against the bars of the small chamber, intending to remain silent unless Holmes required my assistance. Inspector Lestrade watched from the outside.

"Have these policemen been treating you fairly, Major Bellringer?" Holmes asked.

Bellringer remained silent.

"I know they can be somewhat brutal at times," Holmes continued. "I have often thought that the chief requirement at Scotland Yard is that an applicant must be a large boy who has forgotten to grow up. But I am not one of these ruffians and will not treat you as they do. You may confide in me, sir."

Lestrade, beyond the bars, cleared his throat as he heard Holmes' insult, but a cruel glance from me quieted him. He had known Holmes long enough to understand that everything the detective did, every word he spoke, had a purpose.

Major Bellringer, after hearing Holmes' opening words, turned to his visitor and finally began to speak. His voice was dry, croaking.

"They have not beaten nor taunted me, but I would like some water."

"Lestrade!" Holmes barked. The inspector sighed, shuffled off in search of a drink for the accused.

Holmes turned his attention immediately back to Eustace Bellringer. "The inspector reports that you have admitted to the poisoning of Mr. Cyril Douglas. Is that so?"

"That I did."

"You must have had a reason, Major, for killing a man you had known for more than a half-century."

"I did, but I will not speak of it, not to you or to any man."

"Then surely you will hang for it!"

"Let them hang me. How many more years do you expect I have left? I'm an old man. If they rob me of my few final seasons, so be it. I am quite prepared."

"But if you are resigned to death, Major Bellringer, then what have you to lose by revealing the motive behind this murder?"

"I cannot say."

"Then you fear for the safety of others if you tell the whole story!"

Bellringer was silent then, and he hung his head, as if ashamed. Holmes, seeing that he had struck a nerve, pressed the matter.

"If it is the police you fear to tell your tale to, Major, I can assure you that nothing you wish to have kept confidential will pass from my lips to the ears of Lestrade or any other man of Scotland Yard."

"I cannot trust you."

"Major Bellringer, you seem to be an intelligent man, and I am quite often correct in judging such things. I would assume that you read the daily papers. If so, you must have heard of me and the successes I have had in many matters both public and private. I promise you my complete discretion, no matter what you tell me. Heads of state, kings and queens, admirals and generals, as well as private citizens have all trusted me with secrets of the utmost important and I have never broken any vow I have made to any of them, nor has Dr. Watson, whom I have trusted with my very life on more than one occasion. I beg of you, Major, if other lives will be in danger if you reveal certain facts to the police, then unburden your heart by telling these things to me and I shall do everything in my power to help you."

"Swear to me then, Mr. Holmes," the major said. "Swear that not an ounce of harm will come to them!"

"You have my word, Major," said Holmes. "Now say what you have to say before Lestrade returns with your water!"

"When I lived in Peru," said the major. "I had a wife, a lovely native woman. We had three sons together. One died at a young age, the second grew to be a strong, honorable man but passed away in middle age, but the third, I do not know what we did wrong, is a terrible man, a black-hearted greedy scoundrel! Eduardo is his name. Of all my sons, he, the bad one, is still living! He had a son of his own and that one gave me two beautiful great-grandchildren, little Anna and Raphael. I left them behind when I returned to England and they are now...let me think...twelve years old. They're twins, you see."

"Swear to me then, Mr. Holmes."

"Quickly, Major," Holmes insisted. "Time is running short."

"I received a letter, Mr. Holmes, several days ago, from Eduardo, informing me that he is here in London and that he has brought the twins with him, taken them from their parents and forced them to journey with him across the sea."

"For what purpose has he transported them here?" Holmes asked.

"To force my hand into this terrible crime I have committed!" Bellringer said. "My son…my only remaining son…has caused me to murder my oldest friend!"

"Because he threatened to harm your great-grandchildren if you did not poison Cyril Douglas," Holmes guessed.

Bellringer nodded sadly. "Yes, and now that the deed is done, I pray he will release those poor little ones."

"He has not?"

"Not to my knowledge, Mr. Holmes."

"Do you know where he has held them since his arrival here?"

"I do not."

"Why, Major, did your son wish you to end Cyril Douglas's life?"

"The story is too long, sir," said the major, desperation evident in his voice. "And I care not about that now, only about the lives of my great-grandchildren."

"This letter," Holmes asked, "where is it now?"

"It is still at my home, in the bottommost drawer of my desk."

"Then that is where we shall hope to find our answers, Major. Watson and I must go now. You have my word that we will do what we must for the sake of both you and your great-grandchildren. I beg of you…do not relate any of what you have told me to the police, for doing so may place those innocent children in even greater danger. Say nothing, and trust me to do my very best to help you in this matter."

With that, Sherlock Holmes stood and walked in my direction, calling, "Come, Watson!" as he passed. We hurried out, nearly bowling over the startled Lestrade as he returned with water for his elderly prisoner.

❖ ❖ ❖

Holmes barked the address of Bellringer's home at the cab driver and we were on our way.

"What do you think this is all about, Holmes?" I asked as we rode. "What could compel a man, however cruel he is, to threaten his grandchildren in order to force his father to kill a friend?"

"Let us seek real answers, Watson," Holmes said, "rather than waste time and effort on guesses. But whatever the truth may be, I strongly suspect that greed will be at the heart of it!"

I nodded. Greed seemed to be at the center of many of the matters in which Holmes and I found ourselves involved.

Upon our return to Bellringer's home, we immediately sought out the letter the major had told us of, finding it in the drawer he had indicated. I watched as Holmes took it from its wide envelope.

Holmes stared silently at the letter and finally shouted, "Watson, we will need assistance!" and, with a gesture that implied much frustration, flung the papers into the air. One page of the dozen fluttered like a feather to settle upon my outstretched palm. I examined it and saw the reason for Holmes' annoyance. The letter was written in Spanish, a language neither of us were capable of reading.

◆ ◆ ◆

A short time later, Holmes and I stood in the company of an acquaintance. After agreeing on a small price as well as a vow of discretion, we were assisted by one Fernando Ortega, an immigrant to London and now a Baker Street tobacconist. Ortega stared at the letter for many minutes before speaking.

"This letter tells a strange tale, Senor Holmes," he said. "It begins with the utmost rudeness, 'Father, you superstitious old fool, you have withheld great riches from your poor family! But you erred in leaving behind, when you went off to live out your final days in London, the diary you kept as a young man here in Peru…'"

"Ortega," Holmes interrupted, "you need not translate the letter word for word. I beg you tell us the essential facts of the document first, for I fear we have little time to act on this matter."

And so Fernando Ortega related the story that had been written as a prelude to a dire threat from a son to his father.

The writer of the letter, Eduardo Bellringer, had discovered an old journal that his father had left behind in Peru. This diary, according to the letter, contained Eustace Bellringer's account of his earliest days in South America, when he had been a young officer and fast friends with Cyril Douglas. The two men had gone off leading a patrol through the thick jungles of the region and had been ambushed by a hostile native tribe. The attack had come suddenly and most of the patrol had perished, leaving only the two officers, Bellringer and Douglas, who fled deeper into the jungle.

The two survivors came upon a village occupied by a different tribe, this one friendlier to outsiders. They were given food, rest, and shelter for several days before heading back to rejoin their company. During this time, they discovered a shrine, hidden deep in the jungle, which held idols and trinkets from some long ago civilization. These things, seen as holy relics by the native population, were sculpted from solid, flawless gold, some with jewels embedded in their surfaces.

The tribesmen warned the two Englishmen that the shrine was protected by an ancient curse and that any man who touched it would be struck down by the gods. It was at this point that Douglas and Bellringer quarreled. Bellringer, it seemed, believed that the curse may have been true (and his son called him a superstitious coward in the letter because of this), while Douglas scoffed at the idea and wanted to steal some of the gold from the shrine. In the end, Bellringer had won the argument and the two had returned to their duties with no gold or jewels in hand. Douglas, however, had made a detailed map of the shrine's location, which he, Eduardo Bellringer assumed based on the contents of the journal, may have still possessed all those decades later.

Eduardo had come to London to find out, from Cyril Douglas, what had become of the map. He had brought his two grandchildren with him as insurance that his father, the old major, would assist him. But before sending the letter, he had bribed Cyril Douglas's solicitor for information.

The last will of Cyril Douglas, it seemed, had two possible outcomes. From the description in Eduardo Bellringer's letter, it was a very strange document. There were different results specified dependent upon the age at which Mr. Douglas would die. If he lived past his hundredth birthday, everything he owned, all his property and money would go to his granddaughter Pamela. Yet, if Douglas passed from this world before reaching the centennial of his birth, while his house and its contents and any money he had accumulated would still be left to our client, a certain collection of documents would go not to Pamela, but to Eustace Bellringer.

The letter went on to include Eduardo Bellringer's assumption that the map noting the location of the Peruvian shrine of gold and jewels was among the papers that his father would receive in the event of Douglas's earlier death.

The message concluded with another harsh warning that harm would surely come to the two innocent children, Anna and Raphael, if the elder Bellringer did not do as his son insisted and take the life of his oldest friend. Below the signature were the words, as Fernando Ortega translated them to us, "What you need to do this will arrive tomorrow."

"And that," Sherlock Holmes said as Ortega read the final words, "would have been the vial of the Blue Eternity."

"What a cruel and callous scoundrel this Eduardo Bellringer is," I said, "to threaten his own grandchildren to force his father to murder an old friend!"

"Indeed, Watson," Holmes said as we left Ortega's shop. "It is, as we guessed earlier, greed that is the core of this affair."

"But why," I asked, "if indeed the map to the shrine is among those certain papers, would Cyril Douglas wish it to go to his granddaughter only if he reached the age of one-hundred? Would not he give it to her under any circumstances or else respect the wishes of the Peruvian natives and never reveal its location? What conflict went through his mind to cause him to have such an odd will made?"

"The superstitious fears of an old man," Holmes said. "Perhaps he believed in the supposed curse more than he let on to Bellringer, or at least entertained the idea that there could be some speck of truth to it. Numbers, Watson, have magical meanings in the minds of the superstitious. Reaching the age of one-hundred would be perceived as good fortune by such a man and might make him think that the ancient gods and their curse could have no effect on him. It seems that when one grows old the mind wanders in strange circles and clings to phantom reassurances and fantastic dreams. We have no way of ascertaining precisely what went through the mind of Cyril Douglas, but that approaching centennial surely meant many things to him. However, Watson, we must put aside our speculations, for now that we know the whole story, I see that we must act quickly!"

"Act in what way, Holmes?"

"Don't you see, Watson? By now, Eduardo Bellringer surely knows of his father's arrest. A man held by the police and likely to be imprisoned for murder will not soon receive the documents left to him in Douglas's will. In that case, those papers will still, despite the early death of their owner, go to Pamela Douglas. What this means, Watson, is that Eduardo Bellringer has no need to keep his grandchildren safe as insurance!"

"But Holmes, surely you don't think this man would simply discard his own grandchildren like rubbish!"

"You heard the man's words when Ortega read us the letter. Is there any cruelty you do not now imagine the fiend to be capable of? I tell you, Watson, we must find those children as quickly as we can!"

"But how can we find them when we have no idea where in London they might be?" I asked.

"We will discover a way, Watson, as we always have," Holmes said, "but there are other avenues we must also attend to. There are too many strands in this tapestry of greed for us to follow them all. We require trusted allies. I must make a closer examination of this letter if we are to find the children. You, Watson, must gather our friends. The hour is late, but we have no time to squander. Go to Lestrade and tell him I must see him at once. Then find Shinwell Johnson and bring him with you to Baker Street. I will meet you all there!"

With that, Holmes rushed off and I ran in the opposite direction.

❖ ❖ ❖

I found Inspector Lestrade about to go home for the night, but persuaded him to detour to Baker Street instead. I then got to the more difficult task of locating Shinwell Johnson.

Johnson, a former criminal who had spent two terms at Parkhurst Barracks prison, now occasionally aided us on our cases. A tough, sly man, Johnson knew his way in and out of every dark corner of London and had proven himself a valuable assistant. He had a knack for finding the right information at a crucial moment and, perhaps even more importantly, knew how to handle himself in a dangerous situation. After a few discreet questions directed toward the women who patrolled certain shadowy sections of the city, I had my answer. I hurried to the gambling den where Johnson was said to be spending his evening.

The air was heavy with tobacco smoke and cheap perfumes as I made my way through the crowd of men and woman, wary of pickpockets as I proceeded. The shuffling and slapping-down of cards was the most prominent sound of the place, the background chatter occasionally broken by a cry of either delight or disappointment. The mood was tense as it was clear in such places that violence was possible at any moment due to either excessive drink or the merest hint of an accusation of cheating. I wished to spend as little time as possible there and craned my neck to better my view of the tables and players.

I finally spotted Johnson at one of the back tables, accompanied by several large, rough looking men and a dwarf. I made my way further through the crowd so that I was within shouting distance of him and cried out, "Hey Porky! Mr. Baker wants that fifteen you owe him!"

Johnson looked up from his cards and called back to me, "Tell him he can have thirty if he can wait another day! Now shove off!"

I turned and walked out of that place, satisfied that I had accomplished my task. "Porky" was what Shinwell Johnson was called in the streets and alleys of London by those who knew him. "Mr. Baker" of course, referred to Holmes and his address. The "fifteen" which would sound like an amount of currency to anyone who heard, meant that Holmes wanted Johnson present in fifteen minutes or as soon as possible. Johnson's response told me that he could be at Baker Street in half an hour.

❖ ❖ ❖

"Not now, Mrs. Hudson! We haven't time for tea and pleasantries!" Sherlock Holmes roared as he waved the startled landlady out of the room.

We were all assembled now: Holmes, Lestrade, Shinwell Johnson, and I. Lestrade stood impatiently. Johnson and I were seated. Holmes looked at us all, his pipe in hand, and began to speak. After giving to Lestrade and Johnson a brief summary of the information we had acquired from the letter found in Major Bellringer's home, he announced, "Although I admit to being somewhat short of absolute certainty, I suspect that the two children are being held aboard a cargo vessel called the Sunbird, which is presently docked here in London."

"How can you know that, Holmes?" Lestrade shouted, incredulous as always of Holmes' seemingly miraculous deductions.

"The smell of this paper," Holmes said, snatching from the table the first sheet of the letter and holding it up for us all to see, "is of a type of oil commonly used aboard sailing ships. This led me to believe that it was written on such a vessel. Referring to various editions of the Times from the past week, I came to find that only one vessel arrived here recently after travelling directly from one of the ports of Peru. That vessel arrived two days before the death of Cyril Douglas, which we now know was a poisoning, and is scheduled to depart and return to Peru one week from today. This stay in London would give Eduardo Bellringer adequate time to fulfill his murderous mission and acquire the map he suspected would be passed to his father if Douglas did not see his hundredth birthday. As for the children still being on the Sunbird, Eduardo Bellringer is, in my estimation based on the contents of the letter, too intelligent to risk bringing the little ones into the city and possibly arousing suspicion. He is also cunning enough, I believe, to have worked out some deal with the captain of the ship so a blind eye would be turned to the kidnapping and other illegal acts."

Lestrade cleared his throat loudly, having once again been put in his place by Holmes. "All right, Holmes, I see you've had this all planned since before we arrived. What do you intend to do?"

"There are, Inspector," Holmes answered, "several fronts which must be attended to if we are to win this battle. I fear for the safety of Miss Pamela Douglas, for if Eduardo Bellringer believes that the document he seeks is now in her possession or is hidden within her home, he may pay her an unwelcome visit. Attention must also be given to Cyril Douglas's solicitor, who I now know is one Phineas Franklin. Eduardo Bellringer has already made one threatening appearance at the lawyer's office and I suspect another may be imminent. That is why I have assembled the four of us here tonight. We must divide our forces wisely and protect all parties involved in this affair."

"That's all well and good, Holmes," said Inspector Lestrade. "The rest of you can go and guard lawyers and young ladies while I go raid that ship and get those children out of harm's way! Let me round up my constables!"

"No, Lestrade!" Holmes barked. "That will not do at all."

"Blast you, Holmes," the inspector shouted back, "you haven't the right to run this case on your terms, not when innocent children are in danger. I'm the only official policeman in this room! I respect your abilities, Holmes, but I've got more right to have my say in this matter than you or a doctor or this common criminal Johnson!"

At that, Sherlock Holmes had heard enough. He put his pipe down on the mantle, strode over to Lestrade, gripped him by the shoulders and stared him straight in the eyes.

"Lestrade," Holmes said in even but forceful tones, "you are a competent policeman, but you have been doing that job, and doing it well, for so long that every aspect of your being shouts out to those who see you that that is what you are. You talk like an inspector and walk like one and the captain and crew of the Sunbird, and Eduardo Bellringer if he is aboard, would spot your kind coming from a mile away and either flee the scene or do harm to their captives before you had a chance to stop them. That ship must be approached carefully. You are not the man for that part of our task, Lestrade."

Lestrade pulled away from Holmes and sat. He waited, as did Johnson and I, for Holmes to reveal his plan.

"This," Holmes said, "is how we shall proceed. You, Lestrade, will go to the attorney, Mr. Franklin. His office and home share the same building. You will ascertain the whereabouts of the documents willed to Major Bellringer. If the papers are in a secure location such as a bank vault, you will leave them there. In either case, whether they are safe or in Franklin's office, you will remain with the man until further notice. But if you should discover that they are stored somewhere in Miss Douglas's home, you must send a message to that residence immediately.

"You, Watson, will be at the Douglas residence to receive that message should the inspector see fit to send it. You will not leave Miss Douglas until you have heard from me. Guard her well."

I nodded my understanding.

"And Watson," Holmes added. "Bring your revolver."

"Porky and I," Holmes continued, "will go to the docks and find this Sunbird. We will save those children. If they need medical attention, you will be informed, Watson. Go to your appointed stations, gentlemen!"

Lestrade and I left together. As I exited, I saw Holmes going into his bedroom and I assumed he was about to don a disguise fit for the task at hand."

❖ ❖ ❖

Miss Douglas was quite surprised to see me at so late an hour. I apologized for the intrusion and quickly explained the details of what Holmes and I had learned so far. It was evidence of the young lady's courage that her immediate reaction was concern not for her own safety but for that of the captive children.

"Those poor little ones," she said. "Do you truly believe Mr. Holmes will be able to find them?"

"I do," I assured her. "Do you recall the things he said about you when first you arrived at Baker Street early today?"

"The way he immediately seemed to know everything about me," she said. "Yes, it was impressive…and somewhat frightening!"

"Yes," I said after a laugh. "Holmes' ways can be disconcerting to those who meet him for the first time, but I suspect he gives such demonstrations to instill confidence in others that his methods are valid. I know for a fact that he does not do it merely to impress people. Information flows from the world around us and into Holmes' mind like rivers and streams to the sea, Miss Douglas. If any man can find those children, that man is Sherlock Holmes."

She smiled at my assurances then offered to brew some tea. I thanked her but declined, insisting that she try to get some rest after her long day. She retired to bed and I sat up on watch, wondering how Holmes would fare.

What was happening to my friend as I sat comfortably in Miss Douglas's home, I can only relate secondhand, based on what Holmes told me when next I saw him.

❖ ❖ ❖

Holmes had disguised himself as a man of the streets, bearded and wider of shoulder with a long scar down one side of his face. His companion, Shinwell Johnson, needed no alteration of appearance for he was already a tough and intimidating sort of man.

The pair made their way to the docks and located the Sunbird, a medium-sized cargo vessel. A lone sailor stood on deck so late in the night. Holmes called out to him, requesting permission to board. After some back and forth banter, the two visitors were admitted and managed to convince the watchman to wake the captain. Knowing Holmes, I suspect this was done with a coin or several placed in a greedy hand.

The ship's commander roused, he was soon talked into providing Holmes and Johnson passage to Peru on the upcoming journey after Holmes assured him that a fair price would be paid for such a service. Holmes had concocted a story of accusations, painting a vivid picture of him and Johnson as fearful fugitives in flight from Scotland Yard. The captain, used to dealing with the criminal class and as lustful for money as his men, instructed his two new acquaintances to hide in the hold and keep silent. They did as told, bedding down and feigning sleep. When all around them was quiet, Holmes whispered for Johnson to remain where he was but keep his ears open for a signal. Holmes, being the more agile of the two, then stealthily proceeded to leave his berth and stalk about the ship, taking care not to wake any slumbering crewmen he happened to pass.

He came upon one more sailor who was not at rest. This one, a tall man with an ear that looked as if it had been mangled in an accident of some sort, stood leaning against a closed door some distance down the corridor from where Holmes and Johnson had been told to hide.

"What's behind there?" Holmes asked in a voice altered to match his disguise.

"What do you care?" the guard responded.

"I'm hungry," said Holmes.

"We eat in the morning on the Sunbird," the guard said, "not in the middle of the night. That's how the captain wants it. Get back to your bunk!"

"I think not," said Holmes as he reached past the man and tried to push open the door.

Holmes' suspicion that something more than food was concealed in that room was confirmed by the guard's violent reaction. He shoved Holmes back and produced a knife from his belt.

Holmes, quick even with the cumbersome beard about his face and padding to make his shoulders broad, tore off his scarf and wrapped it around his hand. He stepped forward to meet the knife-wielding sailor and caught the man's hand, the scarf forming a barrier between blade and flesh, and twisted the wrist to disarm the attacker.

Both men weaponless now, Holmes' speed gave him the advantage. He plowed one fist into the guard's belly, then the other against the jaw, sending him crashing back against the inside of the ship's hull, head striking wood with a raw thud.

His foe unconscious, Holmes returned his attention to the door. He forced it open and discovered, to his delight, the sleeping bodies of two children. He crept over to them, knelt down beside where they lay in a heap of old blankets, and whispered, "Anna, Raphael, I am a friend. Do not be afraid."

The children stirred, looked up at their visitor, and, failing to understand the words he spoke, muttered something in Spanish.

Holmes could now hear, in the distance, the footsteps of approaching crewmen, probably awakened by the sounds of the scuffle. He had no time to gently rouse the children from their dreams.

"Johnson," Holmes cried out, "to me at once!"

Holmes heard Johnson shouting as he rushed down the corridor. The sound of bodies being slammed into walls and bunks shattered the night's quiet and all the Sunbird's men leapt to their feet and followed the noise to its source. Shinwell Johnson met Holmes outside the door of the small cabin and each man picked up a frightened child and carried them clumsily away with all possible haste. Through some miracle, they managed to avoid a deadly skirmish with the ship's crew and reached the deck safely. When the moonlight shone down upon them once again, Holmes, who had been armed the entire time, drew a revolver and fired a shot of warning into the air. This held the sailors back for a moment despite the captain's orders to slay the intruders. Johnson and Holmes reached the docks and ran, still burdened by the Peruvian children who now struggled against their rescuers in their confusion and fright.

A long, straight run along the docks, then a quick turn down a shadowed alley, and the four escapees from the Sunbird had managed to evade their pursuers. Holmes then doffed his false whiskers and padding so that at least one among the party would look presentable enough to convince a driver to give them transport. And so the four of them rode away from the port: two brave men and two ragged, terrified little refugees.

❖ ❖ ❖

My night at the home of Miss Douglas passed without incident. The sun was just beginning to rise when I heard a knock upon the door. I opened it to find Sherlock Holmes and the two children, each of them grasping one of the detective's hands as they shivered from the early morning chill.

A short time later, I had done a basic examination of each of the children and found them unharmed save for a few minor bruises. But they were quite hungry and so Miss Douglas set to work on breakfast. As they ate, Holmes related to me the events on the Sunbird. He had sent Shinwell Johnson off now, having no further need of his services. I was much relieved, as was Holmes, though he would never admit it, that no serious harm had come to little Anna and Raphael.

Although we had both gone without sleep, I insisted that I would be the one to make the trip to the home and office of the lawyer Franklin, to see how Lestrade's night had gone. I had merely rested while watching, while Holmes' night had involved an altercation and a desperate chase while carrying the burden of a struggling child. Before I departed, it was decided that I would send Fernando Ortega and his wife to collect the children; better that they would be kept safe by those who could understand their language, and Holmes and I trusted the Ortegas fully.

❖ ❖ ❖

I found Lestrade nearly asleep when I reached Franklin's office. Franklin, however, was wide awake, the sort of man likely to be made nervous, it

Holmes then doffed his false whiskers.

seemed, by the slightest alteration to his routine. Having a police inspector for a guard and all the potential danger that such a precaution might imply must have seemed a terrible ordeal for such a man.

The documents in question were, as Holmes had guessed they might be, locked away in the vault of a nearby bank. Nothing of an outright alarming nature had happened during the night, though Lestrade, once I had woken him fully, did report that a man had passed by on the street several times in the dark hours. Lestrade was certain it had been the same man, tall and thin and wearing a long coat with a scarf wrapped around his face. We both suspected that it may have been Eduardo Bellringer, but could not be certain.

I was growing worried now. With the elder Bellringer in police custody and the two children safe, Eduardo Bellringer would have two clear options: he could make his move to get his hands on the map he so desperately wanted, or he could flee the area. I hoped he would do the former, for I wanted very much to catch the wicked man who had forced his father to commit murder and stolen his grandchildren from their home.

I left the lawyer once again under Lestrade's watch and hurried back to the Douglas residence to report to Sherlock Holmes.

◈ ◈ ◈

"Describe this Phineas Franklin to me, Watson! Give me every detail! Search your mind and memory and recall all you can of this man's appearance and demeanor!"

Holmes had grown quite excited upon my return. As soon as I had mentioned the bank vault and the cloaked man passing by repeatedly, I could see that Holmes was forming a plan in his sharp mind.

I sat down, closed my eyes, and tried to recall every bit of information my mind had stored on the subject of Mr. Franklin.

"He is about forty years of age," I began. "A fairly tall man, thin of build with a pale complexion. His hair is of a light brown color and his face is quite plain. He wears spectacles. His disposition is a nervous one. He seems timid and easily upset. When I was in his presence, he continuously paced back and forth across the room as if determined to wear a deep rut in the carpeting. Such a rut would have matched the furrow on his brow caused by his excessive worrying."

"That is enough, Watson," Holmes said, snapping me out of my self-induced trance. "In your opinion, would the similarities be enough that

I might pass as Franklin from a distance after having applied certain adjustments to my appearance?"

"With the skill I've seen you demonstrate on so many past occasions, Holmes," I assured him, "you might easily accomplish such a change."

❖ ❖ ❖

Several hours later, the plan was set. We had sent word of our intentions to Lestrade and Franklin by means of one of the messenger boys often employed by Holmes. Once that was done, we escorted Miss Douglas to Baker Street where she would remain with Mrs. Hudson until we were certain she would be safe in returning to her home.

Holmes packed the things he would need and we soon left for Franklin's building.

Upon our arrival, we entered through a rear door that could not be seen from the street if the man from the night before happened to be lurking nearby. Once Holmes and I were safely inside, Lestrade remained in the front office where he could watch through the windows. The rest of us gathered in the back quarters where Holmes observed Franklin's appearance firsthand and then set about concocting a disguise.

Not long afterwards, one might have sworn after a quick glance that two Phineas Franklins stood face to face. Of course, examining them closely would reveal the truth, for even a disguise artist of Holmes' caliber could not perform miracles, but the transformation would suffice for our purposes. Holmes had donned one of Franklin's suits as well as a pair of spectacles. He had put on a partial wig to lighten and thicken his hair and used some powder to give an even paler shade to his cheeks. Height and weight were close enough already that Holmes did not need to stoop or add padding to his clothing to imitate Franklin's size.

I had seen Holmes undergo such metamorphoses many times, often of a more drastic nature than this, but I was still awed by the sight.

Now we had but to wait for the right time to put our plan into motion.

Some hours passed and it was now well into the afternoon when Lestrade gave the word.

"There he is again, wandering up and down the street!"

"Is the scarf still present?" Holmes asked.

"Indeed it is," Lestrade said, "leaving only his eyes visible."

"Perhaps," Holmes replied, "he wears it to conceal his features...or it may be that he is unused to the chill of the London air, being from a warmer climate. This suggests that it is indeed Eduardo Bellringer who pays such attention to the whereabouts of Mr. Franklin. Hand over the key, Franklin, for it is time."

Holmes took the key from the attorney, grabbed Franklin's black leather case, donned a hat, which he pulled down in such a way that it cast a shadow over his face, and proceeded out the front door. Lestrade and I watched through the window. Holmes walked rapidly down the street. When Holmes was nearly out of sight, Lestrade grew excited and spoke.

"There, Doctor, is our faceless friend!"

As Holmes had predicted, the strange watcher had noticed his departure and, presumably thinking it was Phineas Franklin leaving the office, began to follow. That was my cue to spring into action. I darted out the door, my hand pressing against my coat to make sure I had my revolver. As I left, I heard Lestrade mutter, "Take care with that one, Doctor. He's got the look of a dangerous man."

It was a distance of just under a mile from Franklin's office to the bank. Holmes walked at a brisk pace. Our mysterious stalker followed Holmes while I followed him. Holmes reached the bank and went inside. Our cloaked suspect stopped across the street from the bank's entrance and waited. I watched him from some thirty feet away.

When a quarter of an hour had passed, Holmes emerged, taking care not to look up or straight ahead for more than an instant lest he give away his true identity to his watcher. He had a handful of papers as he exited the bank and let one sheet fall from his fingers as he tucked the rest into his case. Having put the papers away, he began to walk again, going in the opposite direction than from which he had arrived.

Holmes' follower stopped, bent to pick up the paper Holmes had dropped, examined it, and continued his pursuit. I guessed what Holmes had done; surely he had dropped something that would identify the papers he had taken from the bank as belonging to the deceased, Cyril Douglas.

The chase resumed. Holmes walked, our mysterious friend followed, and I took up the last position, keeping both men in sight but remaining inconspicuous.

Holmes made a left turn some blocks later, going down an alley that separated one building from another. Holmes was followed into that alley and I knew what would happen next. I got to the place where the corner of the first of the two buildings stopped and looked down the alley.

Holmes paused and turned to face his pursuer.

"Eduardo Bellringer, I would guess!" Holmes shouted.

"You…you are not the lawyer!"

By this time, I had spotted a stack of wooden crates propped against one wall of the alley. I crept closer to the meeting between Holmes and his pursuer and hid behind those crates, now able to clearly see and hear the exchange.

"I am not," Holmes said. "But you are Bellringer?"

"I am," said Eduardo Bellringer, anger obvious in his voice, his words coming out in thickly accented English. He tore his scarf away, revealing a rough, tanned face full of hatred. "Give me what is in that case!"

"I will not," said Holmes. "Give up this mad quest, Bellringer. Enough people have suffered because of your greed. One man is dead, a woman has lost her grandfather, and your own father sits in prison after being forced to murder his closest friend. Your grandchildren have been put through a terrible ordeal: stolen from their home and carried across the sea! This series of events has gone on long enough. Come with me and give yourself over to the police. Perhaps then the true mastermind of all this carnage will pay the price and the court will show mercy to the poor old man who sits locked in a cell because of you."

"Give me the case!" Bellringer repeated. His voice was a rabid growl now. I watched with worry as his hand went into his coat and came out grasping a revolver.

Holmes let the case fall to the ground, raised his hands, but spoke again as he did so.

"You should know, Bellringer, that while you watched the home of Mr. Franklin through all the hours of the night, I went aboard the Sunbird and freed your grandchildren from their captivity. They are safe and I will make sure that you will not see them again. Any leverage you held against us is now gone. The advantage is mine, despite the weapon in your hand."

Bellringer raised his gun. I knew the motion; it was the change in posture of man about to fire. I had my own revolver of course, and I aimed as quickly as I could. I fired first.

Eduardo Bellringer howled out in pain as my shot struck his forearm. His fingers opened, his gun clattered to the hard ground, but he did not fall, nor did he turn to see who had fired the bullet that had disarmed him. Instead, in his madness and rage, he lunged at Sherlock Holmes, tackling the detective. The two men began to roll about, locked in a struggle of strength. Holmes was younger and would have been stronger under normal circumstances, but Bellringer was, at that moment, driven by pure anger.

I ran to the scene, stood watching as Holmes tried to gain the advantage. They rolled and tumbled across the ground, Bellringer taking a swipe at Holmes' eyes with one hand but blocked by Holmes' fist. I finally reached down and grabbed Bellringer by the shoulders, tried to pry him off of Holmes. He turned his head for just an instant to aim his horrible scowl in my direction. Holmes used the momentary distraction to take the upper hand in the fight. He grabbed the collar of Bellringer's coat, stood as he pushed Bellringer to his feet, and shoved the Peruvian criminal across the alley with full force.

Bellringer stumbled backwards, his back hitting the wall. His head hit too, skull bouncing off brick. The impact disoriented him and he fell forward. He landed face down, twitching once as he hit the ground.

Sherlock Holmes stood watching the fall of Eduardo Bellringer, his stance still one of defense, as if he expected Bellringer to rise and charge again. But Bellringer did not move.

"Holmes, are you all right?" I asked.

"Unhurt, yes, Watson," Holmes assured me. "See to Bellringer. I did not think I struck him that hard."

I knelt down beside the unmoving Bellringer. The man who had been so fierce and determined to do us harm only moments earlier was now deathly still. I felt for a pulse. It was weak.

I turned the body over, loosened the collar, and opened the coat. At that moment, I saw the stain spreading across the front of Bellringer's shirt. It was not the crimson color of blood, but a light shade of blue.

"It was not my blow that kept him down then," Holmes said, looking over my shoulder.

"Indeed," I said. I had opened his shirt now and could see the punctures in Bellringer's chest where the glass had broken the skin and the Blue Eternity he'd had in his pocket had now mingled with his blood. "It seems, Holmes, that if this infernal poison is introduced directly into the bloodstream instead of by ingestion, the deadly effects are accelerated. This man will not live more than a few minutes."

❖ ❖ ❖

Eduardo Bellringer died shortly after his struggle against Sherlock Holmes.

In light of the fact that Major Eustace Bellringer had been coerced into poisoning Cyril Douglas, it was unlikely that he would have been sentenced to hang. He would spend the rest of his days in prison, but his incarceration was a short one, for he died of advanced age not long after the strange events I have just related.

The two children, Anna and Raphael, were sent back home to Peru on a vessel manned by a Spanish-speaking crew. I am certain they were delighted to be reunited with their parents.

The papers of Cyril Douglas, including the map to the secret shrine, were given to Miss Pamela Douglas. One year after Holmes' and my involvement in the investigation of her grandfather's death, I received a letter from Miss Douglas. She reported that she had travelled to Peru and followed the map. The area in question had been abandoned by the native tribes due to the ever-widening encroachment of European settlers in the region. The shrine was precisely where the map indicated and did indeed contain generous amounts of gold and numerous jewels of great value.

Miss Douglas would have all the wealth she would ever need to live a life of leisure and happiness. She did not keep it all for herself however, for she saw fit to give a portion of the treasure to the twin children who had suffered so terribly during the events that had led to her finding such riches. Anna and Raphael Bellringer would receive the finest educations and have options available to them that are usually reserved for the children of aristocrats and royalty.

The letter from Miss Douglas was accompanied by a package containing a gift. Holmes could have sold the token of Miss Douglas's gratitude and received a handsome sum, but he chose to keep it instead. For many years, a small golden statue of some South American god whose name I never learned, and quite possibly would not have been able to pronounce, sat on the mantle above the fireplace at Baker Street, beside various other curiosities acquired during the many strange cases upon which I worked with Sherlock Holmes.

The End

The Many Faces
of
Sherlock Holmes

When people learn that I write Sherlock Holmes stories, one of the questions I'm asked most often is which of the actors to have portrayed Holmes is my favorite. I'm happy to report that it's not an easy question to answer.

If you were to ask me that question about many of my other favorite fictional characters, it would be too easy to choose just one. For example, while I think Timothy Dalton was a superb James Bond and George Lazenby did an admirable job despite his lack of previous acting experience, and even Roger Moore and Pierce Brosnan had their moments. Sean Connery is the best, and there's no question in my mind of that.

When it comes to my second favorite literary detective (after Holmes of course), Agatha Christie's Hercule Poirot, only David Suchet achieved perfection in the role. And I could go on and choose a favorite Tarzan or Batman or Superman or any of a number of other characters that have been played by various actors over many decades.

But Holmes fans are lucky in that many actors have played the Great Detective and many of them have done fine jobs, and so choosing one presents some difficulty. So I'm not going to single out one actor. Instead, I'd like to sing the praises of several of the actors who have stepped into the role of Holmes, each with a different style but each of whom left me with a smile on my face each time I've watched one of their TV or movie performances. And perhaps even more importantly than just providing an enjoyable viewing experience, many of the screen's Sherlocks have had some degree of influence on how I think of the character when I write one of my stories about him. No actor, no matter how great, can be put in the same realm of influence as Holmes' creator, Sir Arthur Conan Doyle, but I'd be lying if I claimed to not have been effected at all by the cinematic versions of Holmes' cases.

I can't cover all the actors who have played Holmes, since this is just a short essay, so I'd like to address the five of them who really stand out to me.

Like many, many people, I suspect that the first Sherlock Holmes

I ever saw was probably Basil Rathbone. I watched a lot of old movies with my father when I was a small boy so I'm pretty sure I came across at least one of Rathbone's 14 Holmes movies during that time. However, my strongest childhood memory of Rathbone is his portrayal of Sir Guy of Gisborne in The Adventures of Robin Hood (1938). It was only in recent years that I've really started paying attention to Rathbone's Holmes films. As Holmes, Rathbone played the Great Detective very well. He looked the part and added a wonderful energy to the role. Those movies are all great fun, although they did play games with the time period, with some of them set in the Victorian era and others in the 1940s (so Holmes could fight Nazis!). Rathbone's work is the strongest part of the series, while its weakness, unfortunately, is in Nigel Bruce's portrayal of Watson. Bruce was a fine actor and his Watson is fun within the context of those films, but it put in the minds of generations of audiences the idea that Watson is an idiot, which is very far from what Doyle wrote in his stories.

If Rathbone was my first Holmes, it was Jeremy Brett whose Holmes meant the most to me and literally changed my life. Brett played Holmes in 36 one-hour episodes and 5 feature-length specials from 1984 to 1994. At some point in the mid-80s, I saw my first Brett-as-Holmes episode (I don't remember which one it was) and grew completely captivated by the character. That was what made me want to read Doyle's original stories and what eventually led me to grow up to write about Holmes. Jeremy Brett was pure perfection as Sherlock Holmes with the vast majority of his episodes being very strict adaptations of the stories upon which they were based. The series looked and felt as if it had been pulled right from Doyle's words and pushed up onto a TV screen. Brett inhabited the role like it was his skin. He was accompanied on his adventures by two very good Watsons. The good doctor was played by David Burke in the first season and Edward Hardwicke (my personal favorite Watson ever) for the remainder of the series.

Another excellent Holmes I discovered over the past few years was Ronald Howard. In 1954, Howard starred in a series of 39 half-hour TV episodes, mostly consisting of original stories rather than adaptations of Doyle's work. Howard was quite good as Holmes. These are short, fun little mysteries that are an excellent way to get a quick dose of Holmes without investing the time it takes to sit through a longer movie. Howard Marion-Crawford was an acceptable Watson who looked a bit like Nigel Bruce but combined Bruce's tendency toward comedy with the more serious Watson of the Doyle stories to create a character who could make the viewer laugh while still being a competent assistant for Holmes.

Of all the Holmes stories by Sir Arthur Conan Doyle, the most famous among the general public is certainly The Hound of the Baskervilles. This particular story has been adapted many times, but my personal favorite version is the 1959 film from Hammer Productions. I adore this version, largely because it stars a man who I'd count among my favorite actors even if he hadn't played Holmes (but I'm glad he did). I can never get enough Peter Cushing! He was superb in all his roles, whether creating monsters as Dr. Frankenstein, battling Dracula as Dr. Van Helsing, or blowing up planets as Grand Moff Tarkin in Star Wars. His work as Sherlock Holmes is no different. Cushing looked like he was born to play Holmes and he did it very well, first in the 1959 "Hound" adaptation and later in a BBC TV series in the late 60s. The Hammer "Hound" movie is great fun, not just because of Peter Cushing but because of the colorful sets, the dark and mysterious atmosphere that made the Hammer movies of that era so unique, and the great supporting cast which includes Andre Morell as Dr. Watson and Christopher Lee as Sir Henry Baskerville.

Finally, for the fifth Holmes actor on my list, I'd like to mention a man who deserves a lot more credit than he is usually given for his portrayal of Holmes. He seems to have been largely forgotten by today's audiences and that's a shame. I'm talking about Arthur Wontner. Wontner made five Holmes films from 1931 to 1937. Unfortunately, one of those movies, The Missing Rembrandt (1932) is considered a "lost film," no longer believed to be in existence.

I discovered Wontner's version of Holmes almost by accident. I had purchased a set of DVDs which included an assortment of early Holmes movies. I bought it mostly for the Basil Rathbone material, at first not paying much attention to what was on the other discs. Then one afternoon I had nothing else to watch so I popped in the disc containing The Sign of Four (1932). From the opening scenes, I was stunned. This was Sherlock Holmes in a way that might even compete with Jeremy Brett! Arthur Wontner looked as much like the original illustrations of Holmes as Basil Rathbone did, only somewhat older. And he acted the part masterfully! It was like finding a hidden treasure right in front of my nose. I sat through the movie shocked by how good it was. Wontner was brilliant as Holmes, his co-star Ian Hunter was a dashing younger version of Watson, and the story was a fairly faithful adaptation of one of my favorite Doyle stories. Basil Rathbone was not the first truly great cinematic Sherlock Holmes. That title must go to Arthur Wontner!

So if I had to choose the five Holmes actors that have meant the most to me as a fan of the character, those are the winners. Of course, dozens of other fine actors have played the Great Detective and I'm sure other Holmes fans and writers would have their own lists that would agree with mine on some names and disagree on others. As I said at the start of this essay, Holmes fans are lucky. The movies and TV have treated us well!

❖ ❖ ❖

AARON SMITH - is the author of over 30 published stories, many of them for Airship 27 Productions. His pulp work includes stories in both volumes of *Black Bat Mystery*, five Sherlock Holmes stories, the Dr. Watson novel Season of Madness, and stories featuring Allan Quatermain, Ki-Gor, Dan Fowler, and his own creations, Hound-Dog Harker and the Red Veil. He has written novels in several genres, including science-fiction, mystery, horror, and spy thrillers. Information about his work can be found on his blog at www.godsandgalaxies.blogspot.com

Sherlock Holmes

in

"The Abominable Merridew"

By
I.A. Watson

"My collection of M's is a fine one. Moriarty himself is enough to make any letter illustrious, and here is Morgan the poisoner, and Merridew of abominable memory, and Mathews, who knocked out my left canine in the waiting-room at Charing Cross."

Mr. Sherlock Holmes, "The Adventure of the Empty House"

Midnight summonses from my eccentric companion were commonplace, but I vividly recall attending on him at the squalid Bar of Gold on January 3rd 1891. The air was heavy with opium fumes. Guttering red lanterns flickered across the addicts' filthy pallets. Some few men, so lost in their dark dreams as to be unaware of their surroundings, still sprawled in unquiet slumber.

Even the blood sprayed across their recumbent forms did not rouse them.

The principal feature of the scene was, of course, the corpse of 'Turnpike' Luke Trippel, operator of that disreputable drug den. It did not require a medical man to know that he was dead; his headless carcass was nailed to the wall panelling by six-inch railway spikes.

I skirted round the pooling blood and examined the murdered man. "He was alive when he was pinned up," I deduced. The man had been spread-eagled before heavy nails were hammered through the thick muscle where wrist meets hand and ankle meets foot; the precise points of crucifixion where the human body can bear its weight without spikes tearing loose and causing instant death. "It took strength to do this, perhaps a pair of men together to hoist him so. And a knowledge of anatomy, to avoid the major arteries."

I examined the bloody neck-stump. The head had been sawed off with some sharp serrated tool. A medical bone-saw would have left a neater cut; this might well have been a garden implement. "Look at the spray pattern on the wall. His heart was still pumping when the decapitation began. And yet he did not struggle much or he'd have ripped his wrists more trying to break free."

I surrendered to the inevitable. I turned to my companion and asked, "What happened, then?"

My friend's keen intellect had already mapped and evaluated the scene. His gimlet glance told me that he had long before drawn the same conclusions; that I was merely plodding behind his own quicksilver thoughts like a backward schoolboy runner trailing a steeplechase champion.

He pointed to the opium house's sealed rear entrance. "Four men entered from the gutter-alley there. One of them was proficient in picking locks, very proficient, leaving hardly any mark of his passing. Trippel was at his desk over there, counting his takings."

I glanced at the grubby table in the corner. An open cashbox still contained some twenty pounds in coin and bank-notes along with folded sachets of poppy resin. "Nothing was stolen?"

"Trippel did not see his attackers until the dart took him in the throat."

Whilst my comrade inspected the packets of dope on the desk, I sponged away the gore at Turnpike Luke's neck. A tiny pinprick was barely visible on the bloody stump. A faint purple discolouration warned that some toxin or venom had been introduced into the victim.

"Forensic tests will be required, of course," my colleague went on as he inspected the scene, "but there are any number of compounds that have paralytic effects. Indeed, I have authored three monographs on the subject relating my observations. Some toxins can deny the brain control of the body, leaving the subject conscious but helpless to command his muscles. I suspect that 'Turnpike' Luke was fully aware of what was done to him."

"And could feel it too?" I have witnessed many cruelties in travel and military service across three continents, but this one made me shudder a little. I thought of the paralysed man, hoisted by his assailants, posed for the hammer and nails that transfixed him, watching his murderer approach with the saw that would sever his head.

"Most likely he could experience all, but I do not wish to draw conclusions ahead of the proper data. That is the error of the amateur. Let us confine ourselves to the facts available by observation. When the attackers entered there were several other people making use of these divans."

I noted the rumpled sheets and discarded hookahs. Some of the glassware still seeped sickly smoke. "Addicts do not readily or willingly abandon their vice."

"I suspect on this occasion they were coerced to do so, simply manhandled to the outer halls. This is not a place where the customers are used to friendly service. Those that were too insensible to stagger away were left to bide."

"Might we get accounts from those who were evacuated?"

"How reliable would be the testimony of an opium fiend? Empirical evidence is our key to this problem. For example..." The floor beneath

Turnpike Luke's desk was rank with the odour of urine. "Trippel lost control of his bladder, possibly a side-effect of the poison dart, perhaps simple terror. He dropped nerveless on his desk, displacing these new packets of poppy. To any customer still sensible to witness he must simply have seemed to fall asleep at his post."

"There are more private places for murder," I argued. "Why enter the Bar of Gold and attempt so public an assault?"

"Because it is public! Trippel's death was gruesome and memorable, intended to make an impression. A warning? A statement? No matter." My companion returned to his lecture. "The killers came prepared. They had blowpipe, hammer, spikes and a rusty common hacksaw missing two teeth in the middle. They knew where to find their prey amidst his addled clientele, suggesting that some recent visitor might have been an agent for the assailants. They took their time beheading Trippel, as the splash patterns across the panelling attest. Afterwards they took his head away with them, for purposes we may currently only conjecture, and locked the rear door behind them when they left."

"Why fasten the door?" I puzzled.

"It is a significant point."

I looked to the bloodstained floor. Several different boot-marks were tracked across the straw matting. "This is how you knew there were four of them," I realised.

"Indeed. Two with common hob-nailed jackboots, lengths of eleven-and-a-half and thirteen inches respectively. A third in almost-new pointed-toe half-boots of the style popular two decades ago; that one wielded the cutting tool, I fancy. You will further note that the fourth intruder remained apart from the others and did not get covered in gore. The only prints number four leaves are mud-marks from the alley-slime. He hovered by the exit door, shifting his weight nervously from foot to foot, and took no part in the execution. His well-mended work-boots have a distinctive nick on the left heel that will be easy to recognise again. The entire party wore heavy overgarments which they doffed when their work was done, see this stain here where bloody fabric has trailed over the floor, but took the garments with them to baffle further detection."

"They knew that their work would get messy."

"Which in turn suggests a carriage waiting nearby to convey them to some place where they might clean up."

"A hansom in this part of town might be traceable," I considered. "Your network..."

"Will be utilised, I assure you; but I believe this attack to have been cleverly and carefully planned. I do not expect the assailants to have made elementary mistakes."

"We will find them, though? Such a crime cannot go unanswered."

"We will find them. Perhaps there will be additional indications at the scene of a subsequent murder."

I looked up sharply. "Another murder?" Sometimes my friend's deductive abilities verged on the supernatural, but I could not see how he might predict another atrocity from the vestiges we examined in that red-lit hovel. "How can you…"

He made an impatient gesture with those long sensitive fingers, bidding me to silence. "The lock was opened by a master. There are less than a dozen men presently in London who might accomplish it with such élan; including myself of course. This locksmith did not take part in the murder. Likely he did not even realise it was murder he assisted until he witnessed the act. Possibly his cooperation was coerced. It was he who hovered horrified at the doorway while the deed was done. If he was a reluctant participant in tonight's events, what odds would you lay on his survival chances now that his work is done?"

"Not gambling odds," I owned.

"Precisely. Judging by shoe size, stride and gait, I infer he was a young man, which rules out Burlington and Barrows. Nor was he left-handed, which eliminates LeClark. Wharfen is presently working with the Sneed Gang and is unlikely to be available for this venture. Kennedy has a limp. Of the remainder, Gadding and the younger Spearer are the most likely options. Both work in key-cutters that take on cobbling jobs, and number four's boots were well maintained. Both are youngsters of precise habits, who might fastidiously refasten a door behind them even when it is not necessary, especially if distressed or distracted by what they had witnessed. We shall begin our enquiries with Gadding and Spearer."

"What about the body?" I wondered. "Sooner or later these addicts will rouse and the police will be summoned."

"Dispose of the body to our specialist in Houndsditch," my friend commanded me, "I do not presently have time to conduct a chemical analysis of the toxin myself so commission one there. Kill everybody in this building. Then a fire to destroy the evidence, if you please, Colonel."

"As you say, Professor," I agreed.

❖ ❖ ❖

The account of Doctor John H. Watson:

My notes for the closing days of 1890 and early 1891 are perhaps not as ordered as other times when I have assisted Mr. Sherlock Holmes. Regular readers of my chronicles will know that after ten years of accompanying him on sundry cases wherein he was consulted, our partnership faced an abrupt and premature termination in the spring of 1891 with the Great Detective's apparent death over the falls at Reichenbach. Those last frenetic months of enquiry with him, wherein I balanced domestic bliss with my dear Mary, a heavy Paddington medical practice, and Holmes' intensive investigations, left me less time than on other occasions to properly log and file my accounts.

It is for that reason, and due to the recent extraordinary discovery of documents purporting to be papers of the late Colonel J. Sebastian Moran,[1] reports which I have not seen, that I have returned to my rough-books and reviewed again the matter that engaged Holmes and myself from the moment Mr. Nathanial Spearer presented himself to us in Spitalfields Market.

The occasion was an unusual one. At that time, Holmes was conducting a lengthy and complicated investigation into the organisation of crime in the metropolis and beyond. Work of the utmost delicacy for the Scandinavian royal family had led to a complicated and lengthy investigation for the government of France.[2] As New Year was rung in he had exposed the poisoner Morgan[3] and again discerned the hand of some coordinating force behind London's underworld. That subtle intelligence behind Five Orange Pips and the Sign of Four[4] lurked somewhere in the shadows of the city, and Holmes sought him with a growing fervour.

I had been dragged to teeming, bustling Spitalfields in pursuit of Mathews[5] the workhouse superintendent, whom Holmes suspected of

---

1   The Canon does not mention Moran's first Christian name. It was instead revealed as John from memoir papers uncovered in a Leicestershire saleroom by the erudite George MacDonald Frasier and published as *Flashman and the Tiger*. Moran appears twice in that volume (Holmes and Watson make cameo appearances) and as a juvenile in *Flash for Freedom!*

2   As referenced in "The Final Problem".

3   As referenced in "The Adventure of the Empty House".

4   These Canonical cases both featured the behind-the-scenes presence of Professor James Moriarty, 'the Napoleon of Crime'.

5   Also referenced in "The Adventure of the Empty House".

soliciting young girls for immoral purposes. We were interviewing a barrow boy located for us by Holmes' irregular brigade of street Arabs when an old man dashed up and grabbed the sleeve of my companion's coat.

"Mister 'olmes!" he cried out, "Please, sir! You 'as to 'elp me!"

Holmes dismissed the barrow lad with a florin and turned to the agitated plaintiff. "Come, Mister Spearer," he chided, "You must get a grip of yourself. A man with a heart condition must not allow such strong emotions to overcome him, nor run at such a speed all the way from Petticoat Lane."

Familiar with Holmes' methods, I knew he had noted the distinctive splash markings of grey clay on the old man's trousers and from its type and distribution pattern had deduced the location and speed of the man who carried them. As a doctor I had no difficulty detecting a man with a weak heart who was close to seizure.

"Sit on this barrel," I advised the elder. "Take long, deep breaths and force your pulse to slow. Who is he, Holmes?"

"There was a time when Nathaniel Spearer was the third-finest lock-breaker in London, Watson. His was the hand that opened the Sangster Hotel safe and the Winterton Bank back in the '60s. He would have hung except for the remarkable breakdown of the prosecution's case with the disgrace of their expert witness. But that is long past, and after paying his debt to society with fifteen years hard labour Mr. Spearer now operates a lock-repair shop off Wentworth Street."

Spearer was not content to recover his breath nor calm his blood. He reached again for Holmes. "You have to listen, Mister 'olmes. You have to help me!"

"You certainly have my attention, Spearer," my companion assured him. "What assistance do you require?"

"My Harry…" the old man gasped. "They took 'im, and I don't know where."

"Who took him? When did this happen?"

"Last night, it was. Three coves called after closing time. Harry was expecting 'em, seems like, because they handed him a bit of a package and he led 'em into the workshop. 'I'll see to these blokes, our dad', 'e says to me, which is what 'e does when 'e's got a bit of night business arranged on the side."

The florid father glanced up to see if Holmes understood the hint. My friend was already far ahead. "Harry Spearer occasionally does his own consulting, on the practical matter of opening locks on premises that his clients would not otherwise be able to enter. He carries on the family business." From Holmes' tone this was hardly a new discovery for him.

"Aye, well, he's a good lad for all that, and never any rough stuff or the like. Smart and secret, that's my boy, and as good at his trade as ever I were."

"Perhaps not yet," Holmes considered judicially. "Although he shows promise. If he improves much more I fear that he will have to come to my primary attention."

I knew the detective's curious admiration for effective practitioners of the criminal arts. "Mr. Spearer, you're saying that your son went off with these three unknown men last night and has not returned?" I surmised.

"That's the long an' short of it, yes. Mr. 'olmes, it's not like our Harry not to turn up again 'afore morning. Not without word. I don't like it and I don't rightly know what to do."

"But it was not that which sent you racing so suddenly down to Spitalfields to the detriment of your health," Holmes remarked.

Spearer hesitated, then came to a decision. "No, sir. But y'see, when our Harry didn't turn up by morning I got worried, o'course. So I took a peek in the lad's work-box."

"To see which tools he had extracted for his night's business," Holmes surmised.

"That's the idea. There weren't nought missing but his ring o' master-picks, a couple o' torsion wrenches, a hook pick, a pair o' half-diamonds, a snake rake, an s-rake, a double-rounded and a long double-ended, so he weren't doing naught out o' the ordinary. But... in the case I found this." Old Spearer fumbled in one of his many pockets and produced a leather drawstring bag no more than three inches deep.

Holmes received it, there by the Spitalfields arches, and frowned. He hurried Spearer and I to the privacy of a side-ginnel where we might not be observed. Only there did he show me the sinister brown discolouration at the bag's base, then unpick the drawstring that bound the container closed.

A human finger rolled onto his palm. Even my untutored eye could tell that it was a female digit. The bloody stump was wrapped with a stained yellow ribbon.

"Holmes...!" I gasped, horrified by the severed remains. Spearer was deathly pale now.

My friend retained his usual detachment. "A young woman, I see, of the working class. Though this is the left ring finger, no callosity or other mark indicates a missing ring, so the young lady is unwed. Short nails with traces of flour beneath them, an old burn mark to the side of the intermediate phalanx, from which I conclude she worked in a bakery."

"And so does Milly Claxton!" blurted Spearer. "That's our Harry's girl what 'e's walked out with these fifteen months now! And that yellow hair-ribbon's what 'e gave 'er for her birthday!"

"Your son's visitors brought him his lady-friend's severed finger!" I almost choked me with outrage. "And he left with them?"

"What better way to compel the compliance of one of London's finest lock-crackers, Watson?" Holmes turned the leather bag inside-out to examine the stains of its interior. "This terrible token showed at once all that was required: that Miss Claxton was in the hands of ruthless men who would not hesitate to harm her; that her value to young Harry Spearer was well understood; that the lad's only hope of saving her was to comply with her captors' demands."

"I thought it were just another bit o' business!" old Spearer fretted. "He could 'ave told me what trouble he was in, but he kept me out of it so's I wouldn't get hurt!"

Holmes' hawk-like face hardened into that mask of resolve that I have come to associate with the uttermost application of his faculties. "This is a dark business that requires my immediate attention. I think we have enough evidence regarding Mathews now to lay his case before Scotland Yard, so we are free to pursue Miss Claxton and young Spearer with a good conscience."

"You'll find our Harry, then?" Spearer pleaded. "And Milly?"

Holmes was already striding away through the crowded market.

❖ ❖ ❖

The account of Colonel J Sebastian Moran:

James Moriarty is a precise and meticulous man. As one might expect of the scholar who rewrote binomial theory while still only twenty-one, the celebrated author of "Dynamics of an Asteroid" and other works of high mathematical genius, he is capable of far greater planning and foresight than others. Alterations to his schedules and diversions from his prepared instructions disturb him.

It was for this reason that the passing of Turnpike Luke Trippel troubled him. The Bar of Gold had been ceded to my friend some four years earlier for his assistance in extricating a client from the Bishopgate Jewels scandal,[6] but Trippel's opium hell was an insignificant fraction of the criminal operations that my friend and employer operated. With another man I might venture that the stale stinking den would not even have been worthy of remembrance, simply another line in a thick accounting ledger; but the Professor was as aware of it as he was of every minute part of his vast enterprise.

Once the Professor's mind grapples a problem he becomes as unstoppable as a force of nature.

"Where is your son?" he had demanded of the old locksman Nathaniel Spearer, transfixing him with that serpentine gaze that sees through every evasion and deception.

"Not... not back yet, Professor," the quivering man behind the counter admitted. "'E's... working."

"For whom?"

"I don't know. Three blokes as came last night after dark. They showed 'im some token and 'e took his tools and went off with 'em. I'd 'ave expected 'im home by now."

The Professor's head swayed from side to side as it often did when he was thinking. "Describe the men."

Spearer was a bumbling old fool. Whatever he'd been in his prime was long gone. Under my friend's incisive interrogation he described two roughly-dressed bravos who might have been any of thousands of the idlers of London's lower classes and one fellow with a better cut of suit, but told nothing of further value.

"Tell me then," my companion pressed on, "of your son's boots."

Here Spearer was on better ground. He was able to describe the size and condition of his offspring's footwear, right to the heel-nick that the Professor had observed. Thus we confirmed the identity of the reluctant member of the party that had stormed the Bar of Gold.

"Do you want me to question this idiot more closely?" I asked the Professor. I have some small skill in getting the truth out of men, honed by years in India and the Dark Continent.

He shook his head. "It would avail nothing and waste our time."

Spearer, now a trembling smear cringing behind his counter, almost blubbed to be thus spared.

"You have been honest with me, Spearer, so I shall offer you advice," the smartest man in London told the old crook. "When I have departed, look

6   Watson references this event in *The Sign of Four*, indicating that Holmes played some part in the case's resolution.

to your son's work-box. I fancy you may learn something from it. Then, should you require assistance, hasten to the open market at Spitalfields. You will encounter Mr. Sherlock Holmes there, I believe, seeking information about the workhouse-warden Mathews. By all means lay your troubles before the Great Detective, omitting my involvement, of course."

Spearer nodded vigorously. "I'll do as you say, Professor. Thank you, Professor."

Professor Moriarty strode from the dingy little shop and paused, as he had before entering, to review the marks on the uneven cobbles.

"Why bring Sherlock Holmes into this?" I wondered.

My companion shrugged one bony shoulder. "Mr. Holmes is getting too close to the truth about Mathews' operation; sufficiently so that Mathews must be sacrificed for the blunders he has made. However, if Holmes is distracted by Spearer he will hand his evidence to the Scotland Yard bumbler Lestrade. While the police detain Mathews there will be time to spirit away those account-books and order dockets that might otherwise implicate the other business links in that profitable venture." The Professor's thin lips quirked into a rare smile. "Old Spearer is doing society a great service by diverting Mr. Holmes. Many important men in commerce and politics will continue to enjoy their good reputations as a consequence of it."

How like Moriarty to twist every circumstance to serve his occasions! Not for nothing was he the clandestine master of the greatest and most secret business empire in Europe!

"You always have a reason," I confessed. "I am in awe of it."

"One reason?" The Professor shook his head. "Whoever has the effrontery to perpetrate the outrage against my authority at the Bar of Gold is a cunning and prepared adversary. Let him also have to guard himself against the sleuthery of the consulting detective and he may be diverted at the vital moment. Let Holmes bend his wit and resources to expose the perpetrator. Every contact Holmes uses, every asset he invokes will be logged for my records and can never after be deployed against me. Why set a course of action for one reason, Moran, when many purposes can be simultaneously served?"

"Why indeed? Shall we then allow Holmes to root out Trippel's murderers for us?"

"We shall not. Other avenues of investigation lie open to us."

I would rather be naked and weaponless in a Burmese jungle with a wounded tiger than be hunted by Professor James Moriarty.

❖❖❖

The account of Dr. John H. Watson:

Sherlock Holmes subjected Spearer's shop to a keen and terrible scrutiny. "Your business is chiefly with the insurance trade, I perceive," my companion announced as he ran his gaze over the shelves behind the counter. Holmes had not yet opened the business ledgers.

"Yes," agreed the old man. "Sometimes a bad reputation is a help. 'Set a thief to catch a thief' as the old saying goes. Where the insurers want to be certain there'll be no trouble they come to Spearer."

"And Spearer charges well," responded Holmes. "Perhaps your locks come with a guarantee that men not so retired as yourself won't attempt them in the night?"

The locksmith looked uncomfortable. "I thought we was going to trace our Harry and 'is Milly," he ventured. "I don't do nothing on the wrong side o' the law these days, Mr. 'olmes, I swears it! One brush with the hemp fandango[7] was enough for me."

"You were remarkably fortunate," Holmes judged. "The prosecution laid too much weight on the expert opinion of Dr. Jollydrop. When that was dismissed…"

"It were a long time ago now, Mr. 'olmes. I paid my price. But our Harry…"

Holmes returned to his studies. "The ground outside is too slushy and churned up to offer any clue. The cheap wood planking inside offers no conclusive trace of footmarks." He looked around. "Your property consists of this show-room, a workshop, a kitchen and two sleeping chambers above?"

Spearer confirmed it. "It's enough for two. Maybe three, I was thinking, if Harry and 'is Molly tied the knot."

"They were engaged?" I enquired.

"There was an understanding. From what I 'eard it wouldn't be long."

Holmes moved into the workshop. "How often did your boy undertake his extracurricular activities, Mr. Spearer?"

"Not often. Just… when something special were needed. He's got the knack, sir, just like I did when me 'ands were steadier. Fifteen years o' rock-breaking's ruined me for work that delicate, but Harry's as good as ever I was, and doubtless a deal more sensible with it."

"You cannot tell me who retained his services on other occasions?"

"He wouldn't say and I didn't ask."

Holmes finished his examination of the locksmith's tools, paying special attention to those empty places where an instrument was missing. "Your visitors last night smoked. One used Benson's Naval Tobacco.

7　　Execution by hanging.

"The cheap wood planking inside offers no conclusive trace of footmarks."

Another burned Canterford's Menthol Blend."

"One was a sailor, then?" I checked.

"The former brand is no more restricted to seamen than the latter is to ladies, Watson. We shall continue our search." He passed on to the toolbox where the gory bag had lain. His quick fingers easily found a hidden compartment with a rolled stash of bank-notes.

"The boy's got to plan for 'is future," old Spearer protested.

Holmes examined the wad. A rubber band enclosed a roll of seventy-two pounds. Four ten-shilling banknotes were separate from the rest, hastily stuffed away and abandoned.

"Those were the deposit offered for young Spearer's services," Holmes surmised. "When he demurred, the lady's digit was produced to coerce his assent. He hurried to his workshop to assemble his kit and crammed his fee here by mere habit." The detective meticulously copied down the issue numbers so that the money could be traced.

A series of letters in the night-stand proved to be billet-doux from Miss Claxton. I thought Holmes might take an interest in them, but after a brief glance at the ink he turned away. "Too old to be of relevance to our case," he dismissed them. "The last written some five months ago, you observe? The relationship has progressed beyond the letter-writing stage."

He rose from a futile scrutiny of Spearer's rug and brushed his knees down. "There is nothing else to see here. We must seek a more obscure route." To old Spearer he said, "Wire me at Baker Street should anything new come to light." To me he added, "This case is of special interest, Watson."

"Because a helpless and injured girl's life is at hazard?" I suggested.

"Because of the uniqueness of our client."

"You mean that Spearer is, or was, a criminal?"

"I was speaking of our true client," Sherlock Holmes replied, but said no more.

❖ ❖ ❖

The account of Colonel J Sebastian Moran:

The Professor instructed the carriage to take us a few streets south into the narrow alleys of Shoreditch. Some of the archways were so tight as to almost scrape the coachwork. Scarcely five minutes' travel brought us to the dingy cobbled square that was Kitchener's Yard.

I must have been scowling. "You do not approve of our colleague here," Moriarty observed.

"I do not," I admitted. "Merridew is an abomination."

"Merridew is what I have created Merridew to be," the Professor replied. "You were honed in foreign wars and wilderness adventuring.[8] Merridew was forged in a different crucible, crushed, melted, refined, then cast as I required."

"But still an abomination," I insisted.

Moriarty alighted from the trap and rapped on a peeling cellar door. A spy-hatch slid open. When the visitor was identified, bolts were quickly slid back to allow the Professor access to the laboratory. I followed with a prickling sensation between my shoulder-blades, as I get when an Assagi spear is aimed at them.

"Professor," the creature at the door fawned, bending near double as he bowed. I believe his name was Pretlow, if anyone ever spoke of him. "The doctor did not tell me you were coming."

"The doctor did not know," Moriarty replied, stalking into the cellar.

I kept close to the wall, comforted by the weight of the hunting pistols in my pockets and my shooting-cane, but missing my tiger rifle.

I freely admit that Merridew's domain unnerved me each time I visited it. A hunter notices odours, and that subterranean laboratory was characterised by the stench of bodily discharges unsatisfactorily masked by disinfectant. The gas mantles shed flickering shadows over grotesque medical equipment. A metal chair with stirrups and leather straps stood beside an operating slab; currently the table was occupied by Turnpike Luke's mortal remains. Gleaming trays of silver medical instruments, many of a gynecological nature, were arrayed as if to threaten the visitor with horrors to come. A series of bloody bowls on a drainage grill contained Trippel's vital organs.

Sometimes the Professor sends a man to Kitchener's Yard for questioning. I saw what the Zulus did with the white men they captured at Isandlwana.[9] I'd rather be in the hands of Khozalo's torturers than Merridew's guest.

---

8   According to "The Adventure of the Empty House", Holmes file card on Moran read: "Moran, Sebastian, Colonel. Unemployed. Formerly 1st Bengalore Pioneers. Born London, 1840. Son of Sir Augustus Moran, C.B., once British Minister to Persia. Educated Eton and Oxford. Served in Jowaki Campaign, Afghan Campaign, Charasiab (despatches), Sherpur, and Cabul. Author of 'Heavy Game of the Western Himalayas,' 1881; 'Three Months in the Jungle,' 1884. Address: Conduit Street. Clubs: The Anglo-Indian, the Tankerville, the Bagatelle Card Club."

9   The battle at Isandlwana, South Africa on 27th January 1879 was the first major conflict in the Zulu War. 20,000 Zulus surrounded and overwhelmed a better-armed but overconfident and ineptly led column of 1,800 British and colonial troops and 400 civilians.

The abominable Merridew appeared from a small washroom, wiping his hands clean after his initial examination of the corpse. His long woman's skirts were covered by a stained laboratory coat. His sable wig was set aside on a nearby hatstand, but his face was still rouged and powdered. Those who did not know would let him pass for female.

"Professor Moriarty," the butcher said, "You have come for a preliminary report, I presume?"

"Two questions only," the Professor replied. "I should like to know how long Trippel hung pinned alive to the wall before he was beheaded. And when his head was removed, where was the first incision made?"

Merridew returned to the body. He ran painted fingers over the dead flesh as if caressing it. "I cannot offer other than a best guess, of course," the abomination answered, "but bruising at wrists and ankles suggests several minutes of life after he was pinioned. The cutting of the head began at the thorax, severing windpipe before the major arteries. He would be suffocating to death before he bled his last."

Moriarty nodded, satisfied. "I will require an analysis of the paralytic agent that rendered him helpless. Send a wire using the second Fourier code."

"It will be my pleasure," mewed the doctor.

The Professor rarely bothers with small talk. His business done, he peremptorily made for the exit. Pretlow had to jump to open the door for him.

I trailed behind the Professor to his waiting carriage. I was glad to be away from Merridew's domain. "Why does it matter how Turnpike Luke was beheaded?" I asked.

"The information from Merridew is quite instructive," my friend assured me. "It tells us that the murderer was sadistic in his choice of ends. The selection of a dull hand-saw was suggestive. He prolonged Trippel's death for sheer enjoyment."

"Might Trippel have been tortured for interrogation?"

Moriarty snorted scornfully. "His throat was paralysed by the drug. He could not speak, or his screams would have summoned aid. He had no way of answering questions. Our killer slew Trippel as he did to inspire fear and for personal gratification. Indulgent, too indulgent."

I reviewed what leads might yet remain. "You said the murderers' coach might not be traced. You felt that the surviving opium-eaters might be too addled to offer useful information. And you set Holmes after Spearer."

The Professor climbed into the box and instructed the driver to hasten to Kew. "I told you that empiricism was the key to understanding, Colonel. You have not considered all that we observed at the Bar of Gold. Recall, if you will, that Trippel was at his desk, counting his money, with many bags of poppy arrayed before him."

"I saw that," I admitted, "but..."

Moriarty could be impatient when his student was dull; and to him all students were. "The drug had just been delivered and paid for. 'Turnpike' Luke was putting away the remainder of the treasury with which he had purchased his supply. The new consignment of opium had not yet been opened."

I remembered now that my companion had inspected the resin-bags scattered by the drugged Trippel. "What is the significance of that? Was it the courier who scouted the Bar of Gold to determine that its host was unguarded?"

"Quite possibly. However, the salient fact is that those bags did not contain opium resin."

I was most surprised. "What? Then why...? How?"

"The contents were from poppies, that much is true. But they were not from *papaver somniferum*, the common Eastern garden poppy. The pulp delivered to the drug-house was instead *papaver rhoeas*, the corn rose poppy, which is not an effective opiate. Customers would have been most dissatisfied."

"Then... Trippel was swindled. Swindled by someone who knew that he would not be alive to complain of the deception!"

"And there is our investigation, Colonel. It is to that chain of fakery to which we must apply ourselves."

"It should be possible to find out who sold the Bar of Gold its merchandise."

The Professor snorted. "Trippel was until recently supplied by Amos Morgan." I should have known that the great mind that ordered London's underworld would know such detail. "After Morgan had his encounter with the enthusiastic Mr. Holmes,[10] Trippel switched his business to Crawley of Lichfield Road, adjacent to the Royal Botanic Gardens at Kew.[11]"

"And we are heading to Kew!"

---

10   Referred to in "The Adventure of the Empty House", as quoted at the beginning of our present story.

11   Kew Gardens, purchased by George III in 1781 as a nursery for royal children, was adapted as a national botanical garden in 1840. Its 300 acres are now a UNESCO World Heritage Site.

"Indeed, Colonel. Let us see what the reprehensible Mr. Crawley can tell us of the planned demise of 'Turnpike' Luke!"

◈ ◈ ◈

The account of Doctor John H. Watson:

As I trudged through the sooty London slush after Sherlock Holmes I could not but fret for the wellbeing of Miss Molly Claxton. That undefended young woman had already lost a finger. What horrors would her fiendish captors not perpetrate on her if rescue did not come? My hand crept to my overcoat pocket and touched the Adams .450 breechloader, souvenir of my military days.

"You are right to fret for the lady's safety," Holmes told me without looking over his shoulder at me or breaking his stride. "If Spearer has performed the task which her kidnappers required then they may well have no further use for him or her."

"You fear murder?"

"I do," my friend admitted. "Indeed, I fear that we may already be too late."

Holmes let a hansom cab sweep past us then hailed the one that followed. He directed the driver to Pinchin Lane, Lambeth, from which I concluded that we were to call upon the eccentric taxidermist Sherman, who owned a remarkable hunting dog.

"What trail is there that could be traced by the talented Toby?[12]" I wondered.

"It is not the dog whose help we require on this occasion," my friend answered grimly. "We need the man."

The cab rattled across the Lambeth cobbles and deposited us outside an old-fashioned house-shop near the waterfront. I recognised the lifelike montage in the window, a clever representation of a weasel taking a rabbit. The unkempt Jew who muttered his way round his crowded workroom was a genius in his own field.

As the bell over his door jangled, Sherman greeted us with an odd little bow. "Mr. Holmes! Only the other night I was perusing your wonderful monograph on the properties of tattoo-mark inkings![13]"

"I have recently had further experience of several overseas techniques

---

12   Holmes and Watson previously used the keen senses of the talented mongrel to follow a quarry's trail in *The Sign of Four*.

13   Holmes refers to this essay in "The Red Headed League".

that will require me to substantially overhaul the work," my friend replied.

Sherman cleared a pair of rickety chairs of a glass-eyed barn owl and a cat-with-kitten diorama so that we could sit. He pulled a billy-can from the general detritus of his bench and hung it back over the stove to warm its sludgy brown contents. "Coffee?" he offered.

Thankfully Holmes declined. Sherman's chipped cups appeared to be used indiscriminately for glue-pots, fixative dishes, offal containers, and afternoon tea. "It is business not pleasure that brings me across your threshold today," my friend explained. He produced the drawstring bag that contained the severed finger and handed it to the taxidermist. "This digit was severed with a sharp rounded blade; a cigar cuspidor might be the very culprit. It has been further treated post-removal. I should be grateful of your professional opinion."

Sherman fished a big magnifier from the clutter of this workbench and took the bag over to the window where the light was better. He spent a long time examining both sack and contents. The mongrel Toby, recognising me of old, padded over to lay his head in my lap and have his ears rubbed.

At last Sherman was satisfied. "Your conclusions?" Holmes prompted him.

The taxidermist handed Miss Claxton's ring finger back but retained the bag for now. "It's a pretty piece of work, professionally speaking," Sherman judged. "Quite naturalistic. Only a close inspection would reveal that six-gauge bird wire had been introduced into the flesh to pose the subject."

My stomach turned. "Am I to understand that after that finger was severed someone inserted a wire to crook it in the position it now assumes?"

"Oh yes. Very neat bit of business, Dr. Watson. You can hardly even see the seam where it was pressed in. Of course, it's not a proper bit of taxidermy, only a cosmetic fix. Undertakers use the trick sometimes when a body has been mangled in an accident. I'm not sure why anyone would wish to take such trouble with... with this object."

"That they did is significant," Holmes growled.

"As to the bag," Sherman went on, "you'll have noted the stitching on the interior. Not common thread but raffia, and the seams stapled in with tiny t-pins."

"Common taxidermy supplies," Holmes noted, "But Mr. Sherman, you have not remarked upon the material of the bag itself."

The old Jew fingered the fabric of the drawstring container. "Very soft and pliant," he discerned. "Calf? Perhaps faun?"

The Great Detective shook his head. "I am unsurprised you have difficulty recognising the material. Unless I am very far from the mark that is human hide, Mr. Sherman."

The taxidermist studied the bag in his hands with a fascinated horror. "I believe you may be right, Mr. Holmes! But this skin has been flensed and cured with the greatest skill, treated as carefully as the finest pelts."

"Miss Claxton?" I asked, feeling sick.

"No, no, Watson," Holmes assured me. "The creation of this object was the work of many days."

Sherman scurried back to the window to examine the bag again. "The cross-stitching is in the German pattern. The leather is pricked with a curved surgical needle. The manufacturer was of the old school," he mumbled.

I could remain passive no more. I jumped up and paced the cluttered shop. "Holmes, what does this mean? Has the girl been kidnapped by some mad butcher that he sends such gruesome proofs of his cruelty?"

"He sends a message, for certain, Watson, but the question is for whom?"

"There's something else here!" Sherman exclaimed. "May I apply some chemical stain to the interior of this bag? There is the faintest... yes..."

"By all means apply your chemicals," Holmes urged the taxidermist. "Lives are at stake here."

Old Sherman fished amongst his pots and jars. The vials for which he searched were next to his coffee caddy. He carefully painted them onto the flesh of the bag.

Holmes and I leaned forward. A faint blur darkened and browned, revealing a discernible sigil.

"A tattoo, Mr. Holmes!" Sherman exalted. "Bleached away by the tanning process, but we were able to have her out! This is one for your new monograph, sir!"

My friend clapped the taxidermist on his back. "Excellent work, Mr. Sherman! You have granted Dr. Watson and I the vital clue to continue our hunt and helped shut a case that would otherwise have remained forever unfinished!"

"What case do you mean, Holmes?" I enquired.

Holmes tapped his fingertip on the tiny tattoo. The mark depicted an anchor transfixing a heart, with a crude snake or sea-serpent coiling at the base. "I need hardly consult my notes to recall where this image has been seen before. Your own records cover it, I think, during my investigation into the tired Captain M'Crimmond.[14]"

---

14   Watson comments in "The Naval Treaty" that this was one of "three cases of interest, in which I had the privilege of being associated with Sherlock Holmes and of studying his methods" in "the July which immediately succeeded my marriage"; 1889. Unfortunately, a fuller account of this adventure is missing from the Canon.

His prompt jerked my own memories of a frantic chase through the seedy Limehouse dockyards. I recalled the unfortunate boat-captain who had sought to retire from his smuggling operation, and of the murderous hunter who ended M'Crimmond's life with a powerful air-rifle. And now I remembered his brutal first mate, a giant of a man with just such a tattoo.

M'Crimmond had perished, quieted forever by a crack marksman. The first mate had melted away as well; Holmes had concluded him spirited off by that shadowy mastermind behind the smugglers' schemes. The sailor's name was...

"Barnabus Wells," Holmes supplied. "I had thought it he who informed upon M'Crimmond to his master, but now it seems that Wells also died at that affair's unsatisfactory conclusion."

I could hardly agree with Holmes' pessimistic estimation of a case that ended with handing over a major smuggling ring to the police, and said so.

The detective waved away my praise for his methods. "Wells might have been the key to exposing the coordinator of that business to the forces of the law, but the first mate slipped though my fingers. Now he is gone forever."

I stared at the smoothed hide that had once been a man. "I don't understand how recognising whose skin has been taken to make this bag can lead us to Spearer and Miss Claxton, Holmes."

The Great Detective sat motionless for a full minute, staring past the stuffed wares of the taxidermist's shop into some web of calculation that only Sherlock Holmes could apprehend. His countenance bore that narrow frown which I have learned to associate only with his most troubling cases. Then without warning he sprung up and strode for the door.

"The avalanche has started, Watson! There is no time to lose! Mr. Sherman, our thanks. When you are visited by threatening thugs do not trouble yourself to conceal anything that occurred during our visit. Come, Watson, we are needed!"

He flung himself back into the slushy street, ignored the cab waiting for a fare, and stalked away.

❖ ❖ ❖

The account of Colonel J Sebastian Moran:

I have always disliked Kew, with its broad clean tree-lined streets and neat row houses slumbering amidst carefully-tended garden plots. Give me the wide African Serengeti, tangled with danger and life, or the fierce

The Great Detective sat motionless for a full minute...

rocky Kashmir passages where a red sun rises over steep bandit-haunted slopes. I can endure the seething card-clubs of the City, but the timidity of suburban London is loathsome to me.

Yet it was to docile Kew that the Professor took me. We arrived a little after nine, drawing up not in front of Crawley's residence but rather at the end of Lichfield Road, from whence my comrade could survey the territory.

I was pleased to follow his observations with my own, and I warrant few other men could have traced James Moriarty's diagnosis as swiftly. "The idler by the third elm tree," I noted, "He is watching."

"Very good, Colonel. What else?"

"The two urchin-girls spinning a top. This is not the East End, where ragamuffins play in the street. They have been set to observe also."

The professor nodded. He could not resist playing the tutor. His sunken eyes glinted with cunning. "Mark also the lady with the perambulator who traces a repetitive route up and down the left-hand side of the street, and a young gentleman with carefully-mended trousers pretending to repair a puncture by the post-box behind us. We are expected, Moran."

I felt exposed without my rifle. "An ambush?"

"Say rather a trap. Drive on, Tenney. Take us round to Broomfield Road. The gardens of the houses there abut those of Lichfield Road, and it is through them that the Colonel will gain access to Crawley's house."

It did not surprise me that I would be walking into the situation alone. Although the Professor could be one of the deadliest men alive in a close fight he preferred to remain aloof from such hands-on contact. It was for exactly this kind of undertaking that I was paid six thousand a year.[15]

The carriage rattled round as instructed and halted when the Professor banged his cane on the roof. "Be no more than five minutes," he warned me. "Observe everything but touch nothing. Leave no trace."

I nodded and slipped from the cab. As I dropped to the pavement I cast off that overcoat of manners and decorum that straight-jackets a man in civilised England. I revelled in being Tiger Jack Moran once more, loosed like a big cat to hunt without mercy or apology. There is no thrill like it!

I slipped past the tidy Broomfield Road house, taking the path to the rear, then vaulted the red-brick wall that separated it from Crawley's property. I paused for a moment to check that the reverse of his house was

---

15   Holmes confirms this income in *The Valley of Fear* and notes that it is "more than the Prime Minister gets." This may be another indication of the odd gaps in the Great Detective's knowledge, since the Prime Minister received no salary for holding the post until 1937. In today's money, Moran's annual salary would be around £1.2 million or $1.8 million.

not also watched. I made my way swiftly and silently to the back door and forced the lock.

I'd met Crawley, of course; a fawning, greasy man, eager to give no offence, intimidated by my reputation. At Eton we'd have called him Crawler, but the man had not breeding enough for public school. He used a minor education in horticulture to raise a supply of smoking weed then parlayed that into a thriving business importing substances both legal and illegal for the opium-houses of London. He tithed a fourth part of his earnings to the Professor.

I'd never been in the man's house, though. His conservatory was packed with plants. Their scents almost masked the rank odour of a bachelor with lax housekeeping habits. A paraffin heater stood in the middle of the glass-house to keep the plants warm in these winter days. Its stove was cold.

I nudged the hall door open with my foot, keeping hands free to use my revolvers. The sour stench was stronger away from the greenery.

Howard Crawley was in his living room; or rather his limbs and torso were. He had been nailed above the fireplace just like Trippel. From the look of it he'd died not long after returning from his delivery to the Bar of Gold. They'd known where to find him.

But who? There was no sign of forced entry nor of any struggle, but if Harry Spearer had been with them there would have been no difficulty entering the house without trace.

The only clue was a shattered mug on the floor. I concluded that Crawley had returned from his assignation with Turnpike Luke, no doubt congratulating himself on the deception he'd worked on a man he knew was scheduled for death, indeed, a man he had informed upon so the killers might strike at an opportune time. Crawley had brewed himself a cup of tea and had carried it into his living room. Perhaps he intended to count the money he had received from Trippel? His attackers had awaited him there.

I reached up and checked Crawley's jacket. A blood-drenched envelope of bank-notes was still folded in an interior pocket.

My five minutes was up. I did not even consider ignoring the Professor's instruction. I turned and slipped out the way I had come. Even as I left the conservatory there came a hammering at the front door.

"Open! Open, I say, in the name of the law!"

A convenient policeman had been summoned, doubtless by one of those respectable passers-by in Lichfield Road, to discover a grisly murder and perhaps to catch its supposed perpetrators in the act.

I bounded back over the garden wall and returned to Professor Moriarty.

"We need to get away!" I warned him, outlining in a few terse sentences what I had discovered and how the trap was sprung.

The Professor remained calm and meticulous. "Did you observe Crawley's cat?" he enquired. "A black and white animal of some affection?"

"What? No. No cat. But we must…"

Moriarty picked the fluff-hairs off my jacket and let them blow off in the breeze. "You brushed against a chair, I imagine. The missing feline is not very significant but indicative." He banged on the roof. "Tenney, take us round to Lichfield Road, slow and steady."

"You want us to be seen?"

The Professor peered through those half-lidded eyes. "We have a passenger to pick up," he said, mildly and chillingly.

◈ ◈ ◈

The account of Dr. John H. Watson:

"I'm afraid I must once again utilise the strategy I did in the affair of the Baskerville Hound," Holmes told me regretfully.

"You wish to send me to investigate so that you may undertake some unseen task in the background?"

My friend nodded. "This matter becomes more and more serious, Watson. More lives than you know are imperilled. I can only ask that you trust me to preserve what and whom I may from this murky quag."

"You may count upon me, Holmes. I am certain that I may rely upon you."

Holmes pumped my hand. "Good man! We shall prevail yet!" He drew me round a corner, out of common sight. "You asked how our visit to Sherman and its gruesome revelations might assist in the rescue of Miss Claxton. Now that we apprehend the identity of the unfortunate who donated his distinctive hide, we follow on by investigating the circumstances of his disappearance."

"It is eighteen months since First Mate Wells vanished at the conclusion of the M'Crimmond case,[16]" I objected. "You mentioned then that with the destruction of the smuggling ring, M'Crimmond's elimination, and the absconding of Wells there was no further trace to pursue."

"How well I recall your chagrin, my dear Watson. You would have every investigation conclude itself with a neat summary so that you can convert

16   "The Naval Treaty", which references the Adventure of the Tired Captain, took place over 30th July – 1st October 1889 according to most Holmes chronologists.

them into your idealised accounts.[17] Not every case can offer so convenient a finale. Where no evidence exists no conclusion may be drawn."

"Then how do you propose that I take up the trail of the late Barnabus Wells now?" I asked, perhaps a trifle huffily.

Holmes handed me the gruesome bag. "That tattoo will unlock lips for you, Watson. Those who remained silent for fear of the fierce Wells' reprisal will know that they need no longer keep their peace. Those who hid him for affection will now tell what they may to bring his tormentor to light."

"Very well. Where shall I begin?"

Holmes pencilled down a name and address rather than speak it aloud. He was taking particular precautions. "Speak to that young woman," he advised me in a low undertone. "She had nothing but sauce when I interviewed her then, but I expect she will have a different story to tell you now. If she is no longer employed at that location then ask amongst her former workmates where she might be now."

"What if they will not speak?"

Holmes' mouth quirked a little, as it did when something tickled his odd humour. "You might wish to intimate that you are the father of her child, come at last to make financial reparation."

"Holmes!"

"When Barnabus Wells disappeared he left the girl in an unfortunate condition. I am convinced that her silence was spurred by the conviction that he would return for her when the hue had passed. A year of labouring as an unwed mother, abandoned by the man who quickened her, might encourage any young woman to think again about concealing where he went."

"I'll seek her out," I agreed. "What shall I do when I have interviewed her?"

"Return directly to Baker Street," Holmes advised. "And keep your wits about you. Oh, one other thing. I would be obliged if you would pen a brief note attesting that the bearer is one whom you trust."

I opened my pocket-book and scratched out the requested message. "May I ask why this is required?"

"I must ask again for your trust, Watson. I do not keep you in the dark for frivolous reasons, at least not on this occasion, but rather because your

---

17   At this time, literary agent Arthur Ignatius Conan Doyle had sold two Watson manuscripts for publication. "A Study in Scarlet" featured in *Beeton's Christmas Annual* 1887 and "The Sign of Four" in *Lippincott's Monthly Magazine* in 1890. It was not until July 1891, three months after Watson lost Holmes at Reichenbach Falls, that the first short account of a Holmes case, "A Scandal in Bohemia", appeared in The Strand Magazine.

manner and reasoning must not be tainted by my suspicions. Go on your way and do what you can. I must make some urgent arrangements and conduct an investigation of my own."

We parted at that, me to head back into the crowded East End, Holmes striding away through the grimy snow, long-coat billowing behind him. I made my way to the address my friend had provided, a laundry-house in a yard off Lombard Street.

It was not easy to find. I had to pass down a narrow alley into a tiny court, then duck under half-frozen lines of dripping washing. Clouds of steam guided me to a shuttered doorway into a fusty tropical-hot interior.

The contrast struck me like a hot wet towel in the face. The laundry teemed with people hurrying about their industry. A thin Chinaman approached to make me understand that this was the service entrance. Evidently some shop-front was the approved access for visitors. I dredged up what pigeon-talk I recalled from my time in Nanking, showed him the yen coin on my watch-chain, and eventually managed to explain, with the help of a half-crown, that I was looking for a Miss Ginnie Seaforth.

The woman was still there, labouring away with a heavy stirring ladle at a steaming cauldron of whites. My first impression was that she was a mere girl of fourteen or fifteen. It was only when she was called and looked up to us on the gantry that I observed the weary lines etched into her face and old eyes that had seen too much of a cruel world. She came docilely when summoned, handing her pole to the supervising matron and climbing the metal stair to join us.

I tipped my hat. "How do you do, Miss Seaforth? May we speak for a moment?"

She glanced at the Chinaman. He nodded curtly. I took her arm and deliberately led her out of earshot to the end of the gantry.

"What d' you want?" she asked in the defeated tones of a woman who would yield anything.

"Miss Seaforth, I have some most unpleasant news," I warned her. "I must ask you to be brave."

Her eyes widened. "Charlie…?" she squeaked, her hands rising to her mouth.

"Not your child," I assured her, guessing who might be foremost on her mind when warned of danger.

She unhunched a fraction. "Then what?"

I apologised again and showed her the pouch.

"No," she declared, shaking her head and backing away a pace. "No. No, it's… No."

"Miss Seaforth?"

"It's a trick. An 'orrible trick. Ain't it? It must be. No'un would do that!"

"My word that it is true, Miss Seaforth. Some cruel enemy has murdered Barnabus Wells and used his flesh in this manner."

I had expected tears, and they came. I had not expected thanks, but I got them. "He's dead, then. Murdered. He didn't abandon us. He meant what he said!"

"I'm afraid I don't follow you, Miss Seaforth."

The washer-girl knuckled away tears. "You must know about Barney and me, to 'ave come 'ere like this. You must know about our Charlie."

I admitted as much.

"Then you might know that Barney 'ad to run off. It all went wrong, see? The Peelers came to the boat and got all the shipment from LeHavre. I don't rightly know the detail of it. But Barney comes to me that night and warns me as 'e'd got to vanish fer a bit. I'd 'ave gone with 'im only 'e said it were too dangerous."

"You were with child."

She touched her belly. "I was. Only three months, maybe, but I knew. Me mam said I should go see the old woman in Kitchener's Yard, but I wouldn't. Barney said as 'e'd be back for me, see, and afterwards we'd 'ave a life together, me and 'im and the babe. 'E'd got to go, but 'e'd come back, that's what he promised."

"But he never came?"

"Never. I got rounder and rounder and no Barney, and me friends laughing at me for being such a fool, and all the neighbours sneering, as if any o' them's any better. At least I only ever slutted wi' one man, I told 'em, and 'e'd be back for me. Then Charlie were born, sickly but living, and… no Barney. It's a year now. I was telling meself I'd been made a right fool of, that 'e never did care tuppence for me. I was starting to hate 'im."

She stopped to sniff. I gave her my pocket handkerchief.

Ginnie Seaforth reached out and touched her fingertips to the faint tattoo on the humanskin purse. "But that's not why 'e didn't come. 'E did love me, and Charlie. 'E didn't walk away laughing. 'E were done to death!"

It was a curious mix of sorrow and joy. Her lover was killed, but he had been vindicated of the accusations she had allowed to creep into her doubting mind. Miss Seaforth could now mourn a man she'd loved, without the sour taint of suspicion that he'd cared nothing for her.

"Where did Wells run to, then?" I enquired. "It can do no harm to tell me now."

She looked at me sharply. "Can it not? You stand there showing me my Barney's skin all peeled to make a bag an' say there's naught to fear? My Barney were as strong as any three men and 'e could strike down a prizefighter, but look what they did to 'im!"

"Help me to find who did this and bring him to justice."

Miss Seaforth stared down into the steaming pot of scalding sheets. She reached a decision. "That last night when Barney came to me, 'e told me what 'e'd done. Captain M'Crimmond, him as Barney worked for, 'ad turned traitor and intended to tell all 'e knew about the smuggling game to win escape to Canada and an easy retirement. Barney could've peached too an' slipped away wi' coin in 'is pocket, but 'e weren't that sort. So 'e did what 'e should 'ave, and warned M'Crimmond's boss about what the Captain were doing."

"What boss was that?" I asked.

The girl shrugged. "Never 'eard him named, but 'e was the big man alright. M'Crimmond didn't last the night, did 'e? Air-rifle cartridge right between the eyes, they says. Nobody can double-cross the big boss and live."

"But you say that Wells didn't cross him. In fact it was he who alerted that chief to M'Crimmond's desertion." Holmes had always suspected that Wells had turned on his Captain, a contention undermined only by the First Mate's subsequent disappearance.

Miss Seaforth nodded. "That's why Barney expected to come into a bit o' money when 'e was back. 'I 'as to go hide out for a week or two while the rozzers does their snooping,' 'e told me, 'but when I'm back there'll be a nice reward from the big boss for loyalty and initiative. Enough for you and me and the kid.' That's what 'e said, last time I saw 'im."

"That's why you said nothing to Mr. Sherlock Holmes."

"You knows about that? In 'e comes, with 'is beaky nose all a-quivering, staring at me like I'm a piece in a museum, telling me 'ow I got to work and what I 'ad for supper and the like, aye, and telling me that I was up the duff as if I didn't well know it, and expecting me to turn on Barney. Well I'm not that sort, an' I told 'im so. Same when that Scotland Yard blighter turned up a couple o' days later threatening to run me in."

I filed away that description of Holmes' habits for a time when my friend was being particularly annoying. "You really did know where Barnabus Wells had gone, though?"

"Oh aye," the washer-girl confessed. "'E was 'iding out with a mate of 'is at an opium-house on Swandam Lane, name of The Bar of Gold."

❖❖❖

The account of Colonel J Sebastian Moran:

We hardly stopped the carriage, halting only long enough for me to scoop in the young man with the bicycle problem who still crouched tending to his contraption fifty yards down Lichfield Road from where the policeman was sounding his emergency whistle. I hauled the unfortunate fellow into the cab by the scruff of his neck while Tenney lashed up the horses and moved us away from other watching eyes.

"Wha...?" the young man managed to gasp as I pushed him down onto the seat opposite Professor Moriarty.

I pressed the tip of my stick into the youngster's Adam's apple. "This cane contains an ingenious little mechanism by the blind gunsmith von Herder. He guarantees that a brief squeeze of the handle releases an air-pressured .33 pellet at a velocity of two hundred and thirty miles an hour.[18] You may wish to remain completely motionless."

Our captive froze in place.

"Very wise," I assured him. "Professor?"

Moriarty can sit absolutely still for long periods of time, so motionless as to resemble a gaunt brooding statue. When he then moves, sliding his head one way and another, focussing those dark brooding eyes, it can be somewhat disturbing; especially for the subject of his attention.

"An educated young man, but not academically excellent," the Professor adjudged. "Graduated last year, judging by the state of his jacket elbows. Keeble, if his choice of waistcoat and pocket-chain device can tell us as much. Of limited income, according to the imperfectly removed pawnbroker's mark on his coat lining. A gambler, somewhat desperate to recoup lost fortunes, says the pink sporting paper in his inner pocket and the dog-eared betting stubs within his hatband. Dwells near Hampstead Heath with a landlady of shabby domestic habits, since telltale mud-spots remain on his trouser-cuffs. Your name, boy?"

Our passenger stared at the Professor with a mounting horror. I twisted the cane-tip at his throat.

"Kennedy," he choked. "J. P. Kennedy."

"What were you commissioned to do today, Mister Kennedy?"

"Nothing! That is... a fellow offered me ten bob[19] to idle on the street there and bear witness to anything that happened. He said some men might turn up at a house and there'd be an uproar. I should rush and look

---

18   This device is first described in "The Empty House", wherein it shatters a bust of Holmes that is casting a lifelike silhouette at the window of 221B Baker Street.

19   Ten shillings, half of a pound sterling, perhaps equivalent to £100 or $150 in modern currency.

at what was happening."

"To see you and I being caught next to Crawley's body, Professor," I supposed. "Plenty of witnesses to the scene, dragging you into the spotlight."

"Indeed," agreed Moriarty. "That is why we undertook our investigation somewhat differently."

I followed my train of thought to a conclusion. "We were expected at Lichfield Road. Someone knows your deductive abilities and expected you to follow the trail. Turnpike Luke's murder wasn't because of something he had done; it was because he was one of your men, under your protection!"

"Of course it was," the Professor confirmed, as if he was disappointed that I hadn't seen it earlier. "That was why Trippel was executed in so public and noteworthy a manner. Although we eradicated the evidence that might otherwise have led to attention in the newspapers there were plenty of clients who might stagger away with half-remembered impressions, as well as those staff at the Bar of Gold who discovered the murder and summoned us. Word will percolate in the criminal quarters. If I do not address things my reputation will suffer."

Kennedy looked from one to other of us. His ashen expression showed he had realised how deep into trouble he had stumbled. "Look, I just did a favour for a chap in a pub. I never..."

"Be silent until I have questions for you!" the Professor snapped at him. "Moran, you are correct in saying that these assaults were not against their victims but against me. Other snares were laid too. Doubtless there were clues left at old Spearer's shop that would have led me into other ambushes had I not fobbed them off to be triggered instead by Sherlock Holmes."

"Then Holmes is not behind this? Some fiercer attempt from the detective to cause your downfall that..."

"This is far from Holmes' methods. He is a thinker, a problem-solver. His snares are rational and subtle. He does not condone murder nor enjoy it in the brutal manner of our present adversary. Although Holmes might be at the root of the problem, all the same..."

The Professor left his thought unfinished. The carriage hastened along Twickenham Road, heading for Hounslow Heath.

"Why not let me eliminate Holmes from the problem?" I ventured at last. "I have offered before."

"Holmes is not to be touched," Moriarty commanded. "Not yet. No man in Europe stimulates my thinking as he does. I am still enjoying our game of shadows. He might yet become my valued lieutenant."

"Sherlock Holmes?"

"The same. Conjecture a chain of events wherein he is made to understand the absurdity of his moral view. Betrayal by and the subsequent suicide of his companion John H. Watson,[20] for example. Public backlash, ostracisation, disdain. A few simple misdirections to set the police on his trail for some capital crime and he would sour very well. A year after that he would be mine, a worthy operative, a potential successor."

"You have given this some thought, Professor."

"I have given everything about Mr. Sherlock Holmes some thought, Colonel. He tests me as I have never been tested. More, he tests my theories of organisation of the criminal world, and every science must be proved through rigorous peer review. In short, I need Holmes. He must not be harmed." The Professor turned his basilisk stare back to young Kennedy. "This person, however, will not be required much longer."

Kennedy tried to swallow but found my gun-cane pressing hard to his epiglottis.

My colleague went on, inexorable in his deductions. "Mr. Kennedy has lied to me, you see, Moran, and I detest that. He claimed to have been commissioned by 'a man in a pub' for a fee of ten shillings."

"I was!" the graduate blurted before remembering the command to silence.

"A lie of omission is still a lie," Moriarty chided him. "When the man approached you, I would judge last night, given the creases in your trousers and the redness of eye that indicates no sleep, he clearly offered some threat as well as a banknote to solicit your support. What was it?"

"Please..." Kennedy begged. Why do these soft townsmen always beg? "I can't say. He will kill her!"

Professor Moriarty watched the terrified youth with an impassive coldness. "Some menace was implied against a loved one? A relative? No, a young woman of your acquaintance, whose handkerchief you have retained in your inner pocket. Let me see..."

My friend whipped the lacy scrap from Kennedy's waistcoat. The

---

20   Casual Holmes readers are often surprised to learn that Dr Watson's Christian name John is only mentioned three times in the Canon. On a fourth occasion his second wife refers to him as James (in "The Man With the Twisted Lip"). His middle initial H, referenced in "The Problem of Thor Bridge", remains an enigma.
However, the great mystery author Dorothy L. Sayers, writing in *Unpopular Opinions* (Gollancz, 1946) on "Dr Watson's Christian Name", posits that Mary Morstan Watson disliked the name John and so used James as an affectionate alternative. James is the English form of Hamish, so Miss Sayers speculates that Mary choose to address her husband by his Anglicised middle name. If anyone beyond Conan Doyle is to have the privilege of clarifying the good doctor's full nomenclature as John Hamish Watson it is surely fitting that it be the illustrious and scholarly chronicler of Lord Peter Wimsey.

handkerchief was brittle with dried brown stains. A severed finger was rolled inside.

"Hell's teeth!" I barked.

The Professor examined the digit carefully. "It is your friend's finger that is rolled inside this token?" he asked our captive.

Kennedy's voice was tight and low, almost choked. "Yes. If I do not, that is, did not, go to Lichfield Road and bear witness then Claribel would be harmed in worse and viler ways."

Moriarty sneered. "She is already dead. You have been set as another snare for us, Kennedy. Even if the Colonel had not snatched you from the street you would have been eliminated by sunset to prevent loose ends. Our opponent is a curious mix of Guignol cruelty and meticulous planning."

"Dead? No! He promised!"

"He?" I asked. "Describe him."

The interrogation lasted all the way to rural Feltham, by which time we had established a generic description of a well-dressed man who might be anyone. Kennedy had been instructed to remain on Lichfield Road until there was a furore with the police, then appear to testify to the Professor and I entering Crawley's house with menaces. Kennedy had indeed been paid for his pains; Moriarty confiscated the banknote with its unique identifying number.

"A final question," the Professor insisted as we rumbled into the lonely farm that was our destination. "Did your man have any particular odour to him?"

"What? No. Well, perhaps he was well scrubbed, disinfected." Kennedy gabbled. "I… do not know how to… what to… oh, Claribel!"

Moriarty lost interest. "Colonel, you may feed the pigs now," he told me.

The fat porkers of Feltham Farm quite enjoyed Kennedy.

❖ ❖ ❖

The account of Dr. John H. Watson:

On my return that evening to the familiarity of Baker Street the door was opened by a broad pug-faced bruiser who glared at me in open enmity.

"All's well, Mr. Paxon," Mrs Hudson assured the brute, hurrying forward to identify me as a legitimate visitor to my former chambers. To me she added, "Mr. Holmes has arranged for Mr. Paxon to stand watch for a few days, along with some of his fellow boxers."

I could well recognise the signs of a pugilist. One does not need to be Sherlock Holmes to interpret the flattened nose, cauliflower ears, irregular teeth, or calloused knuckles of a habitual ring-fighter. "But why does Holmes feel the need for protection?" I wondered.

Mrs Hudson shivered. "It is not for him. It is for me."

I hurried upstairs to our rooms. Holmes was squatted in his chair, feet on the cushion, scraping away at his Stradivarius. As soon as I entered he laid the instrument aside and jumped up.

"What is going on?" I demanded.

"I told you I needed to do some things, Watson. We face a foe with a penchant for seizing and maiming those close to his targets. I thought it best to ensure that the people most likely to come to harm if our enemy goes for us should be protected."

A chill rippled through me. "Mary!"

"Mrs. Watson is being escorted to Sir Reginald Musgrave's estate at Hurlstone even as we speak, by trusted men identified to her by the note you kindly prepared."

Holmes had told me of his university acquaintance with Musgrave and of his service to that ancient family.[21] It was clear that my friend felt that Mary was safe in West Sussex. Even so, the thought of Molly Claxton's vicious kidnapper turning his malice upon my wife was a terrifying one.

"A precaution only," Holmes assured me, "but better to err on the side of caution." He pressed his long hands together as if in prayer. "Now tell me how you prospered with Miss Seaforth."

I outlined the unfortunate woman's experience. Holmes listened to my account without interruption, then allowed himself a small chuckle. "That is not where the interview ended, though, is it Watson?"

"What do you mean, Holmes?"

"I know my old friend. You were touched by Miss Seaforth's plight, by her sickly child and diminished position. You gave her money and left her your card, inviting her to bring the infant for care at your practice, did you not?"

I confessed that I had. Holmes clapped me on the back. "It is that generosity of spirit which makes you a better man than I, Watson!"

"But her testimony, Holmes! The Bar of Gold!" I had been to that low dive over a year before, in pursuit of an addict patient who had reverted to his habit, and had been surprised to encounter Holmes himself disguised on a case.[22]

The detective shook his head. "The place burned down this morning," he reported, pushing over a Times clipping describing the East-End

---

21   Recounted by Holmes to Watson in "The Musgrave Ritual".

22   In "The Man With The Twisted Lip"

slum fire. "There were several fatalities. Fire inspectors are blaming an overturned oil stove."

"I presume you have concluded differently?"

"I have not been docile while you approached Miss Seaforth, my dear Watson. After making the security arrangements of which you are now apprised I opened up my disguise kit and assumed the identity of a dockland loafer. In that character I traced one of the few staff that survived the drug-house fire. Four pints of brown stout unsealed his tongue and dragged out his shocking story; of how the house manager Trippel was found nailed up and headless in his own den."

"Surely that fact would have come to the police, whatever the damage done by the fire?"

"My drunken bouncer revealed that the anonymous proprietor of the Bar of Gold removed the corpse and arranged to keep matters quiet. That included the elimination of those addicts too fuddled to quit the premises when the flames were set."

"Then that man is a murderer, perhaps the same who killed this Trippel!"

"Not the same. There is more. My sources tell me that a second beheading was discovered later this morning, in the pleasant neighbourhood of Kew. Kindly pass me that dossier marked with the letter C."

I handed the file from Holmes' cluttered bureau.

"Howard Rupert Crawley dropped his pharmaceutical training for the more lucrative career of drug-provider," Holmes told me. "He graduated to London five years back and has come to prominence as supplier of narcotics both legal[23] and exotic. He was amongst those I had hoped to catch from the testimony of Captain M'Crimmond. He was the second man today to turn up pinned to a wall lacking a head."

"I have not heard the paper-boys shouting about this," I noted. Usually such a sensation would be all their cry.

"The matter has been held close by Scotland Yard at the instruction of a Minister of State," Holmes revealed. "My assistance in the matter has been peremptorily declined."

"What reason is there for suppressing news of the outrage?"

"Ask rather, Watson, who has the influence to order such a thing. The same man who might cremate some eight or nine poppy addicts in an East End slum and have the fire marshals proclaim an accident, perhaps?"

---

23   Opium was legal in Victorian Great Britain, and was used both medically and recreationally. There was even a vogue for society opium parties, at which children as well as adults indulged in the smoke. However, addiction was frowned upon, and the dispensation of opium was limited first to prescription by pharmacists, and when that was proved too easy to misuse, was restricted in 1920 to prescription by doctors.

I admit that an unexpected shiver coursed through me. "You mean Professor Moriarty," I said.[24] "Surely this cannot be coincidence?"

"It is not. A single skein runs through everything we have encountered. The bank-notes given to Spearer were withdrawn from the account of Moriarty's confederate Sebastian Moran, though I doubt Moran knows that notes he has spent have been deliberately used to implicate him. The information you gleaned from Miss Seaforth is another confirmation."

"Then you have a solution? Let us go and save Miss Claxton if we may, and the lock-breaker Spearer!"

Holmes held up his hand to caution me to wait. A moment later I heard raised voices in the lobby below, and Mrs Hudson's mollifying tones.

"I believe the final part of our puzzle is now available," my friend declared. "Come in, Wiggins! No need to knock!"

The gangling lad shambled in, wrists and ankles protruding from clothes he had long outgrown. I reflected that it must be ten years now that this likely youth had led that informal gang of urchins who were employed by my friend to "go everywhere, see everything, overhear everyone."[25] He was a young man now; Holmes and I had discussed securing him a footman's post at the Diogenes Club.

"Mr. 'Olmes, sir!" Wiggins said, doffing his soft cap and cupping it in his palms. "We done what you asked us to. You owe Albert Sutter his guinea."

"Indeed?" Holmes replied, leaning forward. "And what has the ingenious Albert turned up?"

"'E talked to Milly Claxton's landlady, like you said, and then to the girl what shares a room with 'er. E's got a winning way, our Albert. Anyways, he got out o' the lass that Milly might be in a difficult situation." Wiggins actually blushed.

"Is that to say that the young woman is with child?" I clarified.

The youth nodded. "That's what 'er room-mate said, anyhow. Milly's young man didn't know though. Milly was thinking about going quiet-like to the old woman in Kitchener's Yard what sorts out things like that."

"And young Spearer might have disapproved?"

---

24   There is an apparent contradiction in the Canon regarding Watson's knowledge of the Napoleon of Crime. "The Final Problem", published in 1893, describes the 1891 events of Holmes' ultimate confrontation with his nemesis. In that tale Watson describes Holmes revealing Moriarty's name and nature to him mere hours before the concluding events of the Holmes/Moriarty conflict play out. However, *The Valley of Fear*, published in 1914-15 but set in 1888, makes clear that Watson was well aware of the Professor at that time, three years before Reichenbach. Most Holmesian scholars have concluded that Watson inserted a much earlier conversation with Holmes about the identity of Moriarty into his Final Problem narrative so as to make the story smoother and more readable.

25   The Baker Street irregulars were described thus by Holmes in *The Sign of Four*.

Wiggins hefted a shoulder to dissociate himself with such things. He turned his cap round in his fingers and looked uncomfortable.

"What else have you for me?" Holmes demanded.

"You asked about coaches last night on Upper Swandham Lane," the lad went on. "Nobody saw nothing. Nothing at all."

"Which means they are too frightened to identify the carriage that arrived to investigate Trippel's death," Holmes concluded. "A useful confirmation, but effectively robbing us of word of any earlier visitors. What else?"

"There's some loafers watching old Spearer's place, like you said they would be," Wiggins reported. "Pugsy got a clip around the ear for hanging about, but e' heard one of 'em mentioning sending word back to Fenner."

"One of the Professor's guard-dogs," Holmes supplied to me. "This is all merely routine. Anything else, Wiggins? You know how I rely upon my Irregulars."

For some reason that brought the youngster nearly to tears. Then he collapsed altogether, dropping to his knees before Holmes' armchair.

"I'm sorry, sir!" he cried, clutching at my friend's smoking jacket hem. "I'm sorry! They 'as Jenny!"

I looked over at my friend. "Jenny? Holmes…?"

The Great Detective patted Wiggins' hands uncomfortably and rose to dislodge the lad's grip on his robe. "Jenny Wheeler of Blenheim Court, Whitechapel," he proclaimed. "In day service, I believe, at the household of Mr. Crosby the tailor. Young Wiggins here has been walking out with her on Sundays, have you not?"

Wiggins didn't bother to ask how Holmes might know. He took it as natural law that the detective would discern all. He merely nodded miserably. "I couldn't send you to your death, sir," he blubbered, "but they 'ave 'er. They've got her and they said…"

"That if you did not feed some detail to me then she would be harmed," Holmes completed the sentence for him. "Ah! See how my enemy turns even my greatest assets against me!"

"How did you learn that Miss Wheeler had been taken?" I asked Wiggins cautiously.

I half-expected him to produce another severed finger. Instead he told of an unremarkable but sly-looking youth of a similar age to himself bringing word and a note of hand. He showed Holmes the letter, wherein a trembling script read, 'I am captured. Help me. Your Jenny.'

"Cheap unbonded paper, common ink, deliberately bland," Holmes observed. "The handwriting suggests genuine distress but offers no

"...they 'ave 'er. They've got her and they said..."

practical help." He turned back to Wiggins. "This sly youth instructed you to tell me about Miss Wheeler's condition, did he not?"

"He told me to ask the room-mate," Wiggins confirmed. "So I 'ad our Albert go in there primed."

"The murderer wants you to know something!" I reasoned. "A trap?"

"Perhaps, Watson. This is not the first time that the old woman of Kitchener's Yard has popped up in this investigation."

"Ginnie Seaforth mentioned her, yes." I was glad now to have given Holmes so meticulous an account of my conversation with Wells' paramour. "A woman who performs abortions for the lower classes might also have some skill in other medical procedures, or perhaps in taxidermy."

Holmes stepped around Wiggins and searched amongst his indexed files again. "M contains more than the obvious Professor," he attested, flicking back and forth through the pages. "Maxwell, Morton, Milverton, Murdoch, Munday-Smythe, Moran... ah, here we are. Merridew of Houndsditch; the very woman!"

Wiggins climbed to his feet. "Will you go to her, Mister 'Olmes?" he worried.

"We shall, Wiggins," Holmes assured the anxious street-lad before returning to his notes. "Let's see... She has been resident in Kitchener's Yard for the best part of twenty years. In addition to her gynecological services she has a long record of treating fugitives who have been injured in ways that preclude them from visiting a hospital. She is one of those protected few about whom no one will testify..."

"One of Moriarty's creatures!" I exclaimed.

"Very possibly, Watson. In any case, we are being urged to pay her a visit. Have your revolver ready."

"Should we not summon assistance from Scotland Yard?"

Holmes' lips quirked. "If only there were assistance to be had! No, Watson, not another jibe at the professional competence of our esteemed colleagues but rather a concern that, where Moriarty is involved, not even every officer in a blue tunic and helmet may be what he seems. The silence about Crawley is telling. We must journey to Kitchener's Yard alone."

"May I come, Mister 'Olmes?" asked Wiggins.

"For you, another task," the detective replied. He snapped shut the dossier. "Events cascade. Nothing can be left to chance. Let us move on to the crescendo!"

❖ ❖ ❖

The account of Colonel J. Sebastian Moran:

Professor Moriarty was no stranger to the corridors and lecture halls of Bart's Hospital, but I had not previously been aware of how extensive his infiltration of that institution had been. We swept through reception, down green-beige corridors, past long sick-wards, into the maze of service tunnels beneath the sanatorium. There, in a dingy specimen room, the genius of crime waited for those he had summoned to attend him.

"Why this place?" I asked as various minions shuffled into our presence.

"Our adversary knows my regular habits and haunts," the Professor replied. If ever there was a hint of enjoyment in his gaunt face it was now; the challenge stimulated him. "There are a few points to confirm before summing up the equation."

I was surprised that so many key men were assembled in one place. There was Kirk, who ran the docklands, Partridge the financier, Gunnell the betting agent, Wenlock from the Foreign Office, Fenner the enforcer, Jenson the forger, and nearly a dozen other big fry.

I listened patiently as the Professor debriefed and dismissed the minor agents he had set to tasks earlier in the day. I was unsurprised to learn that the various coachmen who had ferried Sherlock Holmes and Dr. Watson around were in my friend's employ. Their accounts of the consulting detective's movements and the comments he had passed to his companion pleased Moriarty.

He paid special attention to the investigators that had visited the taxidermist Sherman. It was from this account that we learned the detail of Spearer's woman's finger. "A predilection for stuffing specimens," Moriarty commented. "You will recall Crawley's missing cat."

Fenner summarised how his agents had learned that the Claxton girl was in trouble and how her friend had been properly primed to confess the indiscretion to whichever of Holmes' creatures was sent to enquire.

The cringing Pretlow had been diverted from Moriarty's chambers to our hidden meeting. He brought Merridew's report on the poison used to paralyse Turnpike Luke: an exotic mixture of South American curare and carnitine. Police pathologists working on Crawley had been far less efficient in their diagnosis than our abominable associate.

I perked up when Blackstock came forward to speak. Blackstock was another of us, the inner circle. He knew his job. At Moriarty's behest he had dispatched one of his young Turks to coerce the leader of Holmes' ragamuffin Irregulars.

"It was not our enemy who kidnapped this girl?" I understood. "Rather she is held at Blackstock's warehouse to convince Holmes that his quarry has taken another hostage?"

"Yes," the Professor snapped. "Had I realised that our foe had such a predilection for fingers I would have had Blackstock deliver one of Miss Wheeler's, of course. The omission irritates me. Holmes appreciates detail."

Partridge testified next. I was shocked to find the bank-notes from Kennedy traced back to my account.

"All part of the snare, Colonel," Moriarty sniffed. "Some doxy you spend your earnings on has been suborned to pass the money on to our foe so that you may be implicated."

"What foe, though? Are you now prepared to tell me who has challenged your authority by executing Trippel and Crawley?"

Moriarty often regards those around him as if they were drooling idiots. I dislike it when he includes me. "Is it not obvious, Moran?"

"Not to me," I grumbled. "If everyone was as clever as Professor Moriarty we would not all be your faithful followers."

The Professor relented. "Think, then. The intention was to weaken me, to challenge my command, preferably to expose me to public scrutiny. At a time when Mr. Holmes' investigations press ever nearer to our core, as my lieutenants become nervous that their deeds might be discovered, as criminals whisper that perhaps I have over-reached, our adversary has chosen to strike."

"Someone, then, with hopes of claiming your position?" I speculated, looking at the circle of senior men who had been summoned. "Someone well-informed, certainly, to know of the Bar of Gold, of Crawley's deliveries, of young Spearer and his woman, even of how we would likely investigate the outrages."

The Professor wiggled his fingertips to coax more out of me.

"Someone medically trained, with knowledge of both toxins and surgery, who does not hesitate to maim if required, and who commands several brutal agents."

"Do not forget the salient evidence. I told you at the start that this was a case based on empirical observation. The out-of-fashion almost-new half-boots were the vital clue."

"A boot purchased long ago and seldom worn," I realised, "since its owner then decided that ladies' footwear was more to his tastes!"

Moriarty gave the faintest nod, as a schoolmaster might acknowledge a backward child that has finally mastered a trigonometry problem. "Your abhorred Merridew, of course."

He snapped his fingers. Fenner and Blackstock seized Pretlow. "No!" cried the medical assistant before a gut-punch silenced him. The laboratory assistant still stank of the cleaning fluids used to sluice away autopsy smells, the distinctive aroma that betrayed him as the man in Kennedy's pub.

"Emmanuel Merridew," mused the Professor. "Who would be better placed, whilst repairing those wounds which our followers occasionally receive in the course of their duties, to apply ether and interrogate them without them ever realising it? Once indiscretions were known, a blackmailer's grip may become a stranglehold. Snaring a wretched pervert like Crawley or a feeble-minded lackey such as Trippel would be simple."

"Then why kill them? If they were Merridew's agents, why dispose of useful assets?"

"For the same reason that Barnabus Wells had to die, after he was persuaded by Merridew into urging M'Crimmond's rebellion, then thought again and betrayed his chief to us. That early gambit of Merridew's was thwarted when you gave our tired captain the retirement he craved, Moran. I imagine Porlock's indiscretion was another attempt.[26] Dr. Merridew could not allow vacillating pawns to weaken and tell us all. What better means to dispose of such weaklings than to turn their executions into the finale of a campaign to disgrace and displace me?"

Pretlow shuddered in Fenner's grip. An examination of the assistant's shoes would confirm him at the Bar of Gold.

My hand was already on the gun in my pocket. "Give the word, then. I'll relish ridding the world of the vile Merridew!"

Others in the room had also been listening raptly to the Professor speak. Each of them broke in with offers to destroy the abomination.

Moriarty raised his hand and commanded instant silence. "You still fail to perceive his scheme. These executions and the minor snares to expose me are mere diversions, to keep me chasing round while the master-stroke is struck. Merridew knows well that when my pride is pricked my temper sours. I become vindictive and demonstrative. You know me well, Colonel. What would you expect me to do?"

I gestured to the men in the room. "You'd summon your closest agents, Merridew amongst them. You'd lay out your chain of reasoning, as you have, then turn on the traitor and have him seized. You would make an example of him, for the education of others."

"Merridew calculated likewise," the Professor hissed. "When he received his telegram summoning him to our meeting he would be ready to act."

"The doctor's not here!" Blackstock objected. He stared around the

---

26   Porlock's warning to Holmes about Moriarty's intent came too late in *The Valley of Fear.*

specimen room as if expecting the abomination to be lurking behind some bell-jar or bookshelf.

"That is because, whilst I summoned each of you to meet at this unconventional venue, I told Merridew that the meeting was in my rooms."

"Then he'll go to the wrong place?" I puzzled. "I don't see how…"

"It is not he who will arrive at my chambers," Moriarty scorned. "Why should he? No, it will be Scotland Yard that arrives, equipped with warrants from Sir Tarrant Besting.[27] Merridew hopes that they will come across us all assembled. A search of the premises would doubtless find the missing heads of Trippel and Crawley, previously concealed there by Pretlow during his visit to report on forensic tests, intended to implicate me, and all of you, in those public murders."

"I had no choice!" howled the frantic Pretlow. "You do not know what he is capable of! How much he hates! What he does to those in his power; Trippel, Crawley, Kennedy's girl, Moran's whore…"

Moriarty signalled for him to be silenced for now. Pretlow's confession would be long and final. His accomplices in Turnpike Luke's murder were equally doomed.

"And with each of us locked away or held on suspicion, who but Merridew might step in and reform the underworld?" I snarled.

"Who else but one that has spent the better part of twenty years gathering secrets on each criminal that crosses his path, from the wounded we send him, from the fallen women who seek his services when some agent of ours has been careless with them? I said our adversary was a meticulous planner, for all his flair for gore."

"All the more reason to send me at him now!" I thundered. If the abomination had been present I would have cheerfully strangled him till those painted lips turned blue and cold.

"Do you not imagine that he will have anticipated that also and made his preparations?" my friend chided. "No, Colonel, I have sent another agent to do the deed. Have I not, Blackstock?"

A slow grin blossomed across the intelligencer's face. "Mr. Sherlock Holmes!" he declared.

◈ ◈ ◈

The account of Dr. John H. Watson:

The access to Mrs. Merridew's cellar was a reinforced door down a short flight of outside steps. There was no lock, denoting stout bolts inside.

---

27   An active and enthusiastic Assistant Crown Prosecutor, previously seen in "Dead Man's Manuscript" in *Sherlock Holmes: Consulting Detective volume 1.*

A small spy-hole was let into the peeling panelling.

Holmes made no attempt to gain entry. He produced from a carpet-bag a thick chain and heavy padlock. He wrapped the links around the metal door-handle and fastened it to the stair railings. Opening the door was now impossible.

"There will be other ways in," my friend assured me.

It was almost dark, and Kitchener's Yard had no street lamp. What doors and windows did look out onto the cramped dingy square were nailed up with old boards. Holmes examined each one carefully.

"Here, Watson!" he called. "The nails on this frame have been bent over on the other side. They do not penetrate the jamb. Indeed, the whole is secretly hinged, to swivel away thus! And there, a lock!" The detective dealt with the mechanism adroitly enough to make the Spearers proud.

I checked my service revolver again. "What shall we find inside? There may be three hostages: young Spearer, his Milly, and Wiggins' lass."

"Not Jenny Wheeler, at any rate," Holmes told me. "Did you not discern the difference in her capture and ransom? No, Wiggins was set to point me here by one who has likewise deduced Merridew's guilt."

"You mean Moriarty?"

"Of course. His involvement was clear from the start. How else would old Spearer know to race all the way from his shop to Spitalfields Market?" Holmes pondered for a second. "And now I know to beware the second cab," he muttered.

"Is Moriarty in there, then?"

"Oh no. He will be somewhere else, somewhere public. His alibi will be impeccable, while we do his dirty work."

"But if he has Miss Wheeler…"

"Not he, but men he retains for such purposes. Where do you think I sent young Wiggins? About now, Blackstock's secret warehouse will be besieged by dozens of angry young street-Arabs set to rescue the fair damsel and to deliver the drubbing of a lifetime to bravos as humble but less honourable than themselves. The Charge of the Irregular Brigade! I furnished Wiggins with a full site plan and loaned him my second-best cane-stick."

I couldn't withhold a snort at the thought of the fiendish Moriarty's careful plans encountering scores of whooping scrambling gutter urchins.

Holmes allowed himself a satisfied moment too, then gestured for silence and led me through the secret doorway onto a darkened stair. We trod carefully. Twice Holmes halted to detach alarm wires. Once he hooked aside a gossamer thread that released a dozen darts into the opposite wall.

The steps ended in a low corridor under a barrel ceiling. Holmes indicated that I should tread only in his footsteps. In that manner we progressed around an L bend to a steel door with another lock mechanism.

My friend gestured for the stethoscope from my pocket. He listened intently for two minutes, then spent another two gently drumming his fingers on each section of the door.

"There is a risk," he warned me.

"Take it," I urged him. "Lives may be in peril."

Holmes unwrapped a tool-bundle and selected his instruments. It took him longer than the outer lock had, but at last he was satisfied. He eased the door out towards us no more than three inches, then felt round and unhooked another thread on the inner side.

Only then did he relax. "Merridew is a cautious one, these days," he noted. "Then again, he has reason to know that the world can be a hard place."

"He? I thought we sought the Old Woman of Kitchener's Court?"

"Ah, Watson. It is long since Dr. Merridew decided to eschew the gender of his birth. Most who know him now assume he is the woman his medical instruments have made him."

"Good grief! You know somewhat of her... his past, then?" I ventured.

"Oh, my dear Watson! Have you not understood that it is Merridew's past which has shaped this entire venture? That Merridew is paying off scores and indulging his pleasures whilst pursuing his ultimate aim?"

The door slipped open. Holmes gestured for me to slide the cover from our dark lantern and play it round the chamber. "Be so good as to explain," I asked as we searched.

The room was filled with shelves. Dozens of jars held pickled human foetuses, presumably the product of Merridew's secret trade.

"Merridew was not always Merridew," Holmes advised me. "Once he was a respected medical man, an expert in his field. Surely you recall that Spearer was saved from the gallows when the specialist brought to give opinion against him was discredited?"

"That was Merridew? I thought you to have said the name was Jollydrop?" Then the pun clicked. "Oh! Merry – Jolly – Dew-drop! It's almost funny that..."

I stopped short in mid sentence. The further shelves contained more aborted children; but these had been stuffed and mounted like the animals in Sherman's shop. Some were even posed in grotesque montages, in the way that some taxidermists create dioramas of kittens smoking round a card table or foxes dressed in red hunting jackets riding hounds.

I felt nauseous.

"I do not imagine your readers will want to hear of this," said Holmes soberly.

I fumbled my way after him to the other door from the room. Beside that exit we found a wooden frame with leather strips stretched out on it for curing. I have never seen cow-hide or horse-hide of that colour and texture.

"Dr. Merridew has developed abhorrent hobbies," Holmes observed. "Here is the apparatus that prepared the bag that was once part of First Mate Wells. I do not see a taxidermist's bench in here, however. That ordeal must await us beyond this door."

We eased the wood open and let ourselves into a workshop laboratory. There, carved open on a stone table was the mortal remains of a butchered young woman. Some of her interior organs had already been removed and replaced with straw.

"Milly Claxton," I breathed.

Holmes disagreed. "The hair is the wrong colour and the fingers of a different shape. She lacks the marks of a baker's girl. This young woman was of a higher degree, who wrote a good deal and owned a young ill-tempered cat." He glanced to the sink. "Not the dismembered animal on the draining rack," he added. "That is an older creature."

Thus we located Miss Claribel Stobridge and Howard Crawley's pet.

I forced myself to look away from the atrocity. "What can she have possibly done to Merridew to provoke such treatment?"

"Note the missing ring finger again, Watson. I think this lady was another hostage for some demanded service. Merridew's reduction of the corpse to a display trophy betrays an utter contempt for human sensibilities and a bitter hatred or jealousy of womankind. The choice of digit indicates a singular hostility to the institution of marriage."

"Why would that be?"

"During the time the Spearer case was heard, a scandal was uncovered in Dr. Jollydrop's private life. A proclivity for dressing in woman's attire, and perhaps a favour for male attentions."

"Then… the old woman who performs abortions on those girls of the unfortunate class and the man to whom you are referring are one and the same?"

"Quite so. When Jollydrop's quirk was exposed his reputation was shattered. His family and friends turned against him. His wife sought divorce. His place in society and his tenure at a teaching hospital were lost. He was ruined and perfect prey to be recruited by Professor James Moriarty!"

I swallowed hard. "We must find this fiend. If he has done this to the poor wretch before us then Miss Claxton may suffer the same fate."

I wrenched open the big cabinet by the remaining door we had yet to investigate and cried out.

Holmes hastened to my side to view the stuffed, naked corpse of another dead woman. She had been positioned in a most obscene manner.

"This is not the missing Millie either," Holmes concluded. "This victim was a prostitute of the more expensive sort, but most traces that might identify her have been erased by the process to which she has been subjected."

"Merridew has a sick and filthy mind!" I responded. "We must find him before he does the same to Miss Claxton."

"And so I shall," Merridew proclaimed. He stood at by the door to his laboratory and had a pistol levelled at us. We had allowed our horror to distract us.

Holmes looked intently at the man in sober Victorian matron's garb who glared at us behind wig and powdered cheeks. "You have finally deduced, then, that it was Moriarty who exposed your secret all those years ago, to save his client Spearer?"

I remembered then that the old thief has talked of 'paying the price', and that the Professor was a consulting criminal to whom felons took their problems as detectives resorted to Holmes.

"I know it," Merridew owned. "It is one of many reasons why that black spider must die."

Holmes picked up one of the formaldehyde jars containing a terminated unborn. "Millie Claxton resorted to you in secret to end her pregnancy. It was the spur you needed to begin your masterplan," he proclaimed.

The mad doctor held his pistol level while drawing on a menthol cigarette with the other hand. He seemed as calm as he might be dissecting a frog. "You are too modest, Sherlock Holmes. It was your own probings into the Professor's affairs that gave me the opportunity I needed. I am pleased for this chance to thank you before you die."

"Moriarty had seen through you, though," my friend warned. "He set me on you to divert me from him."

Merridew looked us up and down. "You two will make a fine stuffed montage," the creature promised. "I'll pose you just as you are now, quivering in the hunt, your fawning companion lurking by your side."

"You placed the missing heads in the Professor's chambers, I suppose?" Holmes checked. "They will not be there when the police arrive."

"They will, and so will all the vital men of Moriarty's network. I have done what the Great Detective could not. I have destroyed James Moriarty as he once destroyed me."

"Moriarty is not at his home," my friend replied scornfully. "You may not have learned that all his lieutenants save you were summoned to Barts instead, but my sources run true. That was an hour since. Be sure that by now they will all be sitting in the British Museum's public gallery for the Professor's hastily-arranged presentation on radical celestial mathematics in the European vogue."

That rouged face blanched. The calm façade cracked. "No!" Merridew denied. "I know him. I have studied him these long years!"

"You knew him. He has changed. Now he has to deal with Sherlock Holmes!"

Merridew was frustrated and enraged for one moment too long. Holmes still held the glass jar. He lobbed it. The heavy foetus bottle shattered across the mad doctor's head.

"Now, Watson!" Holmes cried.

I flung the dark-lantern. Oil spilled. The flame touched Merridew's formaldehyde-soaked skirts and caught immediately.

The burning killer flailed backwards, crashing into more of the bottles.

The whole of the workroom was catching fire. The first of the jars exploded. "Quickly!" Holmes called. He hurled himself past the man who was now a mere tower of flame.

I hastened after Holmes, out into a larger surgery chamber. "Shouldn't we go back the other way?" I called. "We sealed the main exit with chain and padlock!"

"You forget why we came!" my friend called back. Under an operating table with a half-dissected headless corpse he found a thick metal cover-plate to a blood run-off drain. "Help me break this clasp!"

I found a pair of bone-cutters that could force the fastening. Holmes hauled up the grate. Trussed and gagged beneath, splattered with the waste from Trippel's autopsy, lay frantic Harry Spearer and terrified Milly Claxton.

We pulled them out and loosed them. The cellar was becoming dangerously thick with smoke.

"He's mad!" Spearer gasped. "What he was going to do with us..."

"I'm sorry!" sobbed Miss Claxton. "I'm sorry, I'm sorry, I'm sorry..."

"This way!" Holmes commanded. "Keep a hand on the person in front of you or you will be lost."

We struggled back towards the blazing workshop. Holmes found a sluice-pump and sprayed the room to dampen the worst of the flames. "Go now!" he told Spearer, then bundled Miss Claxton after the locksmith.

The inhuman Merridew rose from the pyre to reach out at us.

Holmes and I both emptied our revolvers into that terrible creature and ran for our lives.

❖ ❖ ❖

The account of Colonel J. Sebastian Moran:

I don't believe I understood one word in ten of the Professor's address. Then again, I doubt that four-fifths of the Royal Academy members who'd assembled to review his calculations did either.

Blackstock awaited us outside the hall, red with sour anger. He'd been summoned hastily from the lecture that gave us all alibis by news that his warehouse was burning down.

"It'll be a total loss, and all the stock in it," he reported to Moriarty. "A street-gang attack!"

"A rescue," the Professor corrected him. "Do you not detect the hand of Sherlock Holmes behind your misfortune? I presume it was that site wherein you had sequestered Miss Jennifer Wheeler?" When Blackstock confessed that it was, Moriarty patted him on the shoulder. "We shall find you other accommodation. What of Kitchener's Yard?"

"Another blaze," the intelligencer reported. "Whatever evidence there was of Merridew's work is all ashes now."

"And the Professor's lodgings?" I checked.

"Our men in Scotland Yard concealed the heads before any search could find them. There are red faces amongst the senior officers tonight and profuse apologies due from them in the morning."

"Now I cannot be so easily troubled again. No further warrant will be possible without irrefutable evidence against me," the Professor observed. He flexed his neck and twisted his head. "A most satisfactory twenty-four hours, gentlemen. Merridew's treachery is dealt with. No other will dare oppose me. And Mr. Holmes was diverted from personally supervising the conclusion of his Mathews case so that while the guppy is hooked the bigger fish swim free."

Blackstock winced. The Professor interpreted the meaning and focussed his stare.

"It… isn't quite like that, sir," the intelligencer admitted. "Mathews has vanished. Sir Aubrey and Lord Wharfield have both been questioned. Thomas Anderson and Sir Charles Shuttleworth were detained. The house on Cleveland Street has been raided, the children taken away."

Moriarty frowned. "Who was the officer in charge of the case?"

Blackstock winced again. "That's it, Professor. Orders did not come from Scotland Yard, nor any police station. They were sent direct from the Home Office, under the seal of the Home Secretary.[28] Precise, detailed orders that must not to be deviated from, and were not."

"The Home Secretary?" I puzzled. "How and why would he…?"

"Holmes' absence during Dr. Watson's foray to the Seaforth woman!" Moriarty spat. "He sent a runner to his brother Mycroft. 'Occasionally he is the British government.[29]'" The Professor was white with livid rage. "I thought I was diverting Holmes. He was diverting me!"

I wasn't sure what to do. Holmes was becoming an expensive hobby for the Professor.

Blackstock spoke first. "Maybe it's time to silence the detective?"

Moriarty turned on the intelligencer. "Moran," he commanded me, "kill this man."

So I did.

The Professor turned away from Blackstock's body. "He has inconvenienced me," he hissed, meaning Holmes, not the confederate whose death he had casually ordained in a fit of pique. "Merely inconvenienced me. The game continues. The battle of wits has scarcely begun. Before I am done I'll see him fall lower than Merridew. This is but the start…!"

◇ ◇ ◇

The account of Dr. John H. Watson:

Holmes met me on the landing of 221B Baker Street to assure me that word had been sent for Mary's safe return.

"I've seen Spearer and Miss Claxton back to his father's shop," I reported.

---

28   One of the great offices of British government, the Home Secretary oversees domestic issues such as law and order and is responsible for the police force. A serving Member of Parliament nominated by the Prime Minister, he is part of the Cabinet that runs the nation. At this time in the government of the Marquis of Salisbury the office was held by lawyer and Conservative politician Henry Matthews, 1st Viscount Llandaff PC QC.

29   This is Sherlock's own assessment of Mycroft from "The Bruce-Partington Plans".

"I stitched her hand up as best I could." The wounds in the relationship between those young people, with kidnapping, pregnancy, termination, disfigurement, crime, and nightmare in their pasts, would not easily heal. I intended to keep a watch on them, though, as I would on forsaken Ginnie Seaforth. Holmes does his part and I do mine.

"Come then," Holmes invited me, "come into our sitting room!"

In our familiar chambers Mrs. Hudson was serving tea to Paxton the boxer. On the sofa, side by side, were a triumphant, split-lipped Wiggins and a dainty young thing who could only be his Jenny. The radiant expression on the lady's face showed how perfectly she was aware of her Galahad's deeds.

My friend offered introductions and presided over a pleasant tea-party as if it were not two in the morning after we had all endured danger, fire, and fear. To watch him toasting a crumpet at the hearth and handing it to Mrs. Hudson for butter, one might never guess that this was the irritable, unstoppable scourge of crime and injustice. For sometimes, rarely, Holmes would condescend to the common touch.

"I have word from Mycroft," he confided in me as Miss Wheeler recounted again for our landlady and the hulking pugilist how her Wiggins had liberated her. "Mathews is exposed, and his connections with him. By morning a dozen great men will have fallen and good riddance to them."

"Is this the end for Moriarty then?" I wondered.

"Alas no, Watson. A mere scratch. An opening foray. The greatest test is yet to come!"

I have rarely seen my friend look so alive.

❖ ❖ ❖

"You crossed my path on the 4th of January. On the 23d you incommoded me; by the middle of February I was seriously inconvenienced by you; at the end of March I was absolutely hampered in my plans; and now, at the close of April, I find myself placed in such a position through your continual persecution that I am in positive danger of losing my liberty. The situation is becoming an impossible one..."

Professor Moriarty, "The Final Problem"

The End

Equal and Opposite: Rise of the Moriarty

By 1893 Arthur Conan Doyle was growing sick of Mr. Sherlock Holmes. Doyle's literary enthusiasms had wandered elsewhere and he was tired of publishers and public alike being interested only in his accounts of the Great Detective. He therefore decided to write an end to Holmes' career, and in "The Final Problem" he killed off the character at the Reichenbach Falls. Alas for Doyle, Holmes proved too clever and his readers too loyal, and eventually his death had to be revealed as a sham; but for a while there, before public pressure and financial constraint pushed Doyle to revive him, Holmes had met his end – and met his match.

Doyle decided that for Holmes' last battle he should face what would be literally his ultimate threat: a man as clever and capable as he, his dark mirror-image. Professor James Moriarty was Holmes' equal and opposite. Only such an adversary, an archvillain to counter an arch-hero, would offer a satisfying and credible end to the Great Detective's adventures.

In our modern narrative age the idea of an evil counterpart is commonplace. In Doyle's time this was not a well-established trope. In fact, so compelling was the idea to the reading public that thereafter, when a hero meets a villain similar to himself, that malefactor is often described as "his Moriarty".

New readers of the Canon are sometimes surprised that the Professor does not appear more often. In fact he only serves as Holmes' adversary once, culminating in the Reichenbach clash. A quarter of a century later he lurks in the background and makes a brief appearance in *The Valley of Fear*, set three years before "The Final Problem". Moriarty's deadly lieutenant, Sebastian Moran, likewise appears but once, in "The Adventure of the Empty House". Moriarty and Moran are mentioned in passing in some other tales, and certain investigations are revealed to have touched on Moriarty's plots, but on the whole neophyte Holmes fans are surprised how little his "archenemy" features.

Of course, Moriarty's memorable role and character make him much more likely to appear in movie and TV adaptations, where he is far more prominent. In literature he is the inspiration for T.S. Eliot's "Macavity the Mystery Cat". He and Moran are the protagonists in Neil Gaiman's "A Study in Emerald" (in which Holmes and Watson are the villains). John

Gardner, Antony Horowitz, and many others have further chronicled the Professor's infamy.

It occurred to me that - since these *Consulting Detective* volumes aim to offer Holmes stories in the same spirit and continuity as those of Doyle's original work - it might be possible to once again touch upon the Napoleon of Crime without disturbing the delicate parsimony of his original encounters with Sherlock Holmes. Aiding the legitimacy of this we have Moriarty's own statement, reproduced at the ending of "The Abominable Merridew", about Holmes' escalating interference.

Having decided (with some editorial consultation) that it would be interesting and appropriate to feature James Moriarty, the question then became what to offer, and how to frame it?

What appealed to me was the chance to show Moriarty and Moran in tandem as we so often see Holmes and Watson – a partnership that we had no opportunity to witness in the original Canon. Comparison and contrast between Holmes and Moriarty are common; examinations of similarity and difference between Moran and Watson less so. The juxtaposition of a Holmes/Watson investigation with a Moriarty/Moran investigation would surely offer many new insights into the characters of each?

I determined that this story must, even more than usual, fit well with established material. Better to pick up on and flesh out references to cases already mentioned in Dr. Watson's other accounts than to crowd in more incidents of my own invention. Better to use an established character or resource than create one to fit the same niche.

This in turn opened up new opportunities to feature the taxidermist Sherman and Wiggins of the Baker Street Irregulars. It occurred that Wiggins, who first appeared as a boy in the 1881 adventure *A Study In Scarlet*, would be a young man by 1891. The opportunity to "graduate" him from the street gang was too good to resist.

Likewise, the chance to present "Merridew of abominable memory" as a noteworthy Holmes adversary was too tempting to miss. His passing mention in the Canon offers him the gravitas required to offer a credible challenge to both Holmes and Moriarty. No mere modern creation would have the authority to take on the two sharpest minds of Holmesian England.

I like to assume that some of Dr. Watson's accounts included in the *Consulting Detective* series were not published during his lifetime because of the delicacy of their content. Watson was a respecter of confidentiality, changing names and places to protect the innocent. Several times he mentions events about which the public could not yet know. Watson's modern literary agents may therefore access those cases that the good doctor chose not to send to Arthur Conan Doyle for fear they might be too graphic, too politically or socially sensitive, or otherwise unsuitable for his Victorian audience.

"The Abominable Merridew" would not have seen publication in *The Strand Magazine*. Apart from the graphic nature of the crimes and possible litigation from Colonel Moran (who was alive in prison as late as September 1902; c.f. "The Illustrious Client"), Merridew's sexuality would have prevented the story from reaching print. Likewise Mathews' despicable trafficking of underage girls, while undoubtedly a realistic and common crime of the Victorian age, would not have been deemed suitable fare for a respectable publication. It is good to avail ourselves of modern freedoms and offer the full spectrum of London's criminality and diversity now such restrictions no longer prevail.

My aim as a writer is to tell interesting stories. If they can excite, provoke, entertain, and make readers pause for thought then my work is done. My aim in writing Sherlock Holmes stories is to tell those tales that we wish Conan Doyle had got round to including, while still retaining Doyle's actual output at the core of the mythos. My intention in presenting "The Abominable Merridew" is to offer the preliminary set-up adventure before "The Final Problem" that Doyle might have considered had he not been so keen to rid himself of Holmes so abruptly.

As for Moriarty, he too survived Reichenbach in spirit. He lives on in every evil archvillain opposite. Moran endures as every lethal right-hand henchman who carries out his master's implacable orders. Fortunately we still have heroes with staunch friends who will stand against their frighteningly equal antagonists, no matter the cost. Let us celebrate them all.

I.A. Watson
Yorkshire, England, April 2013

I.A. WATSON -

"What do you make of this chap, Holmes?" I asked my friend, one wet Baker Street morning. "He seems dashed interested in my notes, but I'm not sure he's entirely to be trusted."

Holmes laid aside his Stradivarius and glanced over the letter from the mysterious I.A. Watson. "A man of middle years and sedentary habits," he deduced. "I see from the list of published works he has provided that he has previously reported our cases in four volumes under the general name of *Sherlock Holmes: Consulting Detective*. He even received an award for Best Pulp Short Story for one of them."

"Yes, but what of the rest, Holmes? These other nominations for Best Pulp Novel, for this trilogy— *Robin Hood: King of Sherwood*; *Robin Hood: Arrow of Justice* and *Robin Hood: Freedom's Outlaw*— and for this speculative science work *Blackthorn: Dynasty of Mars* and his recent work on *Zeppelin Tales*? Am I to trust my annotations to an author who lists *The New Adventures of Richard Knight* and B*lood Price of the Missionary's Gold: the New Adventures of Armless O'Neil* amongst the anthologies to which he has contributed? Or these lurid-sounding titles *Monster Earth* and *Gideon Cain: Demon Hunter*?"

"Do not overlook *Sinbad: the New Voyages*. It seems your namesake has a taste for the mythological. And I see he has also contributed to the tomes *Blackthorn: Thunder on Mars* and *Sentinels: Alternate Visions* and to the charity volumes *All-Star Pulp Comics #2* and *Grand Central Noir*. I conclude that he is a man with some literary education but a taste for low fiction, who writes more for the enjoyment of the thing than as a full-time career. He is amateur in the original sense of one who does something for the love of it. You may forward your accounts to him without fear, Watson. Trust to your editors to curb his excesses."

"You believe then that he is harmless?"

"Oh, your correspondent is a time-bomb just waiting to go off," Holmes replied with a thin smile. "Best get work out of him while you can, Watson. I'm certain his appointment with the gallows cannot be far away."

I hastened to forward my material as Holmes updated his file index.

A full list of I.A. Watson's lurid publications is available at http://www.chillwater.org.uk/writing/iawatsonhome.htm

Sherlock Holmes

in

"The Adventure
of the
Invisible Assassin"

By
Andrew Salmon

Although the date is indelibly stamped in my memory, I shall state for this account that it was August 29th, 1896 when the black pall of the invisible assassin darkened our lives and threatened the city. Errands concerning the final sale and transfer of my Kensington practice to its new owner, Dr. Verner, had kept me away from the rooms I shared with my good friend, Sherlock Holmes, and a traipsing about town in the midst of baking heat had left me worn out and ready for repose.

Upon my return, however, Mrs. Hudson informed me that Holmes had been called away on a case and begged my indulgence to await his return. This request I gladly complied with, taking to my chair by the cold hearth to sip lemonade and cool my brow for some hours. The closeness of the room won out in the end and I went to stand by the open window to catch the hint of breeze stealing in amidst the noise and clatter of the busy street bathed in the setting sun.

From this vantage point I observed a hansom rein in outside our door in some haste and Sherlock Holmes half fell out onto the pavement. One look at his appearance was sufficient to spur me to action and I dashed down to the street to meet him.

Holmes had partially recovered himself by the time I joined him. His normally impeccable attire was coated in soot as were his sharp, angular features. A racking cough exploded past his thin lips as he endeavoured to address me. He managed an encouraging grimace instead, then tried to speak again with better success.

"I am quite all right, Watson," said he in a voice reduced to a harsh rasp. "I should like to go upstairs."

"Certainly," I agreed readily and offered an aiding hand, which he refused with another grimace.

Inside, I waited with much agitation for Holmes to clean himself up. He re-appeared a half-hour later in his dressing gown, face scrubbed. Under his arm was a bundle of burlap containing the soiled street clothes which were beyond salvaging. I had set out both lemonade and brandy to suit his fancy. He took neither as he lowered himself into his chair and stared at me with eyes blazing. No doubt observing the questions I was anxious to pose playing about my features, Holmes related his ordeal.

The message had come from one of Lestrade's men. The body of a man had been discovered in a stable located in Notting Hill.

"The stable was of moderate size," explained Holmes, "with space to house two dozen horses. It being day when we arrived, all of the animals had been let out in service to the city, which was just as well given the presence of the dead. In a shadowed corner amidst the cloying scent of fresh hay, the body had been displayed."

"Whatever do you mean? Displayed?"

"Exactly that. Lighting a nearby lantern, the tableau presented itself to me. The dead man looked to be middle-aged, in relatively good physical condition; all things considered. The body had been nailed to a cross beam, through the ankles, the feet were bare, so that it resembled a goose in a butcher's window. The head was scant inches from the floor, the hands, palms up, fingers almost interlaced on the dirt floor."

"Did your inspection reveal any significant clues as to what befell this poor man?"

"He had been garroted, a professional job of it," said Holmes. "The nailing had been post mortem as there was no blood about, not even on the exposed feet. The skin of the face and upper torso bore bruises and some burns; most likely from a lit cigar. Flesh pale and waxy, as one would expect, only more so. Given the time of year, I submit that the man had spent a protracted amount of time out of the sun."

"A night laborer?"

"Too well dressed."

"Nothing on the body hinted at his identity?"

"Nothing conclusive. I had no time to look deeper. The fool constable Lestrade sent to guide me fancied a cigar while I made my brief inspection. Struggling to get it going, the match singed his fingers and he dropped it into the tinder-dry hay. The stable became an instant brazier. Adding insult to injury, the man was soon overcome with smoke and I lost precious moments with the corpse while endeavouring to save the constable. We barely escaped with our lives. I turned back after hauling him to safety only to find the stable was a bonfire. Any further secrets the corpse might have yielded were lost. Feeling the effects of the smoke myself, I returned to Baker Street."

His discourse had winded him, I could see. A handkerchief appeared in his hand and he dabbed at his watering eyes as he cleared his throat wetly. Clearly his recent proximity to fire had affected Holmes more than he cared to admit.

"So, that's it then," said I, hopefully. A day or two of rest would do

Holmes much good in the wake of his ordeal. However, I knew better than to prescribe this.

"Whatever do you mean, Watson?"

"The body burned beyond recognition. Any and all evidence destroyed. Why you do not even know the man's name?"

Holmes swiped at his eyes, then thrust the handkerchief into his pocket. He leaned forward, his teary eyes glistening with intent.

"We are a few yards off the pace," said he. "However the race is not finished. Allow me a bite to eat and something to soothe my throat and we shall be off. There's time yet to see this through anyhow. I have theories that need bearing out."

Instructions were passed to the cook and a small plate was prepared. Holmes was slow in eating and I wondered if nausea accompanied his watering eyes and seared lungs. As much as I wanted to press my friend for information concerning the next step in our investigation, I held my silence so that the soothing broth would have the chance to work on his raw throat. Smoke inhalation is a nasty business not to be trifled with and, judging from the ferocity of the paroxysms that had seized Holmes earlier; I feared he'd have to go under an oxygen tent. This, I knew, would be no simple task to pull off when his blood was up on a new problem for that vast intellect. It was easy, sometimes; to overlook the human weaknesses Holmes was as prey to as any of us given the extraordinary feats I had born witness to over the course of our association.

As fate would have it, I would not be able to pose my questions for a messenger knocked downstairs as Holmes finished the last of his meal. The maid entered with a sealed note for my friend. He accepted the envelope but made no immediate move to open it. A quick sniff of the envelope caused him to raise his wiry eyebrows significantly. He extended the envelope to me. It was slightly scented with toilet water. This scent contrasted with the creased and soiled condition of the envelope. Opening the envelope, he glanced at the contents, then tossed it on the mantle. He shot out of his chair, swiped at his eyes and smiled down at me where I sat.

"Although the messenger is lame, we best not tarry too long in following him or he will be swallowed by the throng."

"The message was significant then?"

Holmes waved a hand dismissively. "A trifle. If it is connected to the dead man at the stable, following the messenger is our best bet. Come!"

❖ ❖ ❖

There was hardly time for Holmes to dress for the street. He threw off his dressing gown and sprang for a light coat and hat while I hurriedly prepared myself to depart.

We found the messenger right enough and proceeded to follow the scruffy lad around the next corner. Our course took us north up Camden Town. The messenger unwittingly guided us to a large, tiered stable. Holmes put his hand on my arm at the connection. He said nothing. The sprawling, labyrinthine establishment bore the name Lucilla Yards. The boy we followed approached from the Chalk Farm Road entrance, disappearing inside while we hung back to observe without being detected.

"What do you make of it?" I asked.

"The day's events being connected with stables?" replied Holmes. "In itself, this is not significant. With three hundred thousand horses kept within the city limits, one could not throw a stone without striking a stable wall. There are deeper meanings, which we shall get to in due course. We have the boy's location; that is sufficient for the moment. Let us be off."

"Should we not question the lad?"

"Now is not the time. If the message and his involvement are pertinent to the body in the stable, we lack sufficient information to ask the right questions. If not, then what facts he could provide will keep until we've made our next stop."

His logic was sound and we stopped a hansom. "What is to be our next destination?"

"To the Diogenes Club," replied Holmes, directing his words to the driver before turning to me as the cab clattered down Regent Street, "and Mycroft. I have a theory."

There would be no elaboration from Holmes on this point until he'd finished collecting the facts he needed so I let the matter go for the present. "How did you know the stable boy was lame?"

"That was simplicity itself, Watson," replied Holmes. He cleared his throat. "The messenger made no haste departing after delivering the missive. There are two things we can learn from this. The first, and most obvious, is that he was ignorant of the contents of the letter in his charge. At the same time, one would not linger on such an errand for fear of involvement in whatever is between the parties; involvement beyond the level of payment received. Still, he departed leisurely. The only conclusion is that the messenger was incapable of making haste. Why is that? The letter creased from being held tightly in his fist is the answer. Given his ignorance and lack of haste, one must conclude he clutched it tightly

"What do you make of it?"

against the discomfort of some affliction. His slow departure pointed at
an injured leg. That said discomfort manifested itself through a clenched
fist tells us that the afflicted could not afford medical attention nor crutch
or cane. If he could, he would be unlikely to take on the task of delivering
letters to strangers. The injury, while painful, is not, as we just observed by
the man's gait, readily visible or else the sender would never have employed
a man limping with a crutch or cane. As I said, Watson, simple."

"For you, perhaps."

"For any with eyes to see."

I confess to some measure of relief at seeing Holmes re-invigorated by
the thrill of the hunt. He was slightly winded following his explanations,
his voice still betrayed the abrasive affects of the smoke and he dabbed at
his watering eyes with a handkerchief yet these seemed the only apparent
symptoms from his earlier ordeal. The state of his lungs would bear
watching however. I vowed to task them no further with questions for the
present.

We reached Pall Mall and started down it from the Waterloo Place end
and had to pass by the Carlton Club. The building housing the political
club had windows ablaze and considerable commotion outside the
building drew our attention.

"My theory is strengthened," commented Holmes, cryptically. "We
need Mycroft's input before we can consider it proven out."

❖ ❖ ❖

I did not know what to make of this and could spare it no further
thought. We had arrived at our destination. Holmes alighted with some
semblance of his usual grace and strode up to the entrance with me a
step behind. Observing strict silence upon entering, as was the rule, we
scrutinized the faces of the men occupying the luxurious room on the
other side of the glass panelling. I did not see Mycroft Holmes, which
was noteworthy considering his singular girth yet not surprising as the
room was full to capacity. Holmes and I exchanged glances then I left
him to wait in the Stranger's Room which looked out into Pall Mall while
he entered the club to seek his brother. Sherlock returned moments later
with Mycroft a step behind. My hand disappeared into the massive paw
Mycroft extended in greeting and we sat in the bow window.

"Sherlock, you've been in a fire and are ill as a result," observed Mycroft
as we were free to speak in this part of the club.

"The state of my health is of no matter," said Sherlock. "The fire on the other hand is what concerns me greatly."

"You don't suspect a connection?"

"I do."

Mycroft Holmes remained silent for a moment, his gray, watery eyes held that singularly opaque gaze as that of a scientist not aware of the test tubes on his worktable but rather focused on the contents therein. "Yes, I see it now. I believe you're right, Sherlock. The fire was at a stable?"

Sherlock Holmes nodded.

"This stable is, or rather, was, located on Ladbroke Road, Notting Hill?"

Another nod in the affirmative.

Mycroft snorted. "There's no question then. You were right to come to me."

Sensing the conversation beginning to slip away from me, I interjected. "Would either of you care to explain what has been determined from your exchange?"

"Forgive us, Watson," said Sherlock. "You are not in possession of all the facts. Although I was unable to confirm the murdered man's identity until now, my suspicion as to who he was brought us here. Our presence, given what Mycroft clearly knows, lays the matter out before us."

"The murdered man," Mycroft interjected, "is a cabinet member who has gone missing; a fact many have gone to great lengths to conceal."

"The Right Honorable Stephen Martin," said Sherlock.

"That is he," confirmed Mycroft.

I turned to Sherlock. "You said you did not know the identity of the dead man."

"Not so. I said I was unable to confirm it–until now. The man had been beaten prior to his death, the features swollen and bruised. Even so, in my brief time with the corpse, I found he resembled Stephen Martin. Recall the state of the body: pale, scarred, with torture both fresh and old. This indicated a stretch of captivity. The fine quality of the man's dress and physical condition spoke of good nutrition and breeding. No labourer he, his resemblance to a member of Parliament, in addition to the factors I have just outlined, though persuasive, were not conclusive. We needed Mycroft for that."

Mycroft Holmes took up the explanation. "Mr. Martin went missing a fortnight ago. No stone was left unturned in searching for him. Quietly, mind you. Quietly, yet to no avail. Sherlock's and your appearance here so soon after the close action my brother had been party to bespoke urgency.

As I deal mainly in government concerns at present, Sherlock had to have questions in that area. Martin's disappearance is whispered on the lips of the elite, what else could my brother wish to see me about? Martin's father had also elevated himself via the equine trade and, at the time of his death, bestowed a legacy on the son consisting of several lucrative stables. Sherlock, fresh from a fire, carries with him the faintest odour of hay though he has gone to considerable lengths to wash it away. What other conclusion could be drawn other than Sherlock having encountered Mr. Martin in a stable which burned?"

"Remarkable!" said I.

"There were no remains?" asked Mycroft.

"Bone fragments, perhaps," replied Sherlock. "Nothing useful."

"Accidental, no doubt."

Sherlock suppressed a cough. "The fire was set by a bumbling constable."

"Unfortunate."

"A setback if we could presume upon you for insight into the personality of Stephen Martin as well as the particulars of his disappearance, the trail may grow as warm as that smouldering stable."

"I never met the man," conceded Mycroft. "All I know is that he used opium, was ambitious, and was not adverse to cards and playing the horses occasionally. His marriage was one of convenience, not based on sentiment though he loved his wife once. Well educated, not particularly broad-minded, he tended to sloth in his work habits. He preferred creature comforts as a means to display his position and authority. He did not eat much at breakfast and a deviated septum was the most likely cause of his sleep apnea. I could go on, however I maintain that the facts I have related are solely significant to the matter at hand."

There was no doubt that his observations were accurate in every detail. I could only sit in stunned awe at what Mycroft Holmes could have told us about Stephen Martin had the two ever met face to face. My friend's next comment only cemented my certainty that these two siblings operated on a different plain than the rest of us.

"And the scandal?"

"He was barely touched by the scandal of five years ago. Martin emerged unscathed with reputation intact when all was said and done. He has made no advancement since. Nor would he have had he survived the ordeal which ended his life. I suspect three ministers will resign within two days of the news breaking. One will be arrested and two former minsters will retire from public life to Afghanistan. The resulting void will be a necessary one though the benefits will not be felt for eighteen months; thirty-three months if your investigation lasts longer than sixteen days. You will get it back for us, Sherlock?"

"I shall certainly do my best. You agree with me, then, that Martin was a likely candidate?"

"There is no room for uncertainly in that regard," replied Mycroft. "Please be careful, Sherlock."

"That is most kind," observed my friend. "No word of this will come from us and the utmost discretion will color my investigation."

Mycroft placed his huge hands on his bulging knees. "That settles it for the moment. I place myself at your disposal."

We made our goodbyes and were back on the street looking for a cab minutes later. Although I had lost the thread of the discussion between the two brothers and had no clue as to the parameters of the case, I had understood, and now heeded, my friend's assurances to his brother that the matter would be handled in secrecy. Thus I held my tongue as we climbed into a cab on the busy street.

❖ ❖ ❖

Back at Baker Street I was able to give vent to my pent up queries.

"Forgive me, Watson," replied Holmes when I had finished. "Mycroft is not one to squander words and I thought his concerns plainly stated."

"Hardly."

"Very well. Let's lay the matter out before retiring for the evening. Tomorrow will be a busy day."

Holmes dropped heavily into his chair. I sat across from him and watched him light a pipe. The smoke troubled his still-tender throat and he set the pipe aside.

"Mycroft mentioned the disappearance of Stephen Martin. We have learned that the man was murdered after having been, shall we say, pressed, for information the nature of which we do not know. It is sensitive information, of that we are certain, given Mycroft's desire to keep it from falling into the wrong hands though we can theorize it may well have already. After all, the man is dead and will yield no secrets now."

I found it strange that so public an official as Stephen Martin could disappear without it being discovered and exploited by the press and gave voice to my thoughts.

"This is not an insignificant aspect of the case, Watson," agreed

Holmes as he made use of his handkerchief. "Public figures do not go missing without someone shouting it from the rooftops. There are several conclusions one can draw from this. I lean towards the crime having been perpetrated by some organization that exacts a high price for speaking out."

"Do you know of such an organization?"

Holmes shook his head. "There is much about this case that proves elusive. We need facts."

"What would they want with Martin?"

Holmes stifled a cough. "Martin was involved in espionage, whether by coercion or full cooperation remains unclear. The man's somewhat wayward habits, the stale marriage around his neck and drug use, these are fertile ground for criminals to exploit and Martin must have made a few blunders in these areas. Escaping the scandal and roundup of five years ago kept him in the good graces of his handlers but left him ostracized from his fellow MPs. For whatever reason, the men to whom he is in thrall have moved against him. It falls to us to find what they are looking for before they do. Or retrieve the information if it is already in the wrong hands."

"Are you sure you're up to the chase after your recent ordeal? Your respiratory system seems to have fallen prey to the fire."

My statements galvanized him and he sprang out of his chair. "I can't help feeling that every minute is precious and fleeting if we are to settle the matter. The perpetrators have the jump on us and we must double our efforts if we are to overtake them. Still, there is wisdom in what you say. It is too late in the evening to continue our investigation by calling on the people involved and we will need to be fresh for our appointments or else all is lost. To rest, then."

❖ ❖ ❖

The new dawn brought with it more questions that had haunted me during the night. I meant to have answers. After fairly wolfing down my breakfast, I eagerly waited for Holmes to do likewise. He was late rising, which surprised me, considering that his typically frenetic energy when starting a case usually left him up half the night and first out the door. When he did emerge from his bedchamber, he did so with customary vigour and excitement for the investigation before us. If the fire and smoke still plagued him, he gave no sign.

Holmes ate little as was his wont during these periods. When the dishes had been cleared away, he wasted no time in laying out our plans.

"We'll go to the Martin residence, I should think."

"Surely the police have been there already."

"They have. I have not," replied Holmes. "Their visits were to no avail regardless. Perhaps the staff will be more forthcoming to citizens with no ties to the police."

"Not if they know their employer has been murdered," I countered. "We have both seen the gulf that opens up in groups attached to an unnatural death. And how these individuals can be struck dumb on the spot when murder is mentioned."

"Too true, Watson," replied he. "Therefore I shan't tell them if you won't."

"It's to be like that, then?"

"There is no other way. Mycroft has entrusted us with the retrieval of secrets damaging to the Empire. Stephen Martin's estate and his businesses are all that's left of the trail that ends at his corpse. We will need answers quickly. If news got out that their employer was dead, it would not be long before they were scattered to the four winds, seeking new situations. We cannot have that until we have spoken to them. Besides, while London believes Martin to be amongst the living, the staff will continue to be retained and will continue to receive wages."

Although I was consumed with questions unanswered and thus unaware of the full parameters of the matter at the time, I had to concede to my friend's reasoning in the end and soon found myself seated beside Holmes as our hansom cut through the morning traffic on the way to Savile Row chambers of the late Right Honorable Stephen Martin.

Holmes excused himself to have a look round the back as we alighted and I went on alone to make our presence known. The staff, by this time, were long accustomed to strangers coming and going through the estate, so that my lack of official credentials was not a hindrance.

Lestrade had left an inspector there, one Paul Kerr, and had instructed him to provide us every cooperation upon our arrival. Clearly the will of Mycroft Holmes was in this development. At any rate, it facilitated our entry into the case and Kerr told me that Holmes was to have a free hand.

"Do you want I should call the servants together?" suggested Kerr, a strapping fair-haired Irish lad.

"That won't be necessary," a voice boomed from the opposite end of the corridor.

Kerr knew the man behind this voice and made the introductions.

"Dr. John Watson, Mr. Cedric Hunter. He's Mr. Martin's personal attorney."

The man before me was short, slight, with hard, sharp features honed by decades of the legal trade. I extended a hand in greeting and the man's cold gaze softened a fraction.

"Ah, quite right," said he. "Dr. Watson. I was a great admirer of your adventurous accountings in the Strand."

I expressed my modest gratitude.

"Your courage is an example to us all in this trying time."

"Well, we'll see this put right. On that you can depend."

A cough sounded behind Hunter. Holmes suddenly appeared behind the lawyer. "You may take my friend at his word."

Hunter whirled, startled. "Sherlock Holmes! I did not expect... I thought you and the good doctor inseparable."

"And so we are." Holmes shook the man's hand, a disarming smile on his face. "As we are here to probe the kidnapping of your master, I thought an informal inspection of the house was in order. Mr. Martin was taken from his bed. Is that correct?"

Still somewhat caught off guard, Hunter stammered a reply. "Y...yes."

"The coal chute at the rear, it was by this means Martin was ferried outside?"

"Exactly." Hunter had regained his icy composure. "How did you deduce this?"

"Elementary. The retaining wall around the rear of the dwelling stands four feet in height. The rear door rests atop a set of six steps. Carrying a resisting man, and we must assume that Stephen Martin was resisting his abductors, through this portal would attract the interest of those windows facing the courtyard behind this dwelling as the door is raised above the level of the wall. The night being sultry, the windows were no doubt open to admit the cooler air. Using the coal chute allows for more private egress though the noise presents a problem. Perhaps the man was rendered unconscious. I detected no signs of tampering with the back door lock however. From the chute, Mr. Martin could have been marched to a waiting coach, the noise of which could easily be misinterpreted as emanating from the various work crews cleaning the city streets nightly."

"That's how we figure it," said Kerr.

"We did not notice his absence until the morning," explained Hunter. "I had papers that needed signing and ..."

"You were here on the night of the abduction?" asked Holmes.

"Yes, the duties of a government official often consume the regular hours of the day, leaving no time for personal affairs. Mr. Martin and I were going over some documents pertaining to his businesses late into the night. When it was time for him to retire, given the lateness of the hour, he offered me the use of a spare bedroom."

"Was this a frequent occurrence?"

"As I said the affairs of state often ..."

"Yes, yes," interrupted Holmes. "Please show us the room you used that night."

Hunter's brow furrowed questioningly though he uttered no objection. "This way."

The bedroom in question was an upper chamber, a corner room at the opposite end of the hall to Martin's room and as far from the coal chute as the structure allowed.

"You heard nothing that night?" asked Holmes.

"The day's labours," Hunter replied. "I slept soundly."

Holmes dabbed at his brow with his handkerchief. "This damnable heat! Only mid-morning and already the upper floors are a furnace."

Hunter fanned himself with the file folder in his hand and we all agreed that autumn would bring welcome relief.

"If no one has any objections, I should like to suffer the heat a moment longer and prowl about in here for a minute," said Holmes. "I'll not keep you though. If you would be so kind as to conduct Dr. Watson to the bedroom of Stephen Martin, I shall join you presently."

We left Holmes and made our way up the corridor. The floorboards along the carpeted corridor gave only the softest of creaks despite the clump of many feet. The door to Martin's bedchamber opened on well-oiled hinges. At the threshold of Martin's bedroom, Holmes called softly to me. "Watson!"

I turned and stepped back into the hall, allowing Martin and Kerr to precede me into the room.

Holmes continued from the doorway of the guest room. "Did you see to the cabman? As we will be here all afternoon, I should hate to think of our cutting into his trade by retaining him so long."

"Yes, he's gone."

"Excellent."

Martin's bedroom was untouched since the man had gone missing. Blankets were strewn about on the four-poster, the throw rug on one side (Mrs. Martin lived in Kent) was curled up and kicked half-under the bed.

Otherwise the room showed the normal signs of daily maintenance.

Holmes rejoined us by the time I'd had my look around. He cast his gaze about the room, peered under the bed, moved the small carpet this way and that with the toe of his shoe. "Some signs of a struggle," he spoke more to himself than the rest of us. "No blood, however. Curious."

This continued for some minutes then, at the suggestion of Holmes, we gladly quit the close atmosphere of the upper floor for the still shaded parlour off the main entrance. Lemonade was provided for our refreshment.

"I could not help but notice that the garden fountain round back is in a disassembled state," observed Holmes.

Hunter set down his empty glass. "Yes, since that terrible night, we've asked the construction firm to hold off finishing the work."

"A work crew was at it in the hours prior to Mr. Martin's disappearance?"

"That is correct."

Holmes turned to Kerr and raised his eyebrows expectantly. It took a moment for the lad to grasp the meaning.

"Oh, yes, Mr. Holmes," said he at last. "We spoke with the team," He withdrew a notebook and flipped back several pages. "Tapley and Sons: A family concern. They were all clean as a whistle."

"Good. We shall eliminate them as suspects."

"Just like that?" asked Hunter.

"Just like that," replied Holmes. "Judging from the mess they left, the repairs to the fountain were to be extensive, I'll wager. Cinder blocks, bags of cement for shoring. That narrow door to the courtyard would not permit the Tapley wagon to be pulled up into the yard. It would have to stay in the courtyard, the men coming and going through the small door."

"That was the way of it," confirmed Hunter.

"The door is on a spring lock," continued Holmes. "It would have to be fixed open for expediency's sake, I should think. Is it known if the men locked it when they broke for their luncheon? Or at the end of the work day?"

Hunter made his explanations. "It cannot be determined if the door was locked during the day. The Tapleys did not have a key so we might guess it was left unfastened. The gardener claims he checked that the door was locked before retiring for the evening. The workers had long since departed by that time."

"The gardener does not live on the premises?"

"No," interjected Kerr. "He checked the door from outside the yard. It was locked."

"I see," said Holmes. "No doubt the latch has been handled numerous times since then."

Kerr nodded. "Inspector Lestrade had us all over the house and grounds like ants, Mr. Holmes."

"Pity. There will be no useful fingerprints now."

"You suspect the fiends to have entered through the rear of the house in the night?"

"It is one possibility."

"Well, they did not walk through the front door," said Hunter. "Given the station of the occupants of Savile Row, there are regular constable patrols."

"Who report nothing unusual that night," finished Kerr.

"What time did you and Mr. Martin call it a night?" asked Holmes of Hunter.

"Ten. Perhaps a quarter past the hour."

"You were the only two awake at that time?"

"I suppose so."

"The butler, sir," said Kerr. "He told us he was up reading in his room in case Mr. Martin might need something or other."

"Where is his room located?"

"East side, Mr. Holmes, ground floor."

"And he recalls no unusual sounds that night?"

"He has said as much."

"I should like a word with him anyway."

"At once." Hunter gestured to the maid and the sprightly young girl was off like a shot.

"Starting with the butler, I should like to speak with the house staff individually. May I indulge you gentlemen in asking that I speak to them privately?" asked Holmes.

Hunter rose up out of his seat. "By all means. My duties await me. I shall leave word for the staff to report in turn." Kerr nodded eagerly and stepped outside for a cigarette and the hope of a breeze. The butler appeared before us, his presence announced by a judicious clearing of his throat.

"You wished to see me, gentlemen." The butler was a portly fellow of not inconsiderable height. A widow's peak stabbed down between deep-set black eyes and his somewhat fish-like countenance.

I made the introductions and Holmes began his inquiries.

"We have been told your room is above the coal chute?"

"Indeed it is, sir," Barclay replied, for that was the man's name.

"And you heard nothing out of the ordinary the night your master was taken?"

"Nothing, sir."

"What time did you retire that evening?"

"I put my light out shortly before eleven."

"We have it on good authority that your master turned in just after ten. What kept you up so long after the house had retired."

Barclay looked uncomfortable.

"Out with it, man," urged Holmes. "A man's life is at stake."

Barclay's shoulders slumped. "I have been diagnosed with diabetes insipidus."

I picked up the thread of this admission. "What have you been prescribed: oil of roses? Dates? Gruel?"

"All of these, Doctor. And they have not agreed with me. There is a servant's water closet off the kitchen. I'm sorry to say that on the night in question, I made considerable use of it."

"I understand," said Holmes. "And so you were not in your room for an extended period of time before finally retiring?"

"You have the way of it, sir."

"Very well, let us move on from the night in question," said Holmes. "Did Mr. Martin have any visitors who gave you pause?"

"He did much entertaining in keeping with his station," Barclay replied. "Government officials mostly or well-placed gentlemen seeking favours. Such goes with the territory of public office."

"No one outside this realm?"

Barclay paused to consider.

"Understand," began Holmes, "we are here to assist through unofficial consultation. Keeping details from us will only prolong the matter."

That settled Barclay's mind. "There was one individual, an older gentleman. He was 80 if he was a day. Still spry, mind, still spry. Tall, thin fellow with a great grey mustache."

"Did the man have a name?"

"I never heard it, sir. Mr. Martin used to admit the man himself and they would retire to the study. My orders were to have a tray and decanter prepared in advance and to leave said in the study. I had strict instructions to not enter the room after they had closed the door."

"Was he a frequent visitor?"

"Once a fortnight, I should say."

Holmes was about to speak but saw that Barclay had recalled something he wished to impart and stayed quiet.

"The man had once been a butler," said he. "He said as much to me once though he did not elaborate as to how he elevated himself."

"That is significant," said Holmes. "Anything else about the man you can tell us?"

Barclay dipped his head in thought. "He had an air of the stables about him, which lead me to believe he held some connection to Mr. Martin's business interests; the stables were his second home. I'm afraid the trivial is all that I can recall at this moment."

"You have been a great help," said Holmes.

"Most kind." Taking his cue, Barclay proceeded to the door. He paused at the threshold and turned back. "If it is within your power to return the master to us, we would be forever in your debt."

I caught the eye of Holmes before my friend replied that we would do all we could in that regard.

"How long does he have?" asked Holmes after Barclay had left us.

"Perhaps five years," I replied. "If his condition does not worsen too rapidly. Poor devil."

"Well, we're all of us living under a death sentence," observed Holmes, philosophically. "Only the particulars vary."

◈ ◈ ◈

The afternoon of staff interrogations passed with some rapidity. Further enforcement of Martin's love of horses, odd work hours, his weak heart and the amyl nitrate he took for it were all extracted by my friend's probing questions. The parlour was relatively cool and shaded which permitted us to endure the hottest hours of the day in some comfort. It was still hot when we quit the house, however, and the breeze through the open window of a hansom was welcome once we were able to procure the transport. It was not too late to visit the stables in which Stephen Martin was a majority owner and Holmes gave the Notting Hill address to the cabman.

"What do you make of it, Watson?" asked Holmes. The cacophonous clatter of the city closing up for the day surrounded us with sufficient auditory insulation thus leaving us to speak freely in low tones without fear of being overheard by the driver.

"I think that Mr. Martin's kidnappers may go unpunished."

"Really? We have uncovered Cedric Hunter's involvement after all."

"Whatever do you mean?"

"It is impossible that he could be sleeping across the hall on that night and not heard an abduction taking place."

"You question his assertion that he slept soundly?"

"I think that Mr. Martin's kidnappers may go unpunished."

"This does not even factor into it. The night was hot; his bedroom door must have been propped open. Recall my speaking to you about the cabman as you made to enter Martin's room."

"I remember it. I thought it queer at the time."

"This was to test the acoustics. I called to you in a low speaking tone and you heard me and turned readily. Do you think the scuffle in the bedroom after a man had been roughly awakened in the night escaped the ears of Hunter?"

"It seems unlikely."

"It is impossible," insisted Holmes.

"If what you say is true," said I, "then why was the entire house not awakened at the sound? And how did the men enter undiscovered in the first place?"

"That last part I have already reasoned out. The rear door was left open with the work on the fountain being done. When the Tapleys broke at midday, the kidnappers entered and concealed themselves in the cellar."

"No one saw them?"

"They dressed in workmen's overalls. Men so attired had been coming and going all morning, don't forget. It would be simplicity itself for the kidnappers, mistakenly considered to be the Tapleys by any casual observer, to slip inside, hide and wait for darkness to fall before seizing Martin."

"And what about Hunter?"

"He is obviously involved with the kidnappers given his denial he heard anything. The kidnappers being tipped off about the workmen and the coal chute which is invisible from the courtyard. Hunter was the inside man."

"Even if we concede Hunter's complicity, you still have not shown how Martin was removed without the rest of the house being aware of what was happening within the walls of the place."

"We shall come to that in time. If you let your thoughts wrestle with it, the answer will no doubt come to you. In the meantime, let's set Cedric Hunter aside, confident that he has fooled us, and see what we can get out of that stable manager. Recall Martin's questionable heart, Watson. It's possible; even likely, he died before his cohorts could obtain his secrets. In which case it is vital we root out information apace."

❖ ❖ ❖

Our trip to Martin's Camden stables proved ultimately futile. The manager, we were told, was out of town inspecting potential breeding stock but was expected back sometime that evening. Holmes suggested we wait and we were shown to an antechamber. There I saw that singular half-hooded gaze typical of the Holmes siblings and I knew my friend was putting his vast intellect to the problem and what we had learned this day.

One hour and a half later, we were told by the clerk that a telegram from the manager bore news that he would be spending the night at the hotel near the stable and was not expected back before midday the next day. This setback did not dampen Holmes's enthusiasm. Enthusiasm I shared though I could not help but be concerned for his health. The physical rest appeared to have done him some good and only someone as familiar with him as I could see the fatigue that had settled on his tall frame. I suggested we call it a day so that he could keep his mind focused on the problem while in repose at Baker Street. Holmes wouldn't hear of it. Features strained, a slight rattle in his throat, he insisted we visit the scene of the fire.

Expecting the stable to be deserted, he hoped to prowl for clues. He was not specific as he had, as he put it, theories wanting facts one way or the other. I went along with the suggestion on the condition that he sit for five minutes more while I procured a cab. To my surprise and satisfaction he accepted and managed three minutes of fidgety repose, then we were off.

❖ ❖ ❖

Night had fallen by the time we alighted from the cab in front of the burned stable. Holmes pulled a portable electric light from his pocket and we entered the deserted ruin. The stench of charcoal, sulfur and burned hay assailed our nostrils. Holmes coughed wetly in the darkness from the foul atmosphere and I followed suit shortly thereafter. All about us was vague, charred shadows barely illuminated by the light seeping from the neighbouring windows thrown open by the inhabitants desperate for a breeze. The beam from the hand-held torch gilded the edges of the teetering stalls and piles of ash that were once feed for the horses. The air was stifling.

"Are we searching for anything in particular?" I drily asked in a whisper some time later.

"If it is here, we will find it."

My friend's cryptic reply was of little solace as we eased through the gloom. I was about to ask that he elaborate when I felt his hand grasp my forearm.

"We are not alone," he hissed into my ear.

Straining my ears in the darkness, I heard a faint scraping. Whether the source was hands digging in the dirt or boots scuffling across the blackened stone, I could not say. The pressure Holmes put on my forearm told me that he meant to have this unseen figure.

We separated. Holmes doused the light and our vision, somewhat accustomed to the gloom and aided to a certain extent by the light from the windows outside allowed us a modicum of stealth.

Stepping as gingerly as cats, we closed on the third occupant of the dismal place. From around a fallen beam, I spotted our quarry. It was the youth who had delivered the message to Holmes earlier. As the boy was lame, I relaxed somewhat for he could not elude us.

I was on the verge of calling this discovery out to Holmes who closed from the rear. However an inopportune cough seized Holmes at that moment, betraying our presence. There was nothing for it now but to step forward and seize the lad.

At the sound, the boy bolted with blinding speed. Catching me unawares, he was past my outstretched arm, ducked under a fallen beam and lost to sight.

Holmes was beside me in an instant. "Damn this cough! Come, after him!"

The debris was as much a help as a hindrance in our pursuit. Navigating through the mess slowed the fleeing boy's progress while we closed the gap as best we could. Holmes paused to listen. I did not hear the boy but, rather, a coach drawing up outside.

"Go to the right, Watson," urged Holmes. "Flush him out. I will be waiting."

I did as Holmes bade me, making as much noise as I could in the process. My efforts were rewarded by the scurry of unseen feet. The strategy Holmes had proposed would have worked if his coat had not caught on a protruding nails as he lunged for the boy. This momentary restraint permitted the lad to evade the outthrust hand of Holmes by the width of a fingernail as the cloth held on the iron, then split. By then it was too late. The boy leapt into the open door of the waiting carriage, which was already moving by the time our perpendicular course brought us close enough to peer inside while still unable to reach it. Holmes panted, doubled over from the exertion.

A seamed, wrinkled face glared out at us for a moment, blocking our view of the wide-eyed, panting youth inside. The old man's lips twisted in a cruel grin.

Holmes barked, "It is he!" Then the horses outdistanced us.

The chase and flight had drawn a dozen shadowed figures to their windows to see what all the ruckus was about. A distant police whistle shrilled.

"Come, Watson. Let us away. Mycroft preached discretion and his reasoning is sound. Let us return unobserved in the daylight."

◈ ◈ ◈

Two pipes proved insufficient for Holmes after our return to Baker Street. He next set about sawing at the violin with such ferocity that I was forced to retire early though I wished to discuss the matter. Besides, Holmes had that internalized look about him, of intense concentration that would brook no interruptions.

When I next saw him, Holmes was taking his haggard, drawn form to bed. In the lantern light the affects of the day's work were clearly evident, etched into his features. Despite his outer appearance, he managed a predatory grimace.

"Tomorrow may see the breakthrough we need," said he. "Mycroft will be pleased."

I was at breakfast the following morning when Mycroft Holmes strode in. He saw and understood my surprise at his arrival.

"It has been nearly forty-eight hours," said he, as if this explained all. "Sherlock has tested my conclusions. As time is short, I have come for the verdict."

Evidently his presence pertained to the conversation between the two brothers at the Diogenes Club. There had not been time to receive an explanation from Holmes during the initial flurry of the case. I would get my answers at last.

"Where is my brother?" asked Mycroft.

"Still asleep," replied I. A quick recap of the previous day's work followed along with my professional opinion on the state of my friend's health. Mycroft's brow clouded as I related my tale.

"I feared as much," said he with some intensity.

"Whatever do you mean?"

He took me by the elbow and drew me out of my chair. "Come!"

Together we raced for the bedroom door. Despite his size, Mycroft Holmes could cover ground when it suited him. I could not fathom his motivation for doing so at this particular moment.

Mycroft rapped on the door with one massive fist. When silence and stillness met the summons, he fixed me with a look of such despair that I shall never forget it until my last breath.

I seized the knob and flung the door inwards.

Sprawled unmoving upon the floor, face down, one arm outstretched in a small pool of blood was my intimate friend.

"Sherlock!" I cried and sprang to kneel beside the still form.

I eased him onto his back and ascertained his condition. There was still life within him. His breathing was erratic. His eyelids fluttered open.

"You are better suited to a solitary road than I, dear Watson," he croaked in a voice barely audible. "God protect you." With that he lay still.

My heart froze in my chest. "You've only just returned to us," said I as I lifted his gangling form off the floor. "You'll not be taken away again if I have any say in the matter!"

Placing the languid form on the bed, I whipped off my coat and rolled my cuffs. Taking up the stilled hand I sought the pulse at the wrist. A short time passed as I stilled my palpitating breathing and allowed my vision to clear. Holmes needed a doctor more now than a friend and I marshalled my resolve. I took the rhythm of his heart. Unsteady.

"I knew he was ill, but could not pinpoint the source" said Mycroft at my side.

My bag was beside me. Mycroft must have fetched it though I was unaware he'd left the room. I plunged a hand inside and withdrew the stethoscope and placed the diaphragm against Holmes's chest, listening intently.

"Obvious dyspnoea. Inspiratory and expiratory crackles," said I. I sounded his chest with two fingers and did not like the results. Holmes was bathed in sweat, he had coughed up blood. "Pulmonary oedema likely. Desperate danger of respiratory failure! He'll die without tracheal intubation. We've not a moment to lose!"

Whipping off the stethoscope, I tumbled out the contents of my bag to find some rubber tubing, a small oxygen bottle and carbolic acid. Mycroft snatched up the carbolic while I stretched the length of the tube. Mycroft needed no instruction. He slopped the acid over the tube and my hands, then his own. I required two hands to insert the tube down the throat. I told Mycroft as much and he held Sherlock's mouth open. It was vital to place the tube above the carina in order to feed both lungs equally. The tube in place, I affixed the bottle, and Sherlock's breathing improved readily. This was a temporary measure only. Without the cause, further treatment would be hazardous.

I examined Sherlock thoroughly. There were signs of slight skin irritation at the wrist, ankle and neck. The redness around the eyes and nose were also indicative.

"Not the fire, surely," said Mycroft.

"Unlikely," I replied. "Fire consists of carbon dioxide, water vapour, oxygen and nitrogen. Non-fatal exposure yields the symptoms I observed in Holmes: coughing, watery eyes, minor damage to the throat, vocal chords and lungs. The cause lay elsewhere. The skin irritations are superficial"

"Is there anything more we can do for him?"

"He is stable at present. However we must determine his affliction or his condition will worsen."

❖ ❖ ❖

The next hour was one of desperate activity and mental anguish. Without knowing what Sherlock has been exposed to it was impossible to know what treatment to administer, which meant he might succumb at any moment. Seated at Sherlock's laboratory table, I employed his microscope on samples of the irritated skin. Working feverishly, my mind vacillating wildly, I was continually haunted by the aged visage glimpsed from the carriage the night before. Holmes had recognized the man and there was something familiar about the face. A chemical test on the clothing Sherlock had discarded upon his return from the fire required ten minutes and I hoped we would have our answer in that time.

My mind still a miasma of concern, I joined Mycroft in the bedroom. His cuffs were rolled past his massive forearms, a damp wash cloth in his huge fist to dab at Sherlock's fevered brow. A washbasin lay to one side. I informed him of what little progress I had made.

In reply, Mycroft jabbed a finger thick as a sausage at the room's hearth. Holmes had lay with his arm above his head, his fingers in the soot of the cold fire. I saw hastily scrawled letters in a mixture of blood and ash upon the stones.

M and H.

"Sherlock was on to something," said I. "And in his desperate hour he tried to impart his findings. Whatever do the letters mean?"

"It is imperative we find out."

My first thought was that these were the initials of Mycroft Holmes. That Sherlock, knowing his last hour was upon him, was urging me to bring his murder to his brother's attention so that, together, we could avenge him. This did not ring true. He had told me upon retiring the night before that Mycroft was expected therefore I would not need to go to him.

"Can you make anything of them?"

"I believe the significance of the first is obvious and I shall expound upon that statement shortly," insisted Mycroft. "Sherlock knew I was expected today and we must conclude he wished to convey as much information as possible in the time he had left. Logically, if the first letter was meant for me, the second must have been meant for you."

I probed the depths of my memory in search of the answer. The man glimpsed in the carriage the previous night sprang immediately to mind. Holmes had hit on a connection immediately. I did not possess his singular intellect. My thinking was muddled by concern and a burning desire for vengeance colored my thoughts.

I sprang from my chair paced the room in frustration, my mind racing. I found myself at the mantel, staring at the note card Holmes has so nonchalantly tossed there days before. The deliverer of that card, or his twin, had escaped us at the scene of the fire the night before, leaving no doubt of a connection. I unfolded the single sheet and was dumbfounded as I read the solitary line written upon the parchment:

YOU ARE A DEAD MAN, SHERLOCK HOLMES

The tumblers of my mind clicked into place. In one bound I was at my desk and pawing through the miasma in the drawers. I had it! My notebook from the year 1881. And there was my answer. Under the heading of 'The Adventure of the Locked Room'.

"Gas!" I bellowed as I dashed for Sherlock's bedroom. "He has been exposed to poisonous gas!"

This explained the breathing difficulties, the skin irritation, and the watery eyes. There was not a moment to lose! I thrust a hand inside my bag and pulled out a pair of rubber medical gloves from America. With these as protection from the rare risk of gas residue, I set about irrigating the eyes, nose and throat of my friend with saline. My work completed, I stood and faced Mycroft.

"His body must be scrubbed, head to toe to remove all traces of the gas," I instructed. "Can I count on you to do it while I complete the testing?" Mycroft immediately agreed. "Be sure to avoid skin to skin contact. Here are gloves for that."

I returned to the lab table for the results. Phosgene was the gas that Holmes had been exposed to. The presence of carbon monoxide, chlorine and activated carbon left no room for doubt. One of the simplest acid chlorides, Phosgene was used in chemical dyes for the fabric industry. But how had Holmes been exposed to it?

I told Mycroft my findings and provided him a quick encapsulation of the case. A locked room murder right here in these very chambers fifteen years ago. Twin murderers: Everett and Lucius Hopkins. The former in London, since deceased, the other abroad, presumed dead. Gas then had been the instrument of death. This was the secret of the letter H scrawled in Sherlock's own blood. The old man Sherlock and I had spied in the carriage was the former butler of Everett Hopkins, Douglas Gavin!

Mycroft's broad intellect took up the thread of my thoughts. "The stable," said he. "Unquestionably, the stable."

Having the odour of fresh cut hay, the stable was the most likely place for Holmes to be exposed to Phosgene unawares though the gas was not used in this line of work.

"But how, why?"

"An assassination attempt. That is plain. A deeper connection is implied yet is unclear."

"Perhaps not," said I, flipping through the pages of my current notebook. "The butler at Martin's residence, Barclay, had mentioned a frequent visitor to the house: an older gentlemen who once told him he had formerly been a butler. Gavin was this visitor, I'm certain of it!"

"The note and the messenger, your encounter at the ruined stable; all linked to Gavin."

"We've got it! The original encounter had been spurred on by the murder of the twins' mother, Lucilla Hopkins."

"The Lucilla Stables," offered Mycroft. "Clearly this Gavin is still in the employ of Lucius Hopkins, and is his instrument here in London."

"We must make haste to the stables and have the truth out of the old man."

In reply, Mycroft quit the room. I followed and found him at the desk drawer in which Holmes kept his revolver. The weapon was swallowed by his thick fist before he slid the gun into his pocket.

"Where are you going?"

"A possibility."

"I will accompany you."

"Someone must remain behind," said Mycroft. "You are the most qualified. We shall get at this Gavin before the dawn."

"If you are seeking vengeance, I will not be denied a part in it."

"He is my brother," said Mycroft, simply.

"Mine as well!" I replied.

Mycroft stepped towards me and tenderly dropped a weighty paw on my shoulder. "Pray stay, John," pleaded Mycroft, emotion evident in every word, "and treat our brother."

Despite the thirst for vengeance boiling my blood, reluctantly, I had to yield. My medical knowledge would be crucial should Sherlock take a turn for the worst. I stepped aside and allowed Mycroft to pass.

"I will return presently and, together, we shall have justice."

◈ ◈ ◈

I checked in on Sherlock after Mycroft had gone. There was no change in his condition. Once he awakened, his treatment would consist of copious amounts of water and rest; the latter would most certainly be a tall order. If necessary I would use ether. Rest would ease the respiratory system and permit the lungs to clear. Oxygen may or may not be necessary and would be dependent on the state of his lungs at that time. For the present, I was free to turn my thoughts to other matters.

At first I cursed Holmes for not imparting to me the contents of the note. He was wont to disregard such threats as they were a common occurance in his choice of occupation. This threat, on the other hand, was not only valid it had been carried out. Holmes had been exposed and should be dead as a result. The gas's odour detection value was four times the threshold limit, which meant that for those exposed to the gas to smell the hay-like scent; one had to already be receiving a lethal dose. This meant my friend should have died within hours of exposure and still he lived. Then I had it. The fire! The sudden conflagration had driven Holmes and the constable out of the building. A glimmer of truth revealed itself to me. Holmes had received the letter upon his return from the stable fire and exposure to the Phosgene gas his assassin had left for him. The exposure had been limited which delayed the manifestation of symptoms as much as forty-eight hours. There was no way for the assassin to have known this directly after the fire. Only Hunter and Gavin had seen Sherlock up and around since. Hopkins, thinking he had delivered a lethal dose to Holmes, had permitted the note to be sent in order to gloat over the perceived triumph. It had been blind good fortune, divine intervention, call it what you will, that had prolonged his life. It would be medicine that saved it.

We also had a solid lead. Mycroft and I would take up the torch.

◈ ◈ ◈

Return he did in three-quarters of an hour. He had made a small breakthrough of his own and we sat down to share what we had uncovered. The concern he exhibited for his brother's welfare could not be put off so I went first, explaining Sherlock's limited Phosgene exposure and how this boded well for a full recovery. Mycroft's massive shoulders visibly slumped at this bit of good news. His eyes blazed intently, like his brother's, when I gave him the rest of what I'd reasoned.

"You have done well, Watson," said Mycroft. "For my part I have made arrangements which will confound unless specific information is imparted to you. I had thought Sherlock and I had made the situation plain back at the Club but that does not appear to be the case. That won't do."

Mycroft settled into his seat, his broad form spreading over the cushions. He gave a great sigh before speaking. "The letter M refers to a certain nefarious Professor of our prior acquaintance."

Stunned by this revelation, I could only gasp. "Professor Moriarty is dead!"

"Exactly so. Nature, and the world of crime abhor a vacuum, sir. When Moriarty lost his life to my brother, it sent his vast network into disarray even while they sought revenge."

Mycroft was referring to the assassination attempt against Sherlock, by Colonel Sebastian Moran, which I recounted in 'The Adventure of the Empty House' and I said as much to him.

"Precisely. Sherlock's wax head and quick police action won the day and we caught the man."

I nodded eagerly. "At the time, Sherlock declared Moriarty's illicit reign over and went on to conclude that we would be safe from more reprisals."

"And have you not both been able to continue your work without harassment?"

"Just so," said I as though the matter were settled.

"But, Watson, the shadow army of criminals who once did the Professor's bidding still exist, at least in part. Like autumn leaves, they have fallen from the oak to drift about on the winds of chance and opportunity. Just because Sherlock beat their best and convinced them through his actions that further attempts would be equally fruitless does not mean that members of the Professor's network would be averse to clawing at each other for the vacant spot at the top. A sweeping net of law enforcement the likes of which the world has never seen worked tirelessly to corral Moriarty's minions at the time of Professor's death. Some went to ground and we have not as yet weeded them out."

"What of it?" asked I. "If the rats devour each other, the cat need not leave its place by the fire."

"A vivid metaphor, but an incorrect one. Here is another. We have cut off the head of the serpent but the body coils and twines in its death throes. Moriarty's army will rise again, in time. I imparted my conclusion to Sherlock that a power play is in progress, that the continent and, perhaps, the world could be in jeopardy again when their internal strife has ended and they once more operate as a single unit."

"The death of Stephen Martin is a sign of that re-emergence." I could not believe what I was hearing. "You are certain of this?"

"I am. First old scores must be settled. Then what has been consolidated can advance. Martin escaped the first net thrown over the network five years ago. While others cowered in the shadows, he prospered in the intervening span of time. It does not take a great mental leap for those who suffered to eventually be convinced that Martin bought his way out of the scandal and preserved his prosperity by means of a loose tongue. That tongue has now been silenced."

"Then what is our next move?"

"Martin was a respected member of Parliament. It is a safe assumption that no man so highly placed was a mere lackey. No, Moriarty must have made better use of the man than that. And so, his murder tells us that the power struggle must be nearing its end if operatives so highly placed are being weeded out. The state of his corpse indicates that they were searching for something he possessed. I maintain that he had in his possession documents and secrets the Moriarty hierarchy need to necessitate their return. We must recover this cache and circumstances are against us."

"We are hampered at present," said I. "This may prove impossible."

"Yes, we would benefit greatly from Sherlock's input. There is no alternative but to continue on as best we can."

"It is of paramount importance that we see Sherlock hale and hearty once more."

"To that end, I have arranged for my brother to die."

"What!"

"His enemies think him dead," replied Mycroft. "You have said as much yourself. Gavin witnessed Sherlock's failing health from his carriage window and gloated. Undoubtedly he has reported to his superior. If they remained convinced he is dead, they may become bold. Lured out of their lairs they will be ripe for the picking. Do you not agree?"

I could only admit that I did. "We cannot move him."

"We shan't. London need only be told he is dead. They do not need to see a body. I have spent this past hour calling on certain trustworthy members of the government to gather the resources necessary. An undertaking firm has been secured. They were reluctant at first. When reason was found wanting, I showed them cold steel and all reservations evaporated instantly. The stage is set and the players are on their way. Watson, can the Empire count on you to do your part?"

◆ ◆ ◆

We played out the farce as Mycroft laid it out. The undertaker came and went. Mrs. Hudson had been informed of the situation and was sequestered away from the pressmen who soon arrived on the scene so that she might 'grieve in private.' Mycroft also withdrew into the background to read over my case notes and I, something of a public figure due to my writing up of past adventures, was left to issue a brief statement to the press. Yes, Sherlock Holmes had died of respiratory failure despite my every effort to preserve his life. I have never hankered for a career on the boards but, somehow, my performance was satisfactory to the press. I suppose having 'lost' him for so many years after Reichenbach Falls, it was easy for me to summon up the spirit of the appropriate emotion, refreshed by recent events, for the charade we were playing out. They harangued me with questions which I ignored, leaving them to file their stories with what little I gave them.

By nightfall the reporters had quit the front of the building and calm returned to Baker Street. Holmes was showing some improvement and I judged it safe to remove the tracheal tube. Sounding his lungs and heart while Mycroft and the fate of London awaited swift action. The health of my friend was of paramount importance and I delayed longer to confer with the physician, a cadaverous though capable man, whom Mycroft had arranged to sit by Sherlock's bedside while we traipsed about for Queen and country. When all was arranged to my satisfaction, I nodded my readiness to Mycroft. I sprang for the closet and a light coat and hat while Mycroft waited at the door with singular stoic calm though I knew a cauldron seethed underneath. All that remained was for us to don black arm and hat bands of mourning. It seemed disrespectful to the venerable custom but we had a part to play for the benefit of our enemies. To that end I added one last piece to my attire. My revolver rested in my coat pocket, ready to hand.

◆ ◆ ◆

Being early evening, a conveyance did not come easily. Found one we did in the end and we were off to our confrontation with Douglas Gavin. We did not speak en route. Mycroft's gaze turned utterly inward as he exchanged the reality of what lay before us for the larger implications of the stakes of the game. My sole emotion was a burning desire for revenge on those who had attempted to murder my friend.

Our arrival at the Lucilla Stables was marred by chaos. The vast complex was ablaze. Thick, choking clouds of smoke billowed from every window and door of the facility. Men dashed this way and that amidst scampering herds of horses turned loose by their masters lest they burn within the stone walls. Keening, almost human screams sounded within as less fortunate beasts were consumed alive by the roaring flames. Winds churned like tornados and ash and smoke blanketed all. Bells clanged and a thousand voices sounded a cacophonous chorus to the throaty bellow of the flames.

"Deliberate," said Mycroft. "No question."

I accompanied him to one of the fire brigade wagons. A captain supervised his men's battle with the inferno.

"Did anyone make it out," shouted Mycroft over the din.

"Not many!" came the shouted reply from the sweaty-faced fireman.

"The manager, perhaps, made it to safety? An older gentlemen?"

"Fire started in the Manager's office as far as we can tell! That side of the stables is gone, consumed!"

"Our enemies stay one step ahead," said I when we had stepped away so as not to interfere with the work of the men at the water wagons. "Hopkins must have known we would come here."

"Perhaps. There is a more sinister implication however. It may very well be that Hopkins simply completed his work and is ready for the next stage. Martin is dead. Hopkins believes Sherlock has met a similar fate. In destroying our one link, Gavin, he hopes to be free to work his will from the shadows."

An idea struck me. "We are not without options. I had the 1881 notebook with me. Finding the section I'd consulted earlier, a possibility presented itself. "At the time of the first murder, the Hopkins family resided at 5186 Clanranald Avenue. As I have not written up this early case for publication as yet, this location is not widely known. It is possible Hopkins is using it as a headquarters."

"Excellent! However should we not see Cedric Hunter at once?"

"Whatever for?"

"The diversion may prove profitable."

"I remind you that we are on the trail of a murderer."

"Have you not examined your case notes?" asked Mycroft. "It is all there. That said, I take your point, Doctor, that we should waste no more time in discussion."

I turned to hunt for a cab in the undulating throng. Mycroft gripped my upper arm. "Wait. We are not far from the burned stable of the late Stephen Martin. A quick detour is called for. I'm afraid I must insist as it is there that the sensitive information is to be found."

We had to retreat three blocks from the scene of the fire before securing a vacant cab. I gave the driver the address of the destination Mycroft suggested and we put the horrible fire behind us.

◈ ◈ ◈

Mycroft urged the driver to wait for us and pressed a coin in the man's hand to stiffen his resolve to do so. Somehow, Mycroft was able to survey the ruin and determine the spot where Martin's body had been displayed as part of the trap to ensnare Sherlock. How Mycroft pulled off this Herculean feat of deduction, I cannot begin to fathom. That he did it, I bear honest witness that he did.

A section of the hayloft had fallen over the spot. However, a canted, charred, load-bearing beam jutted from the fetid mess. The wood yielded to my boot and a minute's work exposed the spot. A ragged hole gaped in the earth at the base of the slanted pillar.

"We are too late," said Mycroft.

"Damn and double blast!" I replied, kicking at the muck.

"Berating ourselves is counter-productive," said Mycroft, calmly. "We might still win the day. Let us proceed with all speed to the former Hopkins residence."

Seeing as the apparent death of Sherlock Holmes had made our adversaries bold, but not careless, I suggested we alight from the cab one block over from Clanranald in order to approach the house with stealth. Mycroft, a stranger to adventure, heeded my judgment and we stepped down on a deserted stretch of road outside a closed up baker's. A narrow alley between two tenements opened on a small courtyard and we were granted an opportunity to look over the rear of the Hopkins house from a safe place of concealment. The windows were dark and the sprawling manor house had seen better days. To my eye it seemed uninhabited and I

"We are too late."

began to suspect my brilliant idea was so much stuff and nonsense.

Mycroft raised one paw of a hand and pointed to a cellar window barely discernible through the thick hedge around the property. We moved closer for a better look. There was no sign of movement from any corner of the property other than the flickering candlelight shining through the grimy window.

"That window was not lit a moment ago," said Mycroft.

"We'll not end this affair standing out here," said I, at last. "We must beard the lion in his den."

I withdrew my revolver and we crept towards the darkened house. The backyard was a bramble, which covered our steps and concealed us until we were upon the sagging wooden deck. The wood creaked at the faintest touch of my boot. We could not approach this way. Mycroft had the answer, he tried the cellar door and found it unbolted. Enough grease of indeterminate vintage remained to lubricate the hinges and we were able to enter silently. Mycroft gingerly closed the door after us.

Three steps lead to a loamy, earthen floor. The cellar was a vast nest of shadows. The candle was a feeble stump in the window to our right and it cast a mere foot or two of light against the impenetrable darkness. A wooden chair squatted within the penumbra of the candle. Strands of dried hemp festooned the thing, hanging in tatters.

"This is where they kept Martin," Mycroft read the thought in my mind.

"They worked on him here until he yielded his secrets or succumbed to their ministrations."

"The stairs to the first landing should be to our left," explained Mycroft. "If you could take up that candle we might make our way to them."

"I shouldn't do that!"

This warning came from behind us, from the other side of the cellar doors. The voice was unknown to me. It was followed by the scrape of something along the length of the doors. The candle sputtered and died and we were plunged into darkness. The fall of the black curtain coincided with a tinkling as of glass rattling against itself and small thuds as something fell to the soft earth.

"Lucius Hopkins!" called Mycroft.

"At your service," replied a deep voice tinged by a foreign upbringing.

"In the service to the vile legacy of Moriarty," I added.

"The professor was a great man but he was blind in his obsession to outwit his equal," said Hopkins. "He never did see that a direct approach at eliminating Sherlock Holmes would never work."

"And so Moriarty's lapdogs bark," said Mycroft. "We heard the same from Moran."

"Do you think just because you blunted the Professor's sharpest arrow that none remained in his quiver?" asked Hopkins. "My voice was not heeded while the Professor was alive, but my actions have succeeded now." A faint chuckle reached us through the panel. "It is indeed a shame you did not become aware of the fire grenades sooner," taunted Hopkins. "The candle severed the rope holding the grenades in place. Now they have shattered and you will die in the same manner as the great thorn in the Professor's side, only quicker. Farewell!"

The sound of running feet receded from the door.

I herded Mycroft to the doors. "Those grenades will be the death of us!"

The globes habitually contained carbon tetrachloride for use in smothering fires. The substance was not without its dangers.

"Do you think it warm enough down here for Phosgene to form?" asked Mycroft, seeing the gravity of the situation.

"Shall we loiter and find out?"

We threw our shoulders at the doors. They would not yield. I emptied my revolver into the wood around the handles in the hope of splintering it. The roar of the pistol throbbed in our ears. The doors held. Fate had not abandoned us, however. I detected no odour of hay as yet, which led me to conclude that the fall to the soft earth had cracked but not shattered the fire grenades. The devices were meant to be thrown into a conflagration to shatter, after all. Still, cracked as they were, the gas was slowly filling the cellar. It was simply a matter of time until we were overcome. We redoubled our efforts against the door. The stout wood bent outward with every thrust against it. The doors held. Our last recourse was to grope blindly for the stairs. In the pitch dark we were as likely to step on the hissing vials as find the stairs. We were done for.

The scraping noise in front of our faces, which were mere inches from the doors, startled us. I still clutched the pistol but had fired the gun dry. One of the doors jerked upwards. I inverted the pistol for use as a club as there was no time to reload. The door moved again, then swung upwards. A face peered down at us.

"Sherlock!" exclaimed Mycroft a split-second before I could.

"Up, gentlemen," said Sherlock Holmes. "If you please."

We were up the stairs like a shot. Sherlock banged the door shut and we all stepped away from the trap.

"Good show, brother," said Mycroft. "Your timing is impeccable."

My elation at escaping certain death and seeing my friend up and about was soon tempered by Sherlock's appearance. He appeared stooped, feeble as though a strong breeze would topple him over.

"You are too soon moving around," I cautioned. "Exertion hastens the effects of the gas."

"I am all too aware... " With that Sherlock sagged. Mycroft and I caught him before he could fall. He continued, weakly, "...commend you both... reasoning the thing out."

"It's the oxygen tent for you."

"Forget that, Watson," said Sherlock with considerable difficulty. "Hopkins... off down the alley... Too weak to tackle him. Watched him go. After him!"

Torn between my duty to my friend and duty to the crown, I hesitated.

It was Mycroft who made the decision for me. "Our brother is safe with me."

Without another word I left them and sprinted towards the alley, reloading the revolver as I ran. I glimpsed the tall form halfway up the street as I emerged from the narrow space. A few pedestrians had decided to sample the evening air and Hopkins brushed rudely past them. His destination was a solitary rider on a black gelding that had seen better days. On horseback, he would escape me readily. I could not permit that to happen.

I cast my gaze about in search of a carriage house or private stable from which I might procure a mount. Closed up storefronts were all that presented themselves to my eyes. Salvation came from the representative of the night crews whose job it is to clean the detritus accumulated on the streets between sunset and sunrise. It was a water wagon used to hose filth from the cobbles and keep the dust at bay. A strong, young mare pulled the wagon. I dashed forward and showed the man my revolver.

"Unhook her," I barked. "Be quick about it!"

There was no time for explanation, as a hasty glance over my shoulder showed me Hopkins swinging his horse around the next corner. Dangling from one hand was a square, metal box containing the secrets Martin had died for. Harness creaked and clattered to the street. I thrust the man back and leapt aboard the unfettered animal, winding the long ribbons in my fist and digging my heels into her flanks. She responded smartly and the chase was on.

Swinging around the corner I spied Hopkins up ahead. Various street vendors were coaxing their drays into motion after a long day on the cobbles. These denizens of the carriage-way would not move for Zeus himself and hindered all progress of the miasmic conglomeration of growlers, Hansoms and the ever-prevalent omnibuses racing each other to make better time amidst pedestrians stamping along in every direction past the sandwich-men. I closed the gap until a sudden opening creating by one such plunging omnibus allowed Hopkins to slip between the vendors and the horse-drawn tram. This hole closed by the time I reached it, leaving me no choice but to take to the footpath in order to gain ground.

Hopkins guided his animal towards Hyde Park where he could evade me amongst the trees. Streetlights were on in the green space but their light was little help against the spreading pool of shadows. To avoid this I needed every bit of speed from my mount. If I did not draw closer, I would not be able to keep him in sight.

Meaning to overtake him, I gave my horse her head and drew within a few yards of Hopkins. It was here the crowded thoroughfare got the better of us both. An advertising van had become jammed perpendicular to the flow of traffic when one of its horses had slipped in the muck at the side of the road and fell on its side. The owner seemed in no hurry to have the animal regain its feet as the van's purpose was to remain outside the establishment that had hired it anyway. The result left no room for a cat to pass and a stalled omnibus between Hopkins and myself.

I could only see the back of Hopkins's horse while I heard the epithets he hurled and the thud of his boots as he kicked people out of the way. If he should clear a path before I reached him, all would be lost.

I leapt from my horse to the rear of the omnibus. A rickety, winding iron staircase took me to the top of the viewing platform jammed with patrons braving the clouds of dust everywhere in search of cooler air on the benches on the roof of the conveyance. I pushed through the seated throng then leaned over the edge.

There was Hopkins. I could have knocked his hat from his head. I sprang upon him like a hawk on a hare. We collided and he tumbled from the saddle. Landing atop him, I drove the air from his lungs. He was solid and strong, though, and this did not incapacitate him as I'd hoped it would. He seized my gun hand and we rolled. I drove my knee into his stomach and that took some of the fight out of him. A stout blow to the chin drove him into the red post-box where he smacked the back of his head sharply.

Hate filled my heart. Here was the man who had willfully murdered time and time again, the man who had come the closest to taking the life of my intimate friend and colleague. I raised the pistol and squeezed the trigger.

❖ ❖ ❖

Dirt had clogged the hammer and cylinder. The weapon did not fire.

Hopkins shook his head to clear it. He was tall, thin, a shriveled snake of a man in middle age. I snatched up the dispatch box he'd lost in our fall and faced him.

"My brother died when Holmes drew him from his hideout," said he, out of breath. "And I have murdered your associate. The scales are balanced. And the great game goes on." He leered.

"Sherlock Holmes is alive and well," said I, triumphantly. "It was he that freed his brother and myself from your trap so that the round up of your associates can begin in earnest. You have lost all!"

The smile dropped from his face and with a snarl he lunged at me. A thirst for justice replaced my desire for vengeance and I cracked the dispatch-box along the man's temple. He collapsed and lay still. The police had caught up to us in time and we were both taken into custody where we remained until Mycroft showed up the following morning to secure my release and take possession of the box.

❖ ❖ ❖

Several days afterwards, upon returning to Baker Street after venturing out in search of cigars, I found the place deserted. Holmes was nowhere to be found. My initial apprehension soon gave way to inner calm. Holmes had been in and out of consciousness these last few days. During his periods of delirious wakefulness, I had fairly drowned him with fluids which succeeded in counteracting the affects of the gas. Once he was fully awake, I turned all of my descriptive powers towards relating the adventures Mycroft and I had shared in the hopes of so enthralling him as he lay abed that I might steal a few more hours for him to rest and thus aid his recovery. I have no doubt he knew precisely what I was up to, though at no time did he voice his suspicions. Rather, he delighted in the blows dealt to Mycroft's precious routine for his benefit.

I had a cigar fired to life and was puffing contentedly when Holmes returned at six o'clock. There was a wrapped bundle under his arm.

"Ah, Watson," said he as he removed his coat. "I have just been to see Mycroft at the Club. He reports that the London limb of Moriarty's vile tree of crime has been rightly pruned. Arrests have been sweeping."

"Excellent! I see you feel fit enough to move about."

"Indeed."

"I have questions concerning the matter. Will you indulge me?"

Holmes took his seat across from me, the package in his lap. "Proceed."

"You suspected Hunter's involvement. Mycroft was certain of it. What proof had you both?"

"Recall the acoustics test I performed between the two bedrooms. It showed clearly that it was impossible for Martin to be abducted against his will. Not only did it prove that Martin went willingly and quietly with his captors, as he was in league with them, but also that Hunter had to have been a willing participant due to this fact and one more telling element. Mycroft hit on it. It appears you did not."

"I confess I still do not know what you are referring to."

"When Hunter greeted you at the door to Martin's residence, he commended you on your courage during a trying time and said that he was a great admirer of your recountings of our adventures. Note the tense. He 'was' an admirer, not 'am.' This implied, though did not confirm, that he knew your fanciful depictions would no longer be appearing because I was dead. And he did not ask where I was. Again, for the same reason he misconstrued your display of courage in the face of the loss he believed you had recently suffered. To this add his surprise at seeing me when I came up behind him. Before he was able to conceal his thoughts, he said, 'I did not expect'. Ah, as a reader of your tales, my presence should have come as no surprise to him. He did not expect to see me because he believed me dead."

I nodded, seeing the chain of reasoning the Holmes siblings had followed. "It will take better evidence than this to convict the man."

"He will suffer no such fate. Mycroft has turned him over to the more clandestine elements of our government and Hunter has turned over to them vast amounts of information. With which, Mycroft tells me, the Hydra that is Moriarty's legacy may well and truly be pruned once and for all."

"Very good. A minor matter now: How did the lame boy outdistance us at the stable?"

"Elementary. He was the twin of the messenger. Both are in custody."

"Then the affair is truly behind us."

"It would seem so," agreed Holmes. He held the package out to me. "I return bearing gifts."

"I don't know what to say."

"Open it."

I tore the plain brown wrapping and uncovered Stephen Martin's tin dispatch-box, battered and worn from its ride with Lucius Hopkins. Painted across the top of it were my full name and title to which was added the postscript: 'Late Indian Army.' The box was empty.

"I don't understand."

"Why, it is for your scribblings, Watson," replied Holmes, jocularity in his voice. "You leave them laying about, underfoot and in the way."

"I see."

The tone of Holmes's voice took on a more somber quality as he let his implacable facade slip for a moment. "You must keep them somewhere. After all, if not for your quick action in preserving my life, the box would forever remain empty as our adventures would be at an end."

I could not help but be moved by these sentiments. "I accept your gift with a full heart. As for saving your life, I am only trying to keep pace. You first saved mine years ago when we first took this lodging."

The End

Hitting Close to Holmes

The Holmes tale you've just read and, I hope, enjoyed, is my fifth go-around with the great detective and the resourceful Watson, making this fictional duo the characters I've written more than any other so far in my brief career. As a result, I've gotten to know these men of action rather well - and still hope to know them better as I continue writing of their adventures.

I was new to Holmes and Watson when I started out. Sure, I'd heard of them (who hasn't?) and had read one novel, the odd story or two over the years and had seen various adaptations of the characters via TV and the movies. Immersing myself in the original tales was an eye-opening experience. I was immediately struck by the crime committed on Dr. Watson in portraying him as a bumbling buffoon in early incarnations of the tales. This was as far away from Doyle's depiction as one can get. Reading through the original canon I was outraged. Over time, Watson has become my favorite of the pair. We can all be awed by Holmes's genius but Watson, to me, is the more dynamic and interesting character. It's been great seeing him portrayed correctly in the current Holmes movies and on TV in Sherlock.

That said, all us Holmesians know that the story must, and should, focus on Holmes and that is what I set out to do every time I sit down to bang out another of their adventures. Still, I try to give Watson a chance to shine and no more so than in the current tale where his medical skills are needed as well as his willingness to throw himself into the action. Adding Mycroft into the mix was a first for me. I love how the two brothers interact in the original tales and you can expect more of that from me in future tales. Pairing Watson and Mycroft was fun and I hope it shook up the mix a little without ruining the original recipe that has been so successful for so long.

Another first for me is that "The Invisible Assassin" is a sequel to my first, and award-winning tale, "The Locked Room," which appeared in the first volume of the series. An off-screen character in that first tale seemed to me to be the ideal foil and it was fun to see the man get the better of Holmes - for a while. I'd always wanted to bring the character back and this stage seemed the best suited to pull that off. Will he return again? Could be. Time will tell. The tale also allowed for the return, at least briefly, of Douglas Gavin. Named for a friend and dedicated Holmesian who has read all of the previous editions in the series, it was fun to bring Doug back for one more adventure. The first appearance made his day and I hope the return was equally as satisfying.

The genesis of this tale was born from a simple idea: is it possible to get the jump on Sherlock Holmes? We all know how brilliant he is and how dangerous an opponent he would be for those wallowing in a life of crime. So can he be beaten? Of course, ultimately, he must triumph, but can he be outsmarted? How do you kill someone with the smarts to see you coming? My answer was the Invisible Assassin and a carefully laid trap.

Research into the nature of that trap (no spoilers here for those of you who read the back-up material first) as well as stables, London streets, omnibuses and the medical know-how of the time was a lot of fun. I love delving into the past for its own sake but also it's important to me to get the setting and science right.

Okay, that's five Holmes tales under my belt. My backburner is already heating up a stew for Volume 6 down the line. My thanks to the Airship 27 crew for making these books happen and for allowing me to be part of them. Until next time, there's work before us! Tally ho!

◈ ◈ ◈

ANDREW SALMON – The Pulp Factory Award winner, Ellis and multiple Pulp Ark and Pulp Factory Awards nominee lives and writes in Vancouver, BC. His work has appeared in numerous magazines, including *Pro Se Presents, Masked Gun Mystery, Storyteller, Parsec, TBT* and *Thirteen Stories.*

He has published or appeared in:

The Forty Club (which Midwest Book Reviews calls "a good solid little tale you will definitely carry with you for the rest of your life"), *The Dark Land*, the first of a series ("a straight out science-fiction thriller that fires on all cylinders" - Pulp Fiction Reviews), *The Light Of Men*, which has been called ("a book of such immense significance that it is not only meant to be read, but also to be experienced... a work of grim power" - C. Saunders), *Secret Agent X: Volume One* and *Three, Ghost Squad: Rise of the Black Legion* (with Ron Fortier), *Jim Anthony Super Detective Volume One, Sherlock Holmes Consulting Detective Volumes One, Two, Three, Four* and *Five, Black Bat Mystery Volume One, Mars McCoy Space Ranger Volume One, Mystery Men (&Women) Volume Two, Moon Man Vol. One, The Ruby Files Vol. One, The New Adventures of Thunder Jim Wade Vol. One, Ghost Boy Vol. One,* and *All-Star Pulp Comics #2.*

To learn more about his work check out the Airship27 Hangar at: (airship27hangar.com) and the following links:

lulu.com/AndrewSalmon and lulu.com/thousand-faces.

amazon.com/Andrew-Salmon/e/B002NS5KR0/ref=sr_ntt_srch_lnk_7?qid=1328666769&sr=1-7

The Napoleon of Crime

hen I realized, while compiling and editing the new stories for this, our fifth volume of new Sherlock Holmes adventures, that two of the tales featured Prof. James Moriarty, it was only logical that we devote some time to this truly fascinating villain. After all, the common truism in literature today is that a hero is only as strong as is his or her archenemy: a tenet displayed throughout pulp fiction. The irony of Prof. Moriarty is why he was created by writer Arthur Conan Doyle in the first place and his evolution into a much greater role than Doyle ever could have envisioned.

After years of writing Sherlock Holmes mysteries, Doyle simply became tired of the series and wished to end it, despite the arguments of his publisher and fans. Still, he knew he would need a truly remarkable villain to do away with his near super human detective and so Prof. James Moriarty appears for the very first time in what was to be the last Sherlock Holmes story: *The Adventure of the Final Problem.*

In this gripping tale, Holmes tells Watson of the man he has labeled The Napoleon Crime, a genius college professor of mathematics, one James Moriarty. Moriarty is a crime lord who protects the majority of the criminals of England in exchange for their blind obedience and a hefty share of their ill-gotten profits. Once having learned of his identity, Holmes begins to systematically dismantle the professor's criminal empire and thus becomes the target of Moriarty's wrath. To elude Moriarty's retribution, Holmes and Watson flee to Europe where the brilliant villain confronts the Great Detective high atop the Reichenback Falls. To Watson's horror, both Holmes and Moriarty supposedly fall to their deaths while locked in fierce combat.

Of course, as we all now know, Doyle's hopes of leaving Sherlock Holmes forever were vanquished soon enough by the hue and cry of his many readers demanding he bring him back. Doyle's publisher was unrelenting and won him over by offering more money than he'd ever been paid before for any of his past works. In the end, always a common sense fellow, Doyle relented and set about writing additional Sherlock Holmes tales. But first he had to bring him back from the dead, which he cleverly did in The Adventure of the Empty House.

It is important to note that due to the plot of *The Adventure of the Final Problem*, Molarity had to be referenced if only to explain he had not been so lucky in surviving the plunge as had Holmes. And so the series continued, but now with a wrinkle of sorts. Doyle knew in Prof. Moriarty, he had invented a character of tremendous potential and to use him again he would need to write a story that predated The Final Problem.

The Valley of Fear thus becomes only the second story in which Prof. Moriarty plays a direct role. In the tale, Holmes attempts to prevent the professor's agents from committing a murder. Moriarty does not meet Holmes in the story. In a scene where Moriarty is interviewed by a policeman, a painting by Jean-Baptiste Greuze is described as hanging on the wall; Holmes later remarks on another work by the same painter to show it could not have been purchased on a professor's salary.

In total, Moriarty is mentioned by Holmes in five other stories: "The Adventure of the House," "The Adventure of the Norwood Builder," "The Adventure of the Missing Three-Quarter," "The Adventure of the Illustrious Client," and "His Last Bow."

Doyle was said to have lifted the phrase, *The Napoleon of Crime*, from a real Scotland Yard inspector who used it in reference to Adam Worth, one of several real life criminal models for Moriarty. Another inspiration might have been American astronomer Simon Newcomb, a multitalented genius, with a special mastery of mathematics who had a reputation for spite and malice, constantly seeking to destroy the careers of rival scientists. Des MacHale, in his *George Boole: His Life and Work*, suggest Boole may have been a model for Moriarty. Jane Stanford, in her biography of John O'Conner Power, thought Doyle had borrowed many of Power's traits and background for the villainous professor.

Some surviving Jesuit priests at Stonyhurst claimed to recognize the physical description of Moriarty as matching those of Reverend Thomas Kay, S.J., Prefect of Discipline, under whose tutelage Doyle came as a wayward pupil. According to this theory Doyle, as a private joke, has Inspector MacDonald describe Moriarty: "He'd have made a grand minister with his thin face and grey hair and his solemn-like way of talking." Finally, Conan Doyle did use his former school, Stonyhurst College, as inspiration for many details of the Holmes stories and among his classmates at the institution were two boys named Moriarty.

Regardless from what well of inspiration Prof. James Moriarty was drawn, the reality is that throughout the years he has been given greater prominence and treated as Holmes' primary archenemy. From radio to films and television, hardly a new Sherlock Holmes incarnation has ever been put forth without Moriarty's dark shadow infused somewhere in the tale. Like Holmes, he has swelled in our imaginations to something greater than his creator ever imagined.

Today it is impossible to think of the Great Detective without at the same time giving thought to his evil opposite, Moriarty, the true Napoleon of Crime. Their never ending battles have provided millions of readers with pleasure and that's really not a bad thing, is it?

Ron Fortier

9/22/2013
(Airship27@comcast.net)
(www.Airship27.com)

FIGHTCARD

SHERLOCK HOLMES

BARE KNUCKLE BOXING

Sherlock Holmes vs. Ezekiel Tanner

TONIGHT

The World's Favorite
Consulting Detective
Gets Ready to Rumble...

Jack Tunney

www.ingramcontent.com/pod-product-compliance
Lightning Source LLC
Chambersburg PA
CBHW071238250626
47163CB00001B/237